GHOSTS OF KARNAK

GEORGE MANN

TITAN BOOKS

GHOSTS OF KARNAK

Print edition ISBN: 9781783294169
E-book edition ISBN: 9781783294176

Published by Titan Books
A division of Titan Publishing Group Ltd.
144 Southwark Street, London SE1 0UP

First edition: May 2016

10 9 8 7 6 5 4 3 2 1

What did you think of this book? We love to hear from our readers. Please
email us at: readerfeedback@titanemail.com, or write to us at the above
address.

To receive advance information, news, competitions, and exclusive offers
online, please sign up for the Titan newsletter on our website:
WWW.TITANBOOKS.COM

For Lyla Foy, whose UMi *provided the fuel.*

ONE

Her name was Autumn, and like the season that had invested her with both name and temperament, her appearance heralded the onset of a fall.

She'd been a pretty thing; all auburn curls and heels, her mouth a slash of wicked scarlet, her painted fingernails uniform and precise. She'd been twenty, twenty-two at most. She'd barely commenced her life, and now the city had taken it from her.

Donovan crushed the nib of his cigarette between his fingertips, grinding the ash and embers until it burned, until the butt disintegrated, and he allowed it to dribble away in the wind. How had a young woman like this ended up lying with her face in a puddle in an alleyway?

He dropped to his haunches, studying the shocked expression on her face; frozen, rigid, like an obscene photograph printed in a tabloid rag. She looked surprised. She hadn't been expecting to die, then. Even after everything that had been done to her, she'd clung to the notion that she might somehow find a way out and live, that someone might rush to help her in her final moments, fend off her attackers and sweep her away to safety. And then the moment had come, and she'd been unprepared, terrified, alone. It was a hell of a way to die.

"Ritual, then?"

Donovan looked up to see Mullins standing a few feet from the body, rubbing his sweaty palms on the legs of his pants. His ample cheeks were flushed, and he kept glancing nervously at the corpse, as if he couldn't decide whether he wanted to stare at it, or run a mile in the opposite direction.

Donovan sighed. "Well, given the fact they've carved bloody great icons into her flesh, it's a safe assumption, Sergeant."

"Yeah, well, I suppose it is," said Mullins, redundantly. He ran a hand through his hair; a nervous gesture Donovan had seen a hundred times before.

"Listen, go take a look along the alleyway, see if you can't find anything her attackers might have left behind; a knife, a cigarette butt, a footprint." He knew the chances of turning up anything useful were minimal at best, but he couldn't bear to watch the poor guy suffer any longer.

Mullins nodded gratefully and hurried away. Donovan wondered if the woman reminded him of someone. He'd seen that happen before; watched the most stoic of officers go to pieces over the sight of a dead girl in a familiar dress. Things like that, they brought it all home, made you think it could have been you. That it might have been your wife, or girlfriend, or sister lying there in the gutter, legs splayed apart, stockings torn, blood dribbling from the corner of her mouth. The thought made Donovan grateful he and Flora had never thought about having kids. He was certainly old enough to be this girl's father.

He scratched at his new beard. It felt wiry and unfamiliar, and he was still unsure if he was going to keep it. Flora liked it, though; he could tell from the way he'd caught her looking at him in bed that morning, the little sideways glance when she thought he wasn't paying attention. She'd practically sighed with relief when he'd stepped out of the bathroom, toweling himself down, with the thing still plastered over his face. Maybe he'd give it a few more days. Maybe the itching would stop.

He sighed, took another cigarette from the packet inside his jacket, and pulled the ignition tab. The light was fading now, the long, red fingers of the sunset clawing at the Manhattan skyline, as if trying desperately to cling on. Soon the police trucks would be here with the surgeon, and the stretcher, and the dancing lights, and this poor woman would lose any shred of dignity she had left.

Not that she had much.

Donovan took a long draw on his cigarette, and then gently, cupping the back of her head, rolled her over onto her back.

"You there?" he whispered into the mouth of the alleyway. "If you're watching from the shadows, you can damn well get down here and help."

He waited a moment for a reply, but there was nothing. No subtle shifting of the light, no red glow of night-vision lenses, no quiet, measured observations. He wasn't there.

Donovan balanced his cigarette on his bottom lip, and leaned over, studying the woman's face. There was a mark on her forehead, carved into the flesh with the tip of a knife. The blood had run, mingling with the water to form glossy streaks, but the symbol was just about visible. It appeared to be a circle or disk, resting inside a pair of horns.

There were other marks, too—one just below the soft cup of

her throat, above the curve of her breasts, depicting what looked like a small bird with a long beak, and another on her forearm, a neatly carved succession of nested shapes—a circle inside a square, inside a triangle, inside a larger circle.

Donovan chewed the end of his cigarette. She'd been alive when they'd cut her. He knew that much about corpses. He could tell from the way the blood had swelled to the surface, how the skin had puckered. She'd probably screamed, too. The pain would have been excruciating. He'd have Mullins check that out as well, talk to anyone in the nearby apartments in case they'd heard anything. Trouble was, they probably heard women screaming out here every night. It was that kind of neighborhood.

Mullins had already taken her purse; Donovan would take a proper look at that back at the station. He checked her hands, though. There were rings still on her fingers. Impressive rings, too, with big rocks. She'd been going up in the world, keeping company with someone who could afford expensive presents. The rings meant something else, too—this wasn't just a robbery, with someone trying to cover his tracks or get a cheap thrill from carving her up. Whoever had done this had left her purse, and three rings totaling in the hundreds of dollars. Whoever was responsible—whichever sick bastard Donovan was going to have to find—had targeted this woman for a reason. The symbols were a message. Donovan's first job was to discover for whom.

He saw the lights before he heard the shrill cry of the sirens, and stood, pluming smoke from his nostrils. Two police trucks and a surgeon, just as he'd anticipated. He'd been playing this game for too long.

"Mullins?" he said, cupping his hand around his mouth and calling down the alleyway. "You found anything?"

"No, sir," came the muffled response. "Nothing worth mentioning."

"All right, then get out here and brief the others. I want her bringing straight to the morgue, and I want Dr. Vettel's eyes on her. No one else. Only Vettel. She's not going to like it, but when she's done working up a lather on the holotube, tell her that I owe her one." He flicked ash from the end of his cigarette, watching as Mullins emerged from the other end of the alleyway, wearing a sullen expression. "You got that?"

"I've got it," he said.

Donovan nodded. Uniformed men were jumping out of the trucks, spilling out into the road in a veritable tide of blue.

Shame they couldn't have been here when she needed them, he thought. He knew he wasn't being fair, that he was grouchy and tired and needed a drink, but then what had happened to the woman wasn't fair, either.

He rubbed his palm over his face. There'd been too many girls recently. Maybe it was starting to get to him.

Mullins was already talking to Parkhurst, one of the uniformed boys, issuing instructions about getting the body brought back to the morgue. Donovan decided not to bother him. He'd see him back at the station.

Turning up the collar of his coat, he walked past the parked police trucks, their lights still flashing wildly, and cut down a side street, emerging onto Fourth Avenue. Cars sailed by on the wet road as if skating on mirrors, their tires stirring up puddles close to the sidewalk. Steam curled from a nearby standing pipe, and overhead, the silvery shaft of a searchlight from a police blimp danced across the rooftops, making ghostly shapes amongst the stark silhouettes of water towers and billboards.

Donovan flicked the butt of his cigarette into the gutter, where it fizzed for a moment in a puddle before going out. He figured that was some kind of metaphor for his day.

He took a deep breath, then set out for the station.

TWO

If the splintered ribs weren't enough, now he was bleeding from a gash above his left eye, and he had an awful, dawning notion that his lung was about to collapse.

The Ghost tried to roll onto his side, but even that set off a series of blooming explosions in his head; tiny bursts of fairy lights, dancing before his eyes.

He sucked at the air, and then wished he hadn't. His chest burned. Not just the usual, taken-one-too-many-punches sort of pain, either—this was *excruciating*. The sort of pain that made you think twice about trying to breathe again. He decided that might be his best course of action—to feign death and hope the thing that had done this to him would lose interest in the fight.

His cheek was pressed against the wet concrete. He twisted his head.

It hadn't given up yet. He wouldn't be that lucky.

The Ghost rolled as the Enforcer took a lumbering step, its gauntlet splintering the paving slab where his face had been just a split second earlier. Tiny fragments of concrete peppered his face, drawing stinging beads of blood.

He leapt up, trying to catch his breath. The thing was *relentless*. He'd already buried upwards of a hundred flechettes in the pilot's flesh, but still it lumbered on, undeterred.

The pilot had once been a man, but although it still had the shape and form of a human being, he could see from the dead look in its eyes that any sense of humanity had long ago been driven out by the pain and madness of being incarcerated in such a diabolical machine.

The Enforcer suit was an exoskeleton, of sorts—a bulky, armored frame that encapsulated the pilot, who hung suspended at the heart of it like a puppet. Thick metal rods formed a series of braces, standing proud of his limbs, giving him bulk and presence. This outer skeleton was affixed to his body by means of a series of shorter rods, which were sunk into his flesh, screwed deep into his bones. Its fists were heavy plated gauntlets, which hung almost to the floor, and each leg was supported by a brace of pistons, helping to manage the weight and generate speed.

The man's head was exposed, deep within the chest of the exoskeleton, a knot-work of wires and cables protruding from the base of his skull. His expression was slack and unemotional, and his stare seemed vacant and disinterested. The Ghost supposed the man must have been pumped so full of drugs that he simply couldn't feel the ragged holes in his chest, inflicted by the Ghost's flechette gun. He was more machine than man, now—a living tank, firmly set upon the Ghost's destruction.

The Enforcer swung at him, its immense fist striking him like a wrecking ball and throwing him up and back. He flipped under the force of it, spinning head over heels and crumpling into the side of a nearby tenement building. Something else snapped in his chest, and he slid to the ground, spitting blood.

This wasn't going very well at all. The thing was going to kill him, and he had *nothing* left. He was out of weapons, and out of ideas.

Groaning with pain, he clawed at the wall, dragging himself to his feet. One more punch like that and he'd be out for the count. Worse, if the thing managed to pin him against the wall, it would crack his skull like an egg.

He looked up, trying to see through the fog of blood in his eyes. One of his goggles was cracked, fracturing the sky. He peered through the haze, looking for an escape route, an opportunity for a temporary reprieve.

There. He spotted a platform on a fire escape, about twenty feet above him, out of reach of the Enforcer. He fumbled inside his coat, trying to find the ignition cord for his boosters. The Enforcer was getting closer, pulling back its fist for another strike.

His fingers closed around the cord. He yanked down, hard, and felt the kick of ignition at his heels. The Enforcer leaned in, its massive fist closing on the Ghost's head, just as the power level reached critical and the Ghost shot up on a bright plume of flame. He swung his arms out, catching hold of the railing and taking himself up and over. He came down hard, landing on the platform with a resounding *clang*. He cut the power to his boosters, and sunk to the ground, drawing ragged breath.

Below, the Enforcer struggled to extract its fist from the wall, pulling hunks of the building loose in a shower of dust.

The Ghost pulled himself up into a sitting position. He could feel bubbles of blood popping in his left lung as he breathed. He tried not to think about the pain.

The Enforcer was still down there, furiously trashing a parked motorcar as it tried to figure out a way to reach him. He had to stop it. Somehow, he had to find a way. The Reaper couldn't be allowed to have these things running around the city.

The Ghost had heard stories about the mob boss using the machines to strong-arm other mobsters into bending their knee, decimating their forces and subsuming them into his own growing network. There'd been reports of bank raids, too, in which men piloting enormous machines had simply smashed their way into the vaults and taken thousands of dollars' worth of gold deposits, battering aside any resistance from civilians or police.

The Reaper—so called, the Ghost was given to understand, because of the number of executions he had ordered—was building a powerbase here in the city, and soon there would be no one left, not even the police department, with the resources to take him on.

The Enforcers were a symptom of this, a virus in the system. And the city was sickening.

The world shuddered. Or at least, the building he was resting against. With a sigh, the Ghost shuffled to the edge of the platform on his knees and peered over, just as another blow shook the wall at his back, and caused the iron frame of the fire escape to rattle and creak.

The Enforcer was punching handholds in the side of the building and hauling itself up after him. He watched in amazement as it swung its arm up for another blow, burying its gauntlet deep in the brickwork and levering itself higher. Soon it would be level with the fire escape.

The weight of the thing must have been tremendous. He could see the pilot straining, neck muscles popping as the machine thundered higher. Its feet scrabbled at the ruins of the wall, but could find little purchase. It was taking all of the strain on its arms.

It was determined; he'd give it that.

Hurriedly, the Ghost checked his pockets. He'd already used his flare, he'd emptied all of his flechettes, and he wasn't carrying any explosives. The only weapons he had left were his fists and his booster jets. Neither would do him any good—if he tried to fly close enough to the Enforcer to burn the pilot with his boosters, he'd be putting himself in its reach. If it got hold of him, he'd be dead in seconds.

He'd have to try to use its bulk against it, somehow.

He stood, bracing himself against the railing.

The Enforcer was only a few feet away now, coming up alongside the fire escape. He wasn't taking any chances. He fired the ignition on his boosters, rising up slowly from the metal platform.

The Enforcer, thinking he was about to make good on another escape, launched itself at the gantry, flinging itself across the face of the building and crashing into the wrought-iron structure. It collapsed as the Enforcer struck it, smashing free from the side of the building and clattering noisily to the sidewalk below.

Momentarily in freefall, the Enforcer punched out, shattering a window and catching the edge of the stone frame to halt its descent. The window ledge gave way beneath its weight, but it had served its purpose, and the Enforcer had already buried its other fist in the wall. It slid a few feet in a shower of brick dust, before resuming its steady ascent.

The Ghost continued to rise slowly, keeping his back to the wall. If he could get it high enough, maybe there was a chance he could do some damage.

"Come on, keep up!" he called down to the pilot. "Can't you see I'm getting away?" Blood flecked his lips as he spoke, and he wiped it away with the edge of his sleeve.

They were nearing the upper story now. He'd have to act soon, before they reached the roof. Up there, he'd have no chance of bringing it down.

The drop was around thirty feet. It had to be enough.

With a deep breath, the Ghost fell back against the wall, and then pushed himself away, dipping his head into a dive.

The Enforcer, seeing him hurtling down toward it, pulled one of its hands free and tried to swat him out of the sky. He twisted, narrowly avoiding the metal fist, and caught hold of the back of the Enforcer's frame, swinging himself up and around, so that he was now the right way up again, and clutching onto its shoulders.

It thrashed, trying to shake him loose, its free hand grasping for him, reaching up and around its back, but its shoulder joints wouldn't pivot far enough, and he was able to keep just out of its reach.

This was his chance, his one opportunity.

The Ghost flipped again, turning upside down and aiming his boosters at the wall. Still clinging onto the Enforcer's frame, he gave the ignition cord a second tug, increasing the burn rate. He'd spend precious fuel this way, emptying the canisters, but he couldn't see any other option.

Luckily, the Enforcer didn't appear to comprehend what he was doing, still grappling for him with its free hand instead of trying to keep itself attached to the wall.

He felt a sudden jerk as the force of the boosters kicked out, searing his ankles and wrenching them both away from the building. The Enforcer bellowed as it lost its grip, its hand still opening and closing redundantly, trying desperately to cling on as they launched back into the air

The Ghost let go, releasing his grip on the Enforcer as it tumbled, the momentum sending him spiraling up into the sky, out of control. He fought to right himself, throwing his weight left and twisting, just as he dove at the wall of the opposing building. He struck a windowpane instead, bursting through into the darkened apartment beyond, striking the ceiling, setting the curtains aflame and, seconds later, crashing down into the dining table and sending a candelabra flying. Black smoke curled from his ankles, and the room filled with the stench of burned flesh.

Hurriedly, he clambered to his feet, wrenched the curtains from their rail and tossed them—still burning—out of the open window. They fluttered and billowed on the night breeze, trailing thick smoke, as they slowly drifted to the ground.

He peered after them. The Enforcer was lying in the road, its exoskeleton buckled, the pistons of one leg still firing spasmodically, causing the limb to twitch with a mechanical whirr. Inside, the pilot wasn't moving.

He could hear sirens trilling in the distance. It was time for him to leave. A quick glance at the ruins of his boots told him the canisters had completely burned out. He'd have to take the more traditional route home.

He carefully removed his broken goggles, wiped the blood from his eyes and buttoned his coat. He'd lost his hat at some point during the fight, but it mattered little; like this, he was just Gabriel Cross, the rich playboy and former soldier. No one would give him a second look.

With a final glance at the devastation in the street below, the Ghost hobbled to the apartment door and let himself out into the hallway.

THREE

Gabriel had always adored the sea.

He supposed he'd probably been raised with a predisposition, having grown up on an island, but he loved how the fresh, briny smell of it seemed to pinch his nose, how the water sighed longingly as the waves broke over the shore, how the gulls clacked and squabbled over the small, silvery fish he didn't know the name of.

As a younger man he'd often snuck out of the house during the summer to spend nights on the beach, skinny-dipping with Katherine, the closest he'd ever come to a childhood sweetheart. She'd been his girl next door—quite literally—although next door, in Gabriel's world, was half a mile from his parent's estate.

They'd make clandestine arrangements to meet in the sand dunes, throwing their clothes off with gay abandon and running pell-mell into the frothy water without a single care in the world.

He'd loved the tingle of the cool air on his flesh, the shock of the icy water, and the luxurious curve of Katherine's back. She'd felt so soft beneath his fingers, so pure, and yet, when she bit his lip and played with the tip of his cock, she'd seemed so forward, so feminine, so vital.

He hadn't thought of those days for years, not since he'd

returned from the war to find her gone, moved out west with her family, leaving nothing so much as a forwarding address. He hadn't tried particularly hard to find her, either, but then— what would a girl like that have wanted with a damaged soldier like him? He supposed she was probably tearing up the West Coast these days, a riotous novelist or painter, a notorious and outspoken flapper girl, making a name for herself amongst the usual pantheon of crashing bores who presided over high society.

The thought made him smile, but it was tinged with disconsolation.

Of course, here at the Chelsea Piers, things were a little different to the Long Island beach he remembered; the air reeked of oil and fish, the water was filthy, and the baritone honk of the ships' horns set him constantly on edge.

It was early, and he wasn't feeling his best. He'd downed two Bloody Marys with his eggs that morning, but even they'd failed to take the edge off. He was considering visiting a doctor to see about having his broken ribs strapped. He'd been meaning to have a word with Felix about that—seeing if he couldn't figure out an arrangement with an understanding surgeon who wouldn't ask too many questions. Although, the way things had been going lately, he'd be more likely to need an undertaker than a doctor.

He adjusted his sunglasses, wincing as he brushed the tender flesh around the orbit of his left eye. It was already black and swollen from where the Enforcer had cracked his goggles. He consoled himself with the fact he could still see out of it, and lit a cigarette, searching for distraction.

He was propped against the railing, facing out to sea. In the dock, the *Centurion* sat like a great leviathan, squat upon the water, casting him in its long, ominous shadow. Passengers bustled on the deck, crowding into the wedge of the ship's prow and hanging over the side, waving down to those who had dutifully filed out here to meet them.

Disembarkation ramps were being pulled into place, buttressing the glossy flanks of the steel beast, while wooden cargo crates were already being unloaded from one of the holds, bearing dubious bounty, he presumed, from the East.

An exhibition was coming to town, to be held at the Metropolitan Museum of Art—the resulting plunder from a recent expedition to Egypt. The newspapers were bursting with claims of wondrous finds; how the evidence from the dead queen's tomb would forever change how the Ancient Egyptian religions were viewed. It was, apparently, the find of the century—although Gabriel took such grandstanding with a pinch of salt; the century, to his mind, had barely begun.

No doubt Arthur, up at the museum, would be lost in paroxysms of joy at the prospect of getting his hands on the new finds, but Gabriel wasn't here for that. In fact, all of the flashbulbs going off around him were starting to become an annoyance, newspapermen snapping pictures of the crates, as if the wooden caskets themselves were objects of ancient beauty, deserving of celebration on the front pages.

Gabriel had come down to the docks for one thing, and one thing only: to be reunited with Miss Ginny Gray.

He'd missed her terribly in the months following her departure earlier that year. She'd written him once, a simple postcard, fronted by a sprawling monochrome photograph of Luxor. On the reverse she'd written simply "missing you", and signed off with a kiss. It had been enough, an admission that everything was not finished between them, that she hoped to see him again upon her return. He'd clung onto that, and as the perpetual party had circled on around him, flowing like a melody through his life, he'd thought only of her, and not of the pretty but vacuous women who filled his house each weekend, rich with the musk of desperation, and the search for validation.

He had no idea what to expect upon seeing her again; whether he might hope to rekindle the affection they had clearly felt for one another, or if she'd made altogether different plans in the intervening months. He knew only that he wanted to see her coquettish smile, to brush her hair from her eyes, and to hold her in his arms. Provided she didn't hug him too hard, of course—his ribs might not be able to withstand it.

He glanced up at the ship, searching the deck, but could see no sign of her amongst the press of passengers waiting to be released from their floating prison.

Vessels such as this had a tendency to spark an inexplicable sense of dread in Gabriel, particularly standing there, in its shadow, gazing up at the size of the thing. He couldn't put his finger on why, exactly; something to do with the sheer scale of it, he thought, and the notion that a machine that size had no business defying the natural order of things, ploughing its way across the surface of the ocean. That watery domain belonged to the whales and sharks and other terrible creatures that plumbed its otherwise unassailable depths. Skinny-dipping on a Long Island beach was one thing; propelling an enormous iron leviathan across the globe was quite another.

Ginny, of course, would have taken such considerations in her stride, much as she seemed to face most things in life. To her, long weeks holed up in a tiny cabin would have seemed like an adventure, a challenge to be faced head-on, and an opportunity to experience something new. Indeed, that was how she had faced the news of Gabriel's double life, when it had all eventually come out. More than anything, she had wanted to be a part of it, to show him that the two halves of his existence didn't have to be quite so separate, after all.

Gabriel dropped the butt of his cigarette and crushed it underfoot, blowing the last of the smoke from the corner of his mouth. The passengers had begun to file down one of the ramps now, jostling to be the first to hit dry land. Ginny, he knew, would take her time. She preferred to make an entrance.

He watched the others hit the dock and spread, like an oil slick comprised of fur coats and hats, sharp suits and briefcases. Behind them, men in overalls were lifting further crates down with a crane arm, lowering them tentatively to the dock, from where, he presumed, they would be loaded onto trucks to be hauled uptown to the museum. He wondered which of them contained the remains of the queen herself, and how she'd have felt about being dragged here, all the way to the New World, only to be placed on display in a cabinet before the glassy eyes of a thousand or more New Yorkers.

Gabriel hung back, avoiding the crowd. He was growing anxious. He'd expected to catch at least a glimpse of her by now, a slight wave from the deck, a wicked half-smile. Yet, there was nothing, not even a hint of her. He glanced redundantly at his watch, and then sighed, catching himself. It wasn't as if he could have got the time wrong—the ship was right there, in the dock, in front of him.

He fished another cigarette from his pocket and pulled the ignition tab. The flood of nicotine in his lungs was a reminder of his cracked ribs, and he coughed, wincing in pain. Frustrated, he tossed the cigarette on the ground and began pacing instead.

The crowd was thinning now, with only a handful of stragglers still dragging their cases down the ramp.

It struck him then that she wasn't coming. Her brief telegram, relayed through Henry, had informed him she was planning to return to New York, that she'd bought a ticket for the *Centurion* and he should meet her at the docks when it arrived. That, though, had been weeks ago. There'd been plenty of opportunity for her to change her mind and decide to extend her trip. Surely, though, she would have written ahead?

He watched the last of the passengers file off the ramp, an elderly lady in a wicker wheelchair, pushed along by a smartly dressed manservant. There was no one to meet her, and they disappeared a moment later beneath the stone arches, the wheels of the chair creaking loudly as they crossed the concrete.

Moments later, the dockworkers assembled around the disembarkation ramp and started to wheel it away.

Gabriel hurried over. "Hey there! Excuse me, but I'm still waiting for someone," he said, gesturing to the ramp.

The nearest dockworker shook his head. "I'm sorry, sir, but all the passengers have disembarked. We got word from above." He inclined his head, indicating the ship. "You sure you didn't miss them? It sure was busy down here."

Gabriel nodded. "Yeah, I'm sure I didn't miss her. Thanks." He stood aside to allow them to roll the ramp back toward the storage hangar. Behind them, others continued to unload the cargo, shouting directions to one another as they sorted the crates into neat stacks.

It was surprising how quickly the dock seemed empty again, as the passengers all filed off, melting away into the city as if they'd never been gone.

He wondered what had happened to Ginny. Something had gone wrong and she'd missed the boat, or else she'd had a last-minute change of heart about coming back to New York. Whatever the case, she hadn't been onboard. He was certain he hadn't missed her.

Battling a creeping sense of disappointment, Gabriel quit the dock. It was still early, and he knew a great place nearby to get more coffee and eggs.

FOUR

It wasn't so much the sweltering heat, she decided, but the dreadful taste of the water that was causing her to feel so unwell. Every time she took a mouthful of the tepid stuff she had to fight the urge to gag. Even *here*, in the hotel bar, which was supposed to cater to tourists. She pushed the awful thing away from her, sliding it across the table. She would order a gin and tonic when the waiter returned. She'd been told that alcohol didn't mix well with the heat, but what else was she to do? She'd been here for three days now, and if she didn't drink something soon, she was going to be as desiccated as the mummies she'd seen in the museum earlier that day.

Ginny mopped her forehead with her handkerchief, and tried to focus on her book. She planned to take in the Luxor Temple the next morning, rising in the early hours to journey out into the starlit desert, and so was anxious to read up on what to look for. She'd hired a guide, of course, but she didn't know whether to believe half of the stuff they told her, and she was anxious not to miss anything important.

The words swam on the page before her, all muddled, as if lost behind a shimmering heat haze. With a sigh, she leaned back in her chair, fanning herself with the pages. Had she made a terrible mistake, coming out here alone? It had seemed such a romantic notion, taking a steamship across the ocean to a distant land, steeping herself in its history and mythology. A real adventure, and a chance to get away from everything that had happened back in New York.

She'd been running from that for a while now, and was beginning to think that running wasn't going to be the answer. The creature she'd seen at the fairground still haunted her dreams, and some mornings she woke thinking she must be going mad. To even conceive that such things could exist in the world—the very notion appalled her. She needed time to let it sink in, for her view of the world to shift to accommodate what had happened. This trip was supposed to be that opportunity.

Now she was here, though, she found herself longing to see Gabriel, to be with someone who understood. She might have asked him along, she supposed, although she suspected he wouldn't have come. She doubted anything could tear him away from that city, not now. Not even a woman.

She waved her hand to discourage a fly that had been buzzing around her head for the last few minutes. The bar was busier today than she'd seen it, populated by an array of people of all nationalities and creeds. She'd heard Germans talking in the lobby, met an Englishwoman in the restroom, and overheard the swarthy-looking chap at the next table ordering a drink in French.

The bar itself was luxurious and stately, reflecting the inordinate cost of staying here. The walls were comprised of glistening white arches, open to the elements, each of them adorned with a complex fretwork of interlaced patterns. The roof out here on the terrace was domed, and low hanging fans turned rhythmically, the sound of them leaving her feeling dozy and tired. They barely seemed to stir the hot, still air, and she found herself longing for the cool breeze of Manhattan, blowing in off the water and gusting along the broad canyons of skyscrapers, apartments, and shops.

She closed her eyes for a moment, trying to shut out the dizziness, allowing the darkness to swarm in.

The next thing she knew, she was in the arms of the swarthy Frenchman, who was dribbling cool water on her lips and gently mopping her brow with a serviette. She tried to stand, confused and embarrassed, but he shushed her quiet and carefully propped her back in her chair.

"There," he said. "I fear the heat may have got to you." He was crouched beside her chair, and he reached for a glass from his own, adjacent table, holding it out to her. "Drink this."

She did as he said, bringing the glass to her lips and taking a cautious sip. The water was cool and pure, and she gulped at it thirstily, draining the glass. The man laughed. He stood, taking the bottle and pouring another.

"Where did you get this?" she said. After the tepid stuff she'd been drinking, it tasted like nectar.

"This is your first time, isn't it?" he said, evidently amused. His Gallic accent tumbled wonderfully as he spoke. "No one's told you to ask for the bottled stuff."

Ginny shook her head, finishing the second glass and placing it on the table before her. She glanced around, still feeling somewhat embarrassed, but no one seemed to be paying her any attention. It was probably a regular occurrence around here, with inexperienced tourists passing out from the heat.

The man waved to the waiter, who hurried over. "We'll take another two bottles," he said. The waiter nodded enthusiastically, before rushing off to execute the order. Ginny wondered how he managed to operate so quickly in such heat, particularly dressed in his shirtsleeves.

"Thank you," she said. "I don't know what came over me."

"It happens more than you'd think," said the man. "Pretty ladies swooning by my table."

She looked up at him, and laughed. He was handsome, in a rugged sort of way, with a tanned face and thick black beard. His shirt was open at the collar, and his pale suit was stained around the cuffs with smears of what might have been ocher or rust. His brown eyes were sharp and alert.

"I'm Amaury," he said. "Jacques Amaury."

"Ginny Gray," she replied. She noticed her book had fallen to the floor, and bent to pick it up.

"Ah, the Luxor Temple," said Amaury, with a wry smile. "You're here to see the sights, I see?"

"I suppose I am," said Ginny. She beckoned to the empty chair at her table. "Look, I don't mean to seem forward or anything, but if you'd like to join me? It's the very least I can do."

"Not at all," said Amaury. "What sort of man would I be if I didn't assist a lady in distress. All the same, I would be most happy to join you for a while."

"You're waiting for someone?" said Ginny, as he pulled up a chair. He seemed to sink into it, crossing his legs and leaning back in a surprisingly casual fashion.

"My companion, yes," he said, "but he's English, and so he's always late."

Ginny laughed. "I thought the English were supposed to be punctual?"

"At home, perhaps," said Amaury, "but here, in Egypt, not so much. He's too worried about 'keeping up appearances', seeing to his ablutions, pressing his suit. And then he comes out to visit the dig and finds himself covered in sand and dirt regardless." He chuckled, indicating the marks on his sleeves. "Me, I have learned not to care."

"You're an archaeologist, then?" said Ginny.

"I think that is a grand word for what I am," said Amaury. "A treasure hunter, perhaps, if you were being kind. A grave robber if you were not." He smiled.

Ginny leaned forward, intrigued now. "Have you found anything out here?"

Amaury raised an eyebrow. "You've not come all this way to steal my secrets, have you?"

Ginny fixed him with a withering look. "To be honest, I'm not entirely sure why I'm here. Searching for something I'm unlikely to find, I suppose."

"Ah, then you understand the plight of a treasure hunter all too well," said Amaury. "And yes, I've found something." He looked up as the waiter came rushing over, bearing a tray of fresh drinks.

Ginny reached for one of the bottles as soon as he'd placed them on the table. "Well, aren't you going to tell me?" she said, in a conspiratorial whisper. "You can't leave a girl hanging like that."

Amaury laughed. "I can do better than that. Why don't you come and visit the dig tomorrow, see it for yourself? I promise you'll be impressed."

Ginny frowned. "But the temple," she said.

Amaury waved a hand. "It's been there for thousands of years, and it'll be there for thousands more," he said, pouring himself a drink. "How many other offers have you had to see the undisturbed tomb of an ancient queen?"

Ginny took a sip of her drink. She was starting to feel normal again, despite the cloying heat, although she thought she might retreat to her room for a nap once Amaury's friend arrived.

She met his gaze. Could she trust him? The idea certainly sounded exciting—just the sort of adventure she'd been looking for. And he was right—how many other opportunities would she have to see something so spectacular? "Very well," she said. "I'm intrigued. Let's say I go along with your little plan. What then?"

"Then you meet me and Landsworth in the hotel foyer an hour before dawn, and I'll take you on a guided tour."

She pretended to consider this for a moment, despite having already made up her mind. What was the point in coming all this way if she wasn't going to take the opportunities it presented her with? And besides, how much trouble could she get up to on an archaeological dig? "All right. I'm in. How could I pass up the chance to meet royalty?"

"Excellent," said Amaury, holding his glass aloft. Ginny clinked hers against it. "Ah, and here comes Landsworth, too." He nodded his head to indicate a newcomer to the bar, over her left shoulder.

She turned to see a man in a smart gray suit wending his way through the tables toward them. He looked as out of place as she felt; dressed in the wrong clothes, clearly struggling with the heat, apologizing to everyone as he brushed past their chairs.

Amaury threw up his hand in greeting. "Landsworth! Come and meet my new friend."

The Englishman, huffing a little with the exertion, arrived by their table a moment later. He peered at Ginny inquisitively, and then, remembering his manners, extended his hand, and smiled.

"This is Miss Ginny Gray," said Amaury. "All the way from America. I hope you have no objection, but I've invited her to visit the dig with us tomorrow morning."

She took Landsworth's hand and shook it briskly.

"A pleasure," he said. "And no, of course not. No objection whatsoever. Provided you're not with the press." He frowned. "You're not, are you?"

"No, just a tourist," said Ginny. "I'm not about to spill all of your secrets."

"Good, good," muttered Landsworth. He glanced at Amaury. "Getting a drink, am I?"

Amaury shrugged. "Why not?" A look of impatience flashed across his face. He clearly wasn't as taken with his English companion as she might have expected. Ginny decided it was time to make her exit. She stood.

"Well, thank you, gentlemen. If you'll excuse me, I need to go and make arrangements for tomorrow. I'd hate to leave that poor tour guide stranded."

Amaury stood, offering her a slight bow. "Until tomorrow, then, Miss Gray."

As she left, she saw Landsworth take her seat at the table, and the two men lean in for what appeared to be a rather heated exchange. She would have to be on her guard tomorrow, she decided. She had a sense that there was more to this dig than Amaury had initially let on. All that stuff about the press— perhaps they really had found something special, and were keen to break the news properly, when they were ready.

Whatever it was, she felt her mood had improved somewhat. She would order another bottle of that water, and then retire to her room for the rest of the day, ready for an early start in the morning.

FIVE

"And finally, news this morning of a series of extraordinary sightings last night in and around central Manhattan. It seems the police have been flooded with reports of a bizarre apparition, seen floating above the rooftops of Fifth Avenue around midnight. Initial reports suggest that this is *not* the vigilante known as the Ghost, also known to frequent the skies in this area, but rather a 'glowing figure in white, surrounded by a halo of fluttering ribbons'. The police have issued a statement announcing they are investigating the matter, and that any citizens who do encounter such a character should not make an approach, but direct their reports to their nearest station."

Gabriel turned the knob on the wireless, clicking it off. The room seemed suddenly silent, without even the ticking of a clock; it was early, and Henry had yet to wind it.

"No appetite for the news this morning, sir?" said Henry, as he laid out the morning cutlery on the breakfast table.

"No appetite for anything much," said Gabriel. "Excepting, of course, your wonderful eggs Benedict," he added hurriedly, when he saw the expression on Henry's face. The valet smiled graciously, and continued setting Gabriel's place.

"I must say, that business with a 'floating apparition' sounds most outlandish," said Henry. "Don't you agree, sir?"

"What? Oh, yes," said Gabriel, "although I've come to believe there are stranger things in this world than wailing spirits and ghosts."

"Quite, sir," said Henry, with a look that suggested he could think of a few things himself.

News of the sightings was troubling, though. For the first time in weeks Gabriel had failed to go out on patrol the previous evening. After his beating at the hands of the Enforcer, and the disappointment of Ginny not arriving aboard the *Centurion*, he'd felt the need to come back here, to Long Island, to seek solitude and a chance to recuperate. He supposed, in truth, he was hiding, holing up for a while to lick his wounds, although the one hurting him most was not the cracked ribs or the swollen eye.

It seemed, though, that his night of rest had left him at a disadvantage. He wondered what this new apparition could signify. He and Donovan had broken a cabal of witches a few weeks earlier, putting a swift end to their occult ambitions, but this sounded different. Was it a message, a warning, a haunting? Whoever or whatever it was, they were hanging around his neighborhood. He supposed he would have to go out that night to look for it.

"May I enquire how you're feeling this morning, sir? Recovering well from your 'boxing' injuries?"

Gabriel sighed. "I'm fine, Henry. Really. It's nothing."

"Then perhaps you are troubled by Miss Ginny's failure to attend your rendezvous yesterday morning?"

Gabriel looked at Henry as if he'd slapped him around the

face. "It's unlike her, Henry. That's all. A telegram, a postcard—I can't help feeling she'd have sent word of some kind that she'd changed her mind."

"Perhaps she didn't," said Henry. "Are you sure that she wasn't on the ship?"

"Insofar as I didn't see her disembark," said Gabriel. "If I missed her, she didn't wait for me."

Henry gave a little shrug. "Your breakfast will be ready presently, sir," he said, and left the room.

Gabriel watched him go. What was he getting at? That something might be awry? That Ginny had returned to New York after all, but hadn't wanted to see him? That he was holding himself back for some reason, and hadn't done enough to ensure his assumptions were correct? He supposed there was only one way to find out.

He pulled himself up off the sofa, cringing at the sudden pain in his chest. He could hear Henry clattering pans in the kitchen down the hall. He closed the door and crossed to the holophone terminal on his writing desk. A moment later, and a small, wavering image of Donovan's face began to resolve in the mirrored cavity.

"Gabriel? Where the hell have you been?" he barked, before his image had even clarified.

"Busy," said Gabriel. "I had a run-in with one of the Reaper's Enforcers. It wasn't pretty."

"For you, or for it?"

"For either of us."

"Hmmm. Well, we didn't find anything. The Reaper must have sent in a clean-up crew."

"He might have thought to send a doctor, too," said Gabriel. "I'm pretty beaten up."

"Well, if you're up to it, I could use your help."

"This business with the apparition?"

"What? No, of course not. I'm too busy to be chasing phantoms. Whatever that's about, I'll bet my last dollar on the fact it's a couple of kids out to have us all for fools." Donovan glanced away, looking at something or someone Gabriel couldn't see. He lowered his voice. "No, I have a dead woman on my hands and it's… well, it's complicated."

"All right," said Gabriel. "I'll be there this evening. Usual spot. But I need you to do something for me, too."

Donovan sighed. "I knew this wasn't just a social call," he said. "Go on."

"Ginny was supposed to arrive back in New York yesterday aboard a steam liner called the *Centurion*. She sent word for me to meet her off the ship, but I waited at the docks and she didn't show."

Donovan shrugged. "Maybe she changed her mind, or caught a different boat. There are a hundred reasons why she might not have been there, Gabriel. She might have decided to take an airship home instead?"

Gabriel shook his head. "You're probably right, but something doesn't feel right. That's all. I was wondering if you could get a look at the passenger manifest for the ship, just to see if her name's on it?"

"I'll make a call," said Donovan. "Leave it with me. In the meantime, hasn't she got an apartment somewhere around Midtown?"

"A rented place," said Gabriel, nodding. "She kept it on when she took off, somewhere to keep her stuff."

"You want me to send Mullins over there, just in case?"

"No, I'll take a look myself. Thanks, Felix."

"You won't say that when I tell you about this dead woman."

"You do say the sweetest things."

Donovan glowered. "I'm hanging up now, Gabriel." The line went dead, and Donovan's face, frozen for a split second, fragmented into tiny blue shards, before dissolving away to nothing. Gabriel switched the receiver off and slumped back in his chair. There was a polite knock at the door.

"Yes, sorry, Henry," he said, as the door opened. "I was just making a call."

"Indeed, sir," said Henry. He crossed to the table with Gabriel's breakfast. "I'll bring you some coffee."

Gabriel frowned. "No Bloody Mary?"

"I fear we're fresh out of tomato juice, sir."

Gabriel narrowed his eyes. He didn't have the patience to be mollycoddled by his valet. "Henry, I re—"

"And I'll prepare one of the motorcars for your trip into town," said Henry, cutting him off mid-flow.

"Very well," sighed Gabriel. "You win. Coffee it is."

"Excellent, sir."

Gabriel had only visited Ginny's apartment once before, on the cold January day she'd walked back into his life, dragging him out of the boxing ring and right into a whole heap of trouble. He hadn't paid much attention to the place at the time, having been more concerned with getting her home safely after she'd consumed the best part of a bottle of gin at one of the local bars. He remembered it was situated on a quiet cross street, however, and found it easily enough, noting the familiar flower vendor on the corner.

He parked his car a little way up the road, avoiding an overflowing trashcan that seemed to have attracted an accompanying heap of garbage sacks. He guessed it was trash collection day in Midtown.

It was warm out, and he passed a group of children playing marbles in the street, as well as a small café serving coffee to people sitting out at small chrome tables. They hardly noticed him as he breezed past, intent on their own conversations, and he decided it wasn't worth asking if any of them might have seen Ginny.

The apartment itself was a basement flat in a crumbling brownstone, one of a row of such properties lining the street. The two flats above showed signs of activity; the silhouette of someone moving about behind the uppermost window, and from the ground floor he could hear the strains of a badly played piano, and people's voices, raised above the music.

Ginny's place, however, looked utterly deserted.

He walked down the steps, noting the gathered detritus in the lobby by her door. Decaying leaves, pages from an old newspaper, even an empty wine bottle had tumbled down here, tossed around by the wind. They were piled up against the door, suggesting it hadn't been opened in some time. Abandoned post was wedged in the letterbox, and the faded curtains were drawn shut, meaning he couldn't peer in through the window.

Just to be sure, he rapped loudly on the door, listening for any sound of movement within. When no one answered he tried the handle, but the door was firmly locked.

Despondent, but certain that he hadn't missed anything, Gabriel decided to leave his car where it was and walk the rest of the way to his apartment. He had to make some more flechettes in the workshop before he went out to meet Donovan that night, and then find something to help take the edge off the pain.

SIX

"Don't touch *anything*. Either of you."

Donovan grinned as Dr. Vettel led him and Mullins through the labyrinthine corridors of the morgue to where she was keeping the bodies. She'd finally deemed it fitting to carry out an autopsy on the woman they'd found the night before last, Autumn Allen, and was in the midst of examining a male corpse that had been fished out of the river earlier that afternoon.

He liked Vettel—not in an inappropriate sort of way, although he had to admit, she did have her charms—but because she'd evidently decided early on in her career that she wasn't going to take any bullshit, from anyone, no matter who they were. She had a confident, straightforward manner, and she was damn good at her job. Despite all his years on the job, Donovan couldn't think of another police surgeon who came close.

Mullins, on the other hand, seemed rather intimidated by the woman, and he dealt with this by adopting a rather brusque countenance in her presence. He'd snapped at her on the way in, and now, realizing his error, was walking one step behind Donovan, attempting to keep out of her way. Donovan found the whole thing most amusing.

"Through here," she said, holding the door open for them. She was young for a doctor, or so it seemed to Donovan, who might just have been getting old. She was wearing a pleated skirt and a tangerine blouse, mostly covered by a stained white apron. She had an ample, attractive figure, and wore a small pair of glasses that seemed to pinch the bridge of her nose. Her brown hair was tied up in a casual knot, as if she'd hurriedly pinned it there that morning and forgotten to let it down.

Donovan and Mullins filed into the room. It might have been a large laboratory, if it weren't for the extra workbenches, racks of specimen jars, and operating slabs that had been crammed inside. Over each of the two slabs was a star-shaped cluster of pneumatic spurs, each one bristling with surgical tools. To Donovan they looked like large mechanical spiders, draping from the ceiling, each limb terminating in a deathly blade.

The slabs were both occupied, but thin cotton sheets covered the shapeless mounds. Donovan was grateful; he'd known surgeons in the past so desensitized to death that they could happily eat their lunch whilst finishing up an autopsy.

"The woman, Autumn Allen," said Vettel, allowing the door to swing shut behind them. "I've taken a full body scan. We can bring it up on the terminal over there." She crossed to a fixture on the wall that resembled the mirrored cavity on a holotube terminal, only far larger. She took a series of glass plates from the workbench beside it and slid them into a row of thin horizontal slots, then flicked a switch. The machine hummed for a moment as the bulb warmed up, and then it blinked on, and an image slowly resolved. It was a full-scale replica of the dead woman's body, rendered in sharp blue light.

"That's remarkable," said Mullins, eyes wide with surprise.

Vettel smiled. "Impressive, isn't it? And particularly useful when some of the more squeamish members of the force come down from the precinct."

Donovan wasn't sure whether the comment was aimed at him or Mullins. He went over to join her, seeing now that there were even more symbols carved into her body—one on her thigh, and another on her belly. "They must have hoisted her dress up to do these," he said. "It wasn't torn, or I'd have noticed them on the night."

"And the one on her back?" said Vettel. "Did you notice that?"

Donovan shook his head. She slid two of the glass plates out of the machine and replaced them with others. The image shuddered, and when it resolved again, he was seeing the woman from behind. Just as Vettel had said, there was a symbol on her back, right between the shoulder blades. It was a lozenge with a flattened end, and inside were what appeared to be an ibis, a semicircle, two parallel lines and a seated figure with a bird's head. The lines had been drawn with excruciating, exacting care. Donovan had no idea what they meant.

"This one was done after she was dead," said Vettel. "The others while she was alive. You can tell by the way the lines are all so precise."

"She wasn't struggling," said Donovan.

"Precisely."

"And what's your opinion, Dr. Vettel?" said Donovan. "On what happened to her."

"Opinion? I don't offer opinions, Inspector. I present *facts*. It's up to you how you turn them into theories, suppositions and outright works of fiction after that."

Donovan fixed her with an impatient glower.

"All right, all right," she said theatrically, throwing her hands up in the air. "The truth of the matter is this—Autumn Allen had been out for a pleasant evening in town. She'd dined well, drunk enough to make her tipsy, and then had vigorous sex."

"Consensual?" asked Mullins.

"The evidence would seem to suggest so, yes." Vettel had started pacing, but her eyes were seeing someplace else, watching the events unfolding in her mind. "Sometime later, within a few hours of leaving her lover's bed, she was accosted in the street, beaten into submission, and then held down while those markings were cut into her flesh with the tip of an exceptionally sharp knife. She tried to struggle, but the men were too strong—and I do believe it was men who carried out this attack—pinning her down by the shoulders and ankles as one of their number carried out the deed."

Vettel stopped pacing suddenly, leaning against her filing cabinet, looking at Donovan. "When they'd finished, they throttled her to death, carved the final symbol, and then left her on the sidewalk. It was another few hours before her body was called in, and my ass was hauled out of bed by your sergeant, here."

"We all have our crosses to bear," said Donovan. "It'll teach you to be so bloody good at your job." He reached inside his jacket for his cigarettes, but caught sight of the look on Vettel's face, and stopped, leaving them where they were. He pointed to the wound on the back of the hologram. "Any idea what the markings mean?"

"They're Ancient Egyptian in origin," said Vettel. "Or at least they purport to be, but I'll remind you, *again*, that *you're* the detective. I might be an expert in human anatomy, but I don't know the first thing about dead languages from the other side of the world." She smiled, clearly enjoying herself. "Nevertheless, I've cleaned up all the wounds and photographed them for you. I thought that might make it easier for you to get out there and do some actual 'detecting'."

She picked up a brown paper folder containing a sheaf of photographs, and handed it to Donovan. He passed it straight to Mullins, who regarded it with a plaintive expression, and put it down on the workbench beside him.

"Thank you," said Donovan. "One further question. How many men do you think were responsible?"

Vettel sighed. "Impossible to say for certain. At least five, I'd warrant, judging by the pattern of bruises around her ankles and upper arms. This was no impulsive attack, Inspector. Whoever did this had a plan, and they executed it to perfection."

"You almost sound as if you *admire* them," said Mullins.

"I admire the tenacity, the work that went into it. But if I ever got hold of the bastards responsible, I'd cut off their balls with my scalpel and serve them back to them as moonshine." She pressed her glasses back up to the bridge of her nose. "Does that answer your question?"

Mullins looked at the floor.

"Tell us about this other body, then, the one fished out of the Hudson at lunchtime."

Vettel crossed to one of the slabs, pulling back the cotton sheet with a gesture like a stage magician whisking a tablecloth from under a tea service. Donovan winced at the sight of the pale, bloated flesh, and the man's horrific expression, his lips peeled back from his teeth, his jaws clenched. His eyes were still open, but misted over now, milky and staring. He looked feral, like a rabid dog that had been forcibly put down. He realized that might not have been too far from the mark.

"Interesting one, this," said Vettel. "I've only had him for a couple of hours, so I've not yet been able to render up a scan. But look at these..." She lifted the man's arm and pointed out a series of round puckered holes in the flesh, each around the size of a quarter.

"Good God," said Donovan. "He's covered in them." He could see now that similar holes had been punched into both legs, his chest, even the back of his neck. He suspected if he rolled the body over, he'd see them on his back, too. "What did this to him?"

"The question you're looking for is 'who'," said Vettel. "These holes go right down to the bone. In fact, they go *into* the bone. There's evidence that metal rods had been screwed into the man's skeleton. They would have protruded from the flesh, maybe forming a sort of metal cage, or exoskeleton."

"Were they introduced post-mortem?" said Donovan.

"Oh, no," replied Vettel. "This man's been thoroughly brutalized. These were fitted while he was alive. He's been walking around wearing the fittings for some time. Weeks, I'd say, if not longer. He's undergone multiple surgeries. He'll have been in constant pain, and when I get chance to run the blood report later this afternoon, I expect I'll find evidence of high-caliber painkillers in his system. He couldn't have survived without them."

"And these rods had already been removed when he was found?" said Donovan. He was having a hard time conceiving how anyone could withstand having such equipment bolted *into* his or her body like this.

Vettel shook her head. "Yes. After the victim had died. It seems someone came looking for their equipment and removed it, before tossing what was left of him in the river."

"Salvage?" said Donovan, rhetorically. "Or perhaps simply to prevent us from finding it." Vettel shrugged. "I've heard talk that the mob have been assembling an army of mechanized men such as this. I'd wager a month's salary on the fact we'll turn up some sort of connection between this man and the Reaper." Donovan looked at the dead man's face again. He was going to be almost impossible to identify from facial records; the flesh was too bloated and damaged, and there was evidence that he'd taken a beating. He thought he knew who was responsible.

"Nothing on him that would help us to identify him? A wallet?"

"When he landed here he was as naked as the day he was born," said Vettel. "On his back, there's a bloodied patch of skin that suggests someone's hurriedly removed a tattoo or other identifying mark. They've been very thorough. They don't want us figuring out who he is."

"So what killed him?" said Donovan. "The surgeries? The stress of wearing the suit?"

"No, although that would certainly have killed him after a time. There's evidence he was dropped from a great height, however. Whatever exoskeleton he was wearing couldn't fully absorb the shock. One of the spurs clearly snapped and punctured his chest, and his neck was broken from the fall. Additionally, there are signs he'd been brawling. There are slashes here, here, and here," she said, pointing them out. "Look familiar?"

Donovan nodded. The wounds were little sickle-shaped gashes in his chest—the hallmark left behind by the Ghost's flechettes. That clinched it, then—this was the Enforcer that Gabriel had fought the other night, the one who'd given him a beating. There was no doubt he was associated with the Reaper. The problem was in proving it. He caught Mullins's eye, and a flash of understanding passed between them.

"Have you ever seen work like this before?" he asked Vettel. "Not the wounds, but the other stuff, the surgeries."

"I've seen similar. There was a man named Spectorius, a good doctor, but had a bit of a taste for the macabre. He got himself struck off when some of your boys discovered he'd been experimenting on immigrants and homeless people. He went underground after that, and I think for a time he got mixed up with the Roman."

"I remember," said Donovan. "We never found him when we raided the Roman's mansion. Cleared out his workshop, but there was no sign of Spectorius himself."

"It's just a hunch," said Vettel, "but he might be tied up in all this."

"I thought you didn't offer opinions," said Donovan, with a grin.

Vettel put her hand on her hip. "Go on. Get out of my lab. I've had enough of you now, poking around, asking questions. I've got work to do."

Donovan laughed. "You know where to find me if you turn up anything else," he said.

"What more do you want?" said Vettel. "The culprits all parceled up ready for you, tied neatly with string?"

"That'd be nice," said Donovan.

"Go!" said Vettel, pointing to the door and feigning indignation. Donovan, though, could see the hint of a smile playing across her lips.

"Come on, Mullins," he said, patting him on the shoulder, "before she gets a hold of one of those scalpels and comes after you. We don't want any of that moonshine she mentioned."

Mullins, visibly paling at the thought, didn't look back as he reached for the door, and Donovan, following after, heard Vettel chuckling to herself as he pulled it shut behind him.

SEVEN

The view from the roof of the police precinct was as breathtaking as ever, and for the first time in days, the Ghost felt truly alive.

He was balanced on the low wall that formed a lip around the roof, standing right on the corner, high above an intersection. The updraft was buffeting him, causing his coat to billow out behind him, rippling at his back. He filled his lungs with the scent of the street below: the frying onions on a hotdog stand, the reek of spilled beer from a speakeasy frequented by every policeman he knew, the floral bouquet of a woman who'd indulged in too much perfume.

He held his arms out by his sides, and looked out across the glittering landscape of sweeping canyons, each of them flanked by regimented cliffs of bricks, metal, and glass. From here he could see Atlas—the immense holographic sculpture in Union Square, bearing the weight of the world on his shoulders—and felt a certain kinship with him. All across the city, the fingers of police searchlights reached down from hovering blimps, teasing apart the shadows below.

There was no sign of any glowing phantom, and for that he was thankful; he had enough on his mind, and Donovan—who he could hear crossing the rooftop behind him—was about to add to his burden with talk of a dead woman.

"Come on down from there before you fall," said Donovan. "I'd have to answer some very awkward questions, and there'd be a hell of a lot of paperwork."

The Ghost heard the familiar sound of a cigarette being drawn from its packet, followed by the flare of the ignition tab. He turned, dropping down from the wall to the graveled rooftop. "Evening, Felix."

"Hmmm," mumbled Donovan, around the butt of his cigarette. "You're still alive then."

"I was lucky," said the Ghost. "Those Enforcers aren't like anything we've faced before. The Reaper's building an army, and if we don't find a way to stop them soon, he'll have the run of the place."

Donovan nodded. "Do you ever get the feeling we're already too late? Sometimes, this job… it's like fighting against the tide. There are days when I think I'd be happier if I just allowed it to wash over me. Or put on a mask, like you, and kicked the crap out of something."

"Now that's the lack of sleep talking," said the Ghost. "You're tired, Felix. Take a vacation."

"A vacation? I wouldn't make it off the island before they summoned me back. We're undermanned and overworked, and half the men in the tertiary precincts are already turning a blind eye for a glimpse of the Reaper's dollar."

"Then hire more women," said the Ghost.

Donovan laughed. "You know, that's probably the best idea I've heard yet. I'll put it to the Commissioner." He took a long draw from his cigarette and let the smoke spill out slowly from the corner of his mouth. "We found your man, by the way. His body had been dumped in the Hudson. Washed up this afternoon. All the equipment had gone, but it was obviously the man you told me about. Someone had drilled holes in his arms, legs, and chest. Vettel said she could see where the metal rods had been removed from the bones."

"I had to throw him off a building," said the Ghost, "and he almost survived that, too. Did you manage to identify him yet?"

Donovan shook his head. "He certainly wasn't local. We're thinking maybe he was an immigrant, brought in by the Reaper. It seems he has a line in sneaking people over the border."

"Larceny, murder, bribery and people trafficking—and still we can't touch him."

"He's a wily bastard," said Donovan. "Always does enough to keep his own hands clean. That's why we need you, digging in ways we can't."

"For what it's worth," said the Ghost. "Tell me about this dead woman."

"Her name was Autumn Allen. Her body was discovered on the sidewalk two nights ago. She'd been throttled to death, but not before her killers had held her down and carved a series of icons into her face, arms, and chest." Donovan reached into his jacket and produced a roll of photographs, which he unfurled and held out to the Ghost. "They carved another one on her back after she was dead, too."

He took them, studying them for a moment, then rolled them up again, slipping them inside his own coat. "Egyptian," he said. "Although I don't recognize the one on her arm." He frowned. "You think they have something to do with Ginny and the *Centurion*?"

"The thought hadn't even occurred to me," said Donovan, "but now you come to mention it, isn't there some big exhibition coming to the Met?"

The Ghost nodded. "They were unloading the exhibits when I was down at the docks yesterday. But the ship didn't come in until *after* the woman was found dead. The timing doesn't add up."

"Still, I don't like coincidences," said Donovan. "It seems a little unlikely that we'd turn up a body scored with Ancient Egyptian symbols the night before a new exhibition arrives in the city, and they *not* be connected."

"Perhaps," said the Ghost. "So that's what you wanted to tell me?"

"No," said Donovan. "I wanted you to see if you could find out what the symbols mean. You have… connections. We've already sent copies to the museum, but I was thinking there might be some significance the historians are likely to miss, if you see what I mean?"

The Ghost nodded. "I'll do what I can do."

"There's another thing," said Donovan. "In her handbag she was carrying this." He took a small black card from his pocket. "It's a business card for a jazz club we believe to be connected to the Reaper, Café Deluxe."

"A mob girl?" said the Ghost. That would be a turn-up.

Donovan shrugged. "We're looking into it. But someone had spent a lot of money buying her diamonds. She was still wearing them when we found her."

"The killer didn't take them?"

"Interesting, isn't it? That's what made me think there was something more to the symbols, some religious or occult significance."

"Or the mark of a rival gang," said the Ghost, "striking back at the Reaper. He's made a lot of enemies."

"That too," said Donovan. He dropped the butt of his cigarette and ground it beneath his heel.

"And Ginny," said the Ghost. "Did you manage to get a look at the passenger manifest?"

"Not exactly," said Donovan, "but the Second Mate was very helpful on the holotube. He did a little digging around and called me back. She was definitely on the ship, Gabriel. Cabin thirty-five. You must have missed her somehow."

"You're sure?" said the Ghost. "It couldn't be a mistake?"

"I can't see how. According to the Second Mate she even had dinner with the Captain one night." Donovan looked pained. "I'm sorry. I know it's not what you wanted to hear, but she's back in New York."

Then where was she? Something had happened to her. He was sure of it. "All right, then I need to find her."

"What if she doesn't want to be found?"

"Then I'll walk away. But first, I need to know she's okay. People don't just disappear, Felix."

"You checked her apartment?"

"Still locked up and empty. No one's been there for months."

"I'll tell Mullins to put word out," said Donovan. "Treat it as a Missing Persons."

"Thank you," said the Ghost.

"Least I can do," said Donovan, "but remember—that

woman knows how to look after herself. If something *has* happened to her, woe betide any man who's got in her way."

The Ghost hopped up onto the wall, reaching inside his coat for the ignition cord that would activate the boosters strapped to his calves.

"Where next?" said Donovan, reaching for another cigarette.

"The *Centurion*," said the Ghost. "I'm going to take a look for myself. Ginny, the exhibition, the dead woman—maybe even the Reaper—they all have ties to that ship, one way or another. I'm going to give it a kick and see what falls out."

"Be careful," said Donovan. "You're in no fit state for a brawl."

His words were lost, however, by the roar of the Ghost's boosters, as he shot up into the air on a plume of brilliant flame, streaking across the skyline toward the docks.

EIGHT

The *Centurion* hulked in the dock, ominous and dark.

The Ghost circled high above, observing the deck for any signs of habitation. It was a cool night, and the sea breeze played across his face, making him feel alert and ready, despite the nagging pain in his chest.

He'd expected to find guards or dockworkers patrolling the vessel, but the deck appeared silent and still, and even the lights in the small office on the dock had been put out. The only sounds were the roar of the canisters strapped to his calves, and the rhythmic *shushing* of the ocean.

He cut the fuel line, causing the booster jets to sputter and spit, and then fall silent, guttering to nothing as he slowly descended, feet first, to the deck. He hugged the shadows close to the main funnel, keeping low. If there were any guards down on the dock, he'd sooner not give them cause for alarm. The last thing he wanted was a firefight with a bunch of innocent men.

The upper deck had been packed away since he'd stood on the quayside below, watching the passengers milling around while they waited to disembark. The chairs had been upended on the tabletops and tied into place with lengths of blue twine, and canvas tarpaulins had been stretched over all of the lifeboats. The deck had been scrubbed and polished, too; the boards gleamed, even in the moonlight, and he could smell the oils they'd rubbed into the wood. He guessed the ship would be setting out on the next leg of its journey within a day or two, or perhaps making a return trip to Egypt and the far-off ports of the Middle East.

He took a moment to get his bearings, and then, still clinging to the shadows, crossed the deck to a set of double doors, which he presumed would open up onto a staircase and down into the main passenger areas.

He tried the handle, but, unsurprisingly, found them locked. A quick shove splintered the wood around the mechanism, however, and within seconds he was inside, the door wedged shut behind him.

It was dark in the stairwell, so he adjusted his goggles to their night-vision setting, casting everything in a pale red glow. Cautiously, he crept down the carpeted stairs, still wary of triggering some sort of alarm.

The stairs opened up onto a lower deck resplendent in its finery; crystal chandeliers dripped from molded rosettes on the ceiling, plush red carpets lined the floors, gilt-framed mirrors and portraits dressed the papered walls. It might have been the interior of a top-end hotel, rather than the communal deck of a steam liner. Little expense had been spared.

He could imagine the sort of conversations that had passed here, at the foot of these stairs—the same sort that he heard at his Long Island parties, night after night—vacant of all real meaning, just the petty chit-chat of self-obsessed elitists massaging one another's egos. He couldn't see Ginny fitting in here. She'd probably spent most of the journey up on the deck, taking in the view, or else locked away in her cabin with her books.

Now that he was here, he wasn't entirely sure what he was looking for. There was no point searching for the manifest—Donovan had answered that question. What he needed was some sort of proof that she'd really been here, on the ship, and not just a logged entry in a book.

Donovan had said she'd been registered in cabin thirty-five. That seemed the logical place to start. He'd have to make his way down through the First Class decks until he found it.

Moving swiftly, he crossed the foyer, skirting the lounge and passing through a set of double doors into a lobby area. There were elevators here, but he decided not to risk using them, preferring to seek out the stairs. There was less chance of anyone noticing him if he kept to himself and didn't make use of any of the facilities—lights included.

Three decks further down, a sign directed him through another door to a passageway leading to cabins twenty-nine through thirty-nine. He took it, noting how the furnishings down here were still reminiscent of a New York hotel, with rich carpets and brass fittings on all the doors. He couldn't conceive of how much the whole thing had cost to build, and, likewise, to maintain; there had to be a veritable army of staff and servants onboard when she was at sea.

He found cabin thirty-five within minutes, and this time, was surprised to discover the door was unlocked. It was pitch black inside the room, but his goggles compensated, and he slipped inside, pulling the door shut behind him.

It was a small space for a First Class cabin, despite its

evident luxury; a chaise longue, a fireplace, a small vanity table and a plush double bed, draped in silk sheets. A smaller antechamber proved to house a small bathroom and toilet, now devoid of any toiletries, and twin wardrobes which were equally empty of any effects. A maid had evidently prepared the room for the next guest: the sheets had been changed, the bed made, the carpets brushed. There was nothing of Ginny's here, no hairbrush, no clothes, no evidence she had been here at all. Even the scent of her had been polished out of the woodwork with a liberal application of beeswax.

He checked beneath the bed, just in case; opened the drawers in the vanity unit. There was nothing at all.

He noted that a small door led to the adjoining cabin. It was bolted shut from this side, so he slid the bolt and crept through. The room mirrored cabin thirty-five in nearly every way, clearly built to the same schematic, only reversed. Here, the same was true as in Ginny's room; the maids had done a thorough job erasing all evidence of the previous passenger. All save for a small white patch on the carpet.

Interested, the Ghost dropped to his haunches, removing his glove and pinching some of the powdery substance between the thumb and forefinger of his right hand. It was dry and crumbly. He raised it to his nose and cautiously sniffed, surprised to discover that it wasn't, as he imagined, a trace of some illicit narcotic, but simple white chalk. He ran his fingers through the carpet, causing tiny plumes of dust to form in their wake. It seemed the maids hadn't been quite as thorough as they should have been; there was evidence here that someone had been using the chalk to draw outlines on the carpet. Whatever shape it had been was now long gone, but the realization loosened a tumble of thoughts in the Ghost's mind.

Chalk circles? The witches of Godfrey Place had used chalk circles to enact their foul rituals. He supposed it might be a leap to imagine someone on this ship had been carrying out similar elaborate practices, but the ritualistic murder of Autumn Allen was still preying on his mind. The Egyptian connection just seemed too coincidental. And now he had discovered this, in the room directly connected to the one in which Ginny had supposedly been staying. He didn't like the implication of that one bit.

Rising, he quickly checked over the rest of the room, but again, found nothing save for more vestiges of chalk dust, which the maid had obviously found difficult to properly remove.

The door to this cabin was also open to the passageway—as, he presumed, they all would be, until they became occupied again—and he stepped out, careful to leave the inner door pulled shut behind him.

He considered heading up to the bridge, but suspected he'd find nothing there but further log books and charts. If a conspiracy of some sort had taken place aboard this vessel, it was unlikely the captain would have known about it. More likely, the people involved would have had assistance from among the junior members of the crew.

The crew quarters, then, might be a place to look for answers, but as he'd already established, there would be hundreds of them aboard, and without any indication of whom or what he was looking for, it would be like searching for a needle in a haystack. There was always the risk that one or two of them might still be onboard, too—while most had evidently taken the opportunity to explore the iniquitous speakeasies and jazz clubs of the city, some would inevitably have remained here, and he risked raising the alarm if he started rooting through cabins without any real sense of what he was looking for.

Better, he decided, that he take a look at the holds where the antiquities had been transported, to see if he could find anything that might connect the expedition with Autumn Allen. If so, he and Donovan would then be able to go after the expedition leader in search of answers.

The Ghost moved through the ship like a specter, swift and silent. He hurried through the passenger decks and down into the grubby engineering section of the ship, thick with the mingling scents of oil and rust. He'd been impressed by the scale of the vessel from the quayside, but the sight of the engines themselves left him feeling utterly dwarfed. Enormous furnaces, now cold, warmed pressurized water tanks, which in turn drove huge pistons, each the size of tree trunks, to turn the wheels that powered the ship's rudders.

The hangar housing these engines spanned the entire girth of the ship, and was as tall as a small apartment building. Every footfall he made on the iron gangway as he passed through echoed like a ricocheting bullet.

He reached the first cargo hold ten minutes later to find it empty. There was evidence that heaps of crates had been stored here recently: loose strands of packing straw, scattered sand, splinters of wood. The crates themselves had all gone, carted off the ship and up to the museum. Large metal hooks dangled from chains overhead—used to secure expensive cargo or provide support to the cranes as they attempted to load and unload the crates from the ship.

He cast around, searching for anything at all that might help him to understand what had happened on the ship, but there was nothing. It was just an empty hangar, on an empty ship.

All he'd been able to find was a smattering of chalk dust, which might or might not indicate something untoward. It was tenuous at best.

He supposed he was going to have to call in a favor with Arthur over at the Met, see if he couldn't get a look at the exhibition early, before it opened to the public. Maybe there was some clue in the artifacts themselves.

He crossed the hangar, ducking through a doorway into the adjoining cargo hold. Here, too, there was evidence that a large number of crates had been recently removed; only there was one major difference—a single wooden packing crate still stood in one corner.

It was large, about the size of a small room, presumably containing some significant relic from the dig. A statue, maybe? The head of a colossus? Judging by the size of the crate, it would have to be a centerpiece to the whole exhibition.

It seemed odd that it had been left here unattended while everything else had already been unloaded, but he supposed the dockworkers might have found themselves in need of a bigger crane to take the weight, or an alternative means of transporting it uptown.

He crossed the hangar, circling the crate. The sides were unmarked panels, nailed onto a wooden frame. Around the front, he was surprised to see two freestanding statues, just abandoned in the shadow of the crate. One resembled a human female with the head of a lioness. She was seated on a plinth, which had clearly been damaged at some point in the long forgotten past, so that the hieroglyphics carved upon it were scratched and undecipherable. She had her arms folded across her naked chest, one hand holding an ankh, the other a rod or scepter. She'd been hewn in smooth black stone, and her eyes watched him impassively as he circled around, studying her.

The other statue bore a similar aspect, also seated upon a plinth. This one resembled a bare-chested male with the head of an ibis. Its curved beak was partially absent, and one of its arms was missing, lending it a strangely maudlin appearance. This one also carried an ankh, its surviving arm lowered by its side. It had a sun disc headdress, similar to the one he'd seen carved into Autumn's forehead, and the base of its plinth was covered in neat white columns of pictograms. In the near darkness of the ship's hold, they seemed eerie; things that didn't belong in the here and now, relics from an ancient past that should have remained forgotten. The Ghost couldn't help but feel there was good reason why the old religions had been extinguished; his experience with the Roman had left a deep, unsettling scar.

These, though, were simple statues; artifacts recovered from the hot sands of the past and brought here to be gazed upon by thousands of admiring New Yorkers. Despite their unsettling aspect, they posed no threat.

Nevertheless, it seemed odd that they should have been unpacked from their transportation crates here, in the hold of the ship. Surely the museum would have expected to receive them by now, along with all the others? Perhaps, he decided, they were rejects, too damaged to put on display alongside the more pristine examples that had already been chosen for the exhibition.

Frowning, he approached the crate, looking for a means to see inside. There was a door round the front, cut into the wooden panel and hinged to allow access. It was padlocked shut. He leaned closer, trying to peer through the thin crack between the door and the frame to ascertain what was inside. It was too dark, even with his night-vision goggles. He was going to have to break the lock.

Behind him, something groaned. It was a long, drawn-out sound, like rending metal, and at first he thought it was the hull of the ship, settling with the change in temperature. When it started again a second later, he realized it resembled more closely the sound of grating stone. He turned, his mouth suddenly dry.

The lion-headed statue was getting down from its plinth.

The Ghost edged back, flicking his wrist so that the barrel of his flechette gun ratcheted up and around, clicking into place along the length of his forearm.

The statue lurched forward, its movements jerky and deliberate. He glanced at the other to see that it, too, was now pulling itself free of its perch, raising its remaining arm to hold its ankh aloft, as if calling for divine intervention.

This, the Ghost realized, was why the two statues had been left unguarded on the ship. They *were* the guards. Someone wanted the contents of that crate to remain very much unseen.

The two statues marched toward him, their feet clanging on

the metal floor of the hangar. He wondered what was powering them, whether there was a control mechanism hidden inside of them, like the automatons he'd fought before.

"Um, listen," he said, holding out a placating hand. "I really don't think this is a good idea." He glanced at the one on the left. "I mean—you've already lost an arm. I'm sure you don't want to lose another? Why don't the two of you return to your seats, and I'll be on my way?"

The ibis-headed statue leaned forward, its jaws levering open to reveal a wriggling, barbed tongue. It hissed, and the sound was like a pressure valve releasing. It was one of the most unearthly sounds the Ghost had ever heard, and he felt his hackles rising.

"No, I didn't think so," he said. He raised his arm, squeezed the trigger and released a hail of flechettes at the creature. The tiny blades struck home, but they pinged harmlessly off the stone, failing to leave even a single scratch.

"Ah," said the Ghost. "This is going to be interesting."

The lion-headed statue was close to him now, and it pulled its arm back and took a swing at his head, using its scepter like a glaive. He dropped and rolled, coming back up to his feet and firing into its face. Once again, his flechettes had no effect. The creatures really did appear to be made from stone.

The other one was nearly on top of him now, and he cast around for anything he could use to ward it off. There was nothing, not even a length of pipe. It swung at him, and he raised his arm, twisting it so that the barrel of his flechette gun would take the impact. It connected with a resounding clang, and the vibration in his forearm made him cry out in pain, falling back, clutching at his wrist. Cringing, he flexed his fingers. Thankfully, it wasn't broken.

The statues stalked forward, full of menacing intent. He glanced back the way he had come, wondering if he could reach the door in time, but decided he wouldn't make it. They were slow, but not *that* slow.

They were closing in, trying to shut him down with a pincer movement. His only advantage was the fact one of them was missing its arm, but he couldn't yet see a way to use that against them.

Behind them, the stabilizing hooks hung from the ceiling, dangling on massive chains. If he could get to those…

The bird-headed statue punched out at him, its stone ankh still clutched in its fist like a knuckle-duster. He twisted, and the blow missed his chin, glancing off his chest as he leaned back, trying to dodge out of its way. His broken ribs erupted in pain, and he staggered, dropping to one knee.

He felt another blow connect with his kidneys, and threw himself on the ground, rolling just in time to avoid a cracked skull, as one of the stone feet struck the floor where his head had been just a split second earlier.

Quickly, he forced himself up onto one knee, pain flaring in his chest, and pulled the ignition cord for his boosters, propelling himself up toward the roof.

The lion goddess was too quick, however, and jerked at the last moment, aiming a blow that caught him hard in the back of the knee and sent him spinning wildly off target. He shot across the hangar, trying desperately to alter his trajectory. The wooden crate loomed before him, and he buried his face in the crook of his elbow as he collided with it, unable to gain enough height to clear it. The wood splintered beneath the impact, and he fell through into the void inside, slamming into the far wall and tumbling onto the ground.

Groggily, he got to his feet. He was standing in a small room that resembled the interior of an ancient tomb or temple, complete with piles of gilded treasures and accoutrements inlaid with precious stones. The walls were covered in crudely painted hieroglyphics. Whatever was going on here, the interior of the crate had been carefully constructed to resemble a scene from ancient times.

He didn't have time to worry about it now, though—the statues had continued their relentless pursuit, and he could see them through the hole in the wall, closing in.

He angled his shoulders at the hole, and fired up his boosters again. This time he sailed over the heads of the statues, catching hold of one of the massive stabilizing hooks and swinging himself around, using the weight of it as an anchor. He angled his body, hovering for a moment, waiting for a clear shot. The lion-headed statue was lumbering beneath him, glaring up at him with her pristine black eyes.

The Ghost drew a deep breath, and then, using all of his upper body strength, hauled down on the smaller chain securing the hook. There was a clanking sound from overhead as the chain lurched free of its housing, the links clinking against one another as the massive weight of the hook suddenly took up the excess slack, yanking more and more of the chain free from the reel.

The hook fell like a dead weight, striking the lion-headed

statue right between the eyes. It shattered explosively, hunks of stone tumbling across the floor of the hangar. The entire vessel seemed to shake beneath the impact, and the other statue trembled with the reverberation, almost going over as the hook struck the deck.

The Ghost knew he didn't have long now; the noise would have been heard out on the dock, and people would be dispatched immediately to investigate.

He cut the power to his boosters, drifting slowly to the ground. The other statue turned and lurched toward him, hissing angrily.

He knew he'd only have one shot at this, and he was taking a huge risk, but it seemed like his best shot. He stood his ground as the statue approached, aiming his flechette gun as if he were about to unleash another barrage. Then, at the last minute, as the statue closed the gap between them, he dropped into a crouch, fired his boosters, and grabbed hold of the statue's waist.

He felt its fist slam into his back, the base of the ankh gouging his flesh, but he held on as the boosters fought against the weight, raising the two grappling figures off the ground.

Just a little higher… just a little higher…

He let go, pushing himself free of the statue and sending himself into a spiraling upward motion as the force of his boosters, now suddenly free of their burden, sent him careening toward the roof.

The only force acting upon the statue, however, was gravity. It fell, twisting in the air, reaching out with its good arm in a pointless attempt to protect itself. It struck the floor with a thud, face down, its torso cracking into three, its head rolling free of its neck. Its arm, still clutching the ankh, gave a final, jerking spasm, before falling still.

The Ghost struck the ceiling, rebounding painfully, jarring his shoulder and causing more pain to flare in his chest. He hooked his arm out, catching hold of a bundle of chain, and pulled himself to a stop, panting for breath.

He hovered there for a moment, watching the ruins of the statues on the deck. Then, certain that it was over, he cut the power to his boosters and gently lowered himself to the floor. He was smarting all over, and could feel blood running freely down the crease of his spine, from where the statue had jammed its ankh into him.

He crouched over the remains, tentatively turning over a hunk of stone. There were no visible circuits or brass sub-frame here; the statues appeared to be just that—carved from blocks of solid stone. How, then, had they suddenly come to life to attack him? He wondered if the Enforcer had given him a knock around the head, as well as the chest—if he wasn't imagining it all. The evidence was right here before him, though, and he had the wounds to prove it.

He stood, kicking around amongst the shattered remains for a moment until he found what he was looking for—a hand, broken at the wrist, still clutching an ankh. He stooped and picked it up, slipping it into his coat pocket. He'd have someone examine it later to see if there was something he was missing. There had to be *some* evidence of buried technology there, somewhere.

He crossed to the wooden crate, looking up at the ragged

gash he'd made in the side panel during the fight. Whoever had been trying to keep this thing hidden here was going to be pissed, he was certain of that.

With both hands, he grabbed at the splintered panel around the hole and pulled, prising it open a little further. He tossed the broken piece of wood on the ground by his feet. Then, hauling himself up, he climbed inside.

His initial impressions of the small room had been of a temple or tomb, and now that he had chance to study it properly, he realized it was a burial chamber—or at least an approximation of one. He'd seen grainy photographs of the interior of Tutankhamun's tomb in the *National Geographic* a few years earlier, and the layout here was similar, if more compact: a large wooden casket rested in the center of the floor, decorated in elaborate gold leaf, and vertical columns of hieroglyphs.

Lining the edges of the chamber were piles of gilded grave goods—footstools, headrests, Canopic jars, the wheels from a chariot, spears—while the walls themselves were covered in detailed pictograms, presumably a facsimile of the story of the dead king or queen whose tomb it was intended to recreate.

Most of one wall was missing now, but he circled the chamber, taking in what he could of the story. The lion-headed goddess—the one whose statue had attacked him—featured prominently in the artwork; here at the head of a line of charging chariots; there bestowing gifts upon the workers who had erected great statues in her name.

In one scene she stood before a kneeling woman, her hands held just above the woman's head, glowing light spreading from her fingertips. In another, soon after, the kneeling woman was standing, arms outstretched, head tossed back, ethereal lions billowing out of the darkness behind her.

The ibis-headed god was present, too, along with a symbol the Ghost recognized. He fumbled in his pocket for a moment, withdrawing the sheaf of photographs Donovan had given him on the roof. He spread them out on top of the casket until he found the one he'd been looking for—the cartouche, depicting someone's name. It was here, too, just beneath a painting of the ibis-headed god.

He bundled the photographs up again, returning them to his pocket. Was that enough of a link? If it was simply the name of an Ancient Egyptian deity, then surely it was ubiquitous? He'd have to talk to Arthur or Astrid to be sure.

He turned his attention to the casket. Again, it was nothing but a prop, a hurriedly made approximation of the real thing. He could see where the wood had been hammered together with modern nails, hidden beneath a layer of hastily applied gold leaf.

The script on the outer casket was dense and unreadable, at least to someone so untrained in the art as the Ghost. Cautiously, he tried the lid. It came away easily, constructed from thin sheets of ply that had been covered in a layer of papier mâché.

Inside, he expected to find a coffin, but was surprised to see two pillows and a cotton sheet. It was a makeshift bed. It had been slept in recently, too; the sheets were mussed, and there was a depression in the pillows where the person's head had lain. It couldn't have been very comfortable, unless the person was out for the count. Someone must have kept them fed and watered throughout the trip, too. Was this their game, then?

People smuggling? Donovan had mentioned the Reaper's involvement in such activities. Could this be connected? Had they brought someone back from Egypt who wasn't on the passenger manifest? Or even... someone who was?

He reached in and grabbed one of the pillows. It carried the faint scent of women's perfume, along with a few loose strands of blonde hair.

The Ghost swallowed, his mouth suddenly dry. He recognized the scent immediately. It was one of Ginny's favorites. He'd spent lazy hours in bed beside her, breathing in that scent, tracing his fingers along the curve of her hip while she'd kissed his neck and playfully slapped his hands away.

What had she gone and gotten herself mixed up in?

He threw the pillow back where he'd found it, and replaced the casket lid. Again, there was every chance it was just a coincidence. There had to be hundreds, if not thousands of women out there with the same perfume. He had to avoid drawing conclusions, at least for now, despite everything his gut was telling him, despite the gnawing sense of fear. He needed proof. *Real* proof.

Something occurred to him, and he glanced back at the pictures on the wall. He hadn't noticed it earlier, but the woman kneeling before the lion goddess in the painting was blonde. He'd never seen a blonde Egyptian before.

The sound of distant voices brought his reverie to an end. He had to get out of there, and fast. He reached for the hole in the wall, pulling himself through. The dockworkers, or guards, or whoever was on their way, would be there within moments. The wreckage of the statues would hold their attention for a few minutes—long enough for him to get off the ship and be up on the nearby rooftops before the police were called in, assuming he could avoid running into them on his way out.

With one last glance back at the ruins of the wooden crate, the Ghost melted into the shadows, and slipped away.

NINE

The motorcar purred across the smooth desert sands, leaving two snaking trails across the starlit dunes.

Ginny sat in the back beside Amaury, peering out of the window in wonder. It was beautiful out here—desolate, but beautiful. Light was only now beginning to break over the horizon, a shining red disc shimmering across the glassy sand, like the world was only just waking from a long and restful slumber.

She'd risen shortly after midnight, bathed and dressed, and found the others waiting for her in the hotel lobby. They didn't look as if they'd been to bed, and sure enough, Landsworth had slept most of the way out here in the car, snoring noisily as their Egyptian driver wrestled with the wheel, leading them deeper and deeper into the empty desert.

They'd left Luxor behind them over an hour ago, and Ginny hadn't seen a landmark or settlement since. She had no idea how the driver had any sense of where he was going; he didn't even seem to be consulting a compass.

"It's very…"

"Bleak?" suggested Amaury.

"No, not bleak," said Ginny. "Just… well, I'm not sure, really. Peaceful, but… empty, I suppose. I'd expected to see more buildings, villages, towns, that sort of thing. Ruins, even.

I can't even see the city anymore. It's just… empty." She sighed. "If you were to strand me here now, I wouldn't have any sense of how to find my way back."

Amaury laughed. "The desert is a dangerous place, Miss Gray. You can rest assured that you will not have to find your own way back." He grinned. "Although you might be longing for it, soon enough."

The car was drawing to a stop. "What do you mean? What's going on?" she said, craning to see out of the windscreen.

They'd stopped before what appeared to be a small encampment, with pitched tents, a campfire, and a number of men milling about. On the edge of the camp, tied to a post by coils of thick rope, were four camels.

"Oh, you can't be serious," she said. "Camels!"

"I'm afraid the motorcar cannot take us any further," said Amaury, laughing. "The terrain becomes too uneven as we get closer to the site of the tomb." He shrugged. "And besides, you said you wanted to see the *real* Egypt."

"I said I wanted to see the *Luxor Temple*!" said Ginny, with mock protest. "I'm just glad that I didn't wear a nice dress."

"It'll be worth it," said Amaury. "Trust me. You're only the fourth westerner to visit this tomb. You have a chance to see it before the tourists descend and my friend Landsworth here strips it of everything valuable for his colleagues at the museum."

"What? What was that?" said Landsworth, suddenly jerking awake now that the engine had cut out. He twisted in his seat, looking back at Amaury. He narrowed his eyes. "You were talking about me, weren't you?"

Amaury laughed. "I was telling Miss Gray here that you'll soon have plundered the tomb for your exhibition, is all." He turned to Ginny. "That's why he's worried about the press. Doesn't want them giving everything away before he has chance for a grand unveiling."

"Which museum do you work for, Mr. Landsworth?" said Ginny.

"I'm more of a… freelancer," said Landsworth, "although this particular exhibition is being sponsored by the Metropolitan Museum of Art in New York City."

"My home town," said Ginny with a grin. "I'll make sure all my friends come along."

"Very kind of you," said Landsworth. "Now, what about these ruddy camels?" He clicked the door open and almost fell out of the car as his foot sank into the sand. Ginny stifled a laugh; Amaury wasn't so kind.

"Watch yourself there, Landsworth," he said. "We need you to keep the bank off our back."

"Glad to know I'm good for *something*," muttered Landsworth, before stomping off toward the camp, his feet kicking up little clouds of sand in his wake.

"Come on," said Amaury. "It's not far from here. Just another hour or so."

"An hour, on one of *those* things?"

"You'll be fine," said Amaury, opening his door. "What is it you say? 'It's just like riding a bicycle.'" He clambered out of the car, holding it open for Ginny to follow.

"I never learned to ride a bicycle!" she called after him, but his only reply was another heartfelt laugh.

* * *

An hour later, and Ginny had just about figured out how to remain seated on top of the creature as it lumbered ponderously across the sweeping sands.

The sun had risen now, bringing with it the first indication of the heat to come, and while the men had simply wrapped scarves around their heads—all beside Landsworth, who had insisted on wearing his hat—Ginny had managed to balance a parasol over one shoulder whilst clinging onto the saddle for dear life with the other.

She'd only fallen off twice, and while the others had found this rapturously funny, she was counting it as a success.

The landscape around them had altered, too; now there were rocky formations amongst the dunes, peeking out from beneath the golden sand. They'd passed the ruins of an ancient structure, now just a collapsed pillar and a tumbledown wall, still guarded by the gargantuan feet of the colossus who had once stood here. She was reminded of Shelley's "Ozymandias", and wondered what it had been like here once, in that long-lost era of great kings and bizarre ritual. Perhaps Amaury's tomb might provide some insight, some glimpse into the ancient past, a sense of what it must have been like to live amongst these people.

She watched him now, balanced expertly upon the back of his camel, quietly surveying the landscape. A cigarette drooped from the corner of his mouth, and his hand was raised to his eyes, shielding them from the harsh glare. He was handsome, she supposed, and amusing, and there were clear overtones to his interest in her. Yet she found she could not even consider him in that way. Or rather, she did not *want* to consider him like that.

All the way here she'd thought of Gabriel, and even now, thousands of miles away on a different continent, thirsty and perspiring on the back of a camel, her thoughts returned to him. She would send him a postcard when she returned to Luxor that evening, and begin making arrangements for her return to New York. She'd stay a few more weeks, make the journey back to Cairo to see the pyramids, and after that, take a berth on a steamship home. A month here would be long enough to see everything she wanted to see, to make the long journey worthwhile—and besides, she wasn't sure she could stand being away from him any longer than that. Not if she didn't have to.

She sensed another camel drawing up beside her, and turned to see Landsworth, hunched uncomfortably in his saddle, sweat dribbling down his forehead and staining the front of his shirt. At least he'd made the concession of foregoing a tie that morning, although his pale suit still looked uncomfortably hot, and he was obviously suffering.

"Here," she said, holding out her water bottle. "Take a sip of water. You look as if you could use a drop."

Landsworth nodded gratefully, and took it from her, gulping at it as if it were the first drop of water he'd seen all day. He wiped his mouth on his sleeve, replaced the stopper, and passed it back. "Most generous of you, Miss Gray. Although, if truth be told, I could use a drop of something stronger."

"Ah, well you have me there," she said. "I'm avoiding the stuff."

"Good for you," he said enthusiastically. "Best to keep your senses about you, what?"

"Something like that," said Ginny.

He tugged on the reins of his camel, drawing closer to her. She wrinkled her nose at the smell, which she presumed to be the beast and not the man. "Listen, you seem like a good sort of girl, so I'm going to give you a little bit of advice." He lowered his voice. "Just keep your wits about you around Amaury. That's all. You might want to think about going off to visit the Luxor Temple tomorrow, after all."

Ginny frowned. "Are you driving at something, Mr. Landsworth?"

He sighed. "No, no. Nothing like that. It's just... oh, never mind." He gave a dismissive wave, and then yanked at the reins again, and his camel pulled away.

She watched him clomp away, moving up the caravan to speak with their Egyptian guide. She glanced over at Amaury, but he didn't seem to be paying her or Landsworth any attention—the dig site had suddenly hove into view over the crest of a dune, and the sight was enough to take her breath away.

The guide pulled his camel to a stop, raising his hand and issuing a low, braying sound that seemed to mean something to the other camels, which all juddered to a halt, forming a small group on the top of the dune.

The excavations had clearly been going on here for some time. Amaury had given her a clear impression they'd discovered a tomb, but had failed to mention the vast necropolis that surrounded it. It was the size of a small town, and a veritable army of Egyptian workers crawled all over it, armed with trowels, brushes, and spades. From up here, she could see the broken stumps of a vast colonnade, the ruins of several buildings, the top half of a toppled statue; she hardly knew where to look. Onyx figures stood in a series of recesses sunk into a wall: one with a bird's head, another a lion's, and a third with a jackal's. A plaza, partially unearthed from its sandy grave, displayed great symbols carved into the ground—a series of nested shapes, a circle inside a square, inside a triangle, inside a larger circle.

These were things that no human eyes had seen for millennia, their true meaning lost to posterity. She thought again of Shelley's words, although it was not despair she felt, but elation.

"Impressive, isn't it?" said Amaury, from beside her.

She turned, surprised, to see him standing by her camel. The others had dismounted, too, while she'd been surveying the dig.

"It's... well, it's not what I expected," said Ginny.

Amaury smiled and held out his hand. "You haven't seen the best bit yet. Here, allow me to help you down."

Ginny took his hand, and lowered herself down from the saddle. Amaury handed her the parasol. "You might want to hold on to this," he said. "It gets hot down there when the sun's beating down."

"It's hot *now*," said Ginny, with an exasperated sigh. How much hotter could it get?

"Come along, and watch your footing on the way down," said Amaury, starting off down the side of the dune, his feet splashing in the loose sand like water. The guide set off behind him, and Ginny glanced over at Landsworth, who she noted was regarding her with a curious expression. She'd decided she really didn't like him much, and that his "warning" back there had probably been some sort of veiled pass at her, trying to put her off Amaury in the hopes he could move in on her himself. She shuddered at the thought of it. She'd be on her guard around him from now on—around them both. If either of them did try anything, she knew how to look after herself—especially against a podgy little Englishman like Landsworth.

He beckoned down the slope, as if politely inviting her to go first. Ginny painted on a polite smile, and set off after Amaury and the others.

After stopping to greet the dig supervisor—another Frenchman, named Fabrice, whom Amaury spoke to in urgent Gallic tones—they walked the perimeter of the dig, sipping at their water bottles and marveling at the new discoveries.

Even Amaury, whom she'd imagined to be immune to the effect by now, was like a little boy at Christmas when one of the diggers showed him the head of an enormous statue that had been partially unearthed that morning. Much of it was still buried beneath the sand, but she could see it had the upper torso of a man and the head of an ibis. Remarkably, the long, curved beak was still largely intact, and the blank, staring eyes still showed traces of the thick white paint they had once been daubed with.

The head was on its side, but standing down in the pit, it still towered above Ginny, casting her in its eon-long shadow.

She ran her hands over its smooth surface, awed by the age and majesty of the thing.

"Thoth," said Amaury, coming to stand beside her. "God of knowledge and science, father of language and architect of the heavens. Without Thoth, the stars and planets would no longer traverse the night sky, and we should all be doomed." He grinned. "This site was largely dedicated to him."

"It seems a shame that all the old religions have died," said Ginny. "There's poetry in such ideas."

"Who says they're dead?" said Amaury. "Belief systems change and develop over time, just like languages. Thoth is not forgotten, despite the fact that people no longer congregate to worship at his temple. Every time we marvel at the heavens, or scratch a word in our notebook, we remember Thoth, and honor him."

"That's a beautiful sentiment," said Ginny. "I like that idea very much."

"I am glad," said Amaury. "I believe very much that the old gods still deserve our attention. Only now, they are sleeping, one day to live again." He beckoned for her to follow him. "That is why I dig."

"I thought you were a treasure hunter, or a tomb robber," said Ginny, laughing.

"That too," said Amaury, with a sly grin. "But see the work we are doing here. We are waking the old gods, so that modern man might come to gaze upon them."

"There's certainly something honorable in that," said Ginny.

"I like to think so," said Amaury. "Now, to the main event! I promised you a tomb."

He took her by the arm and hurried her along the colonnade to the very edge of the dig site, toward a large mound, where a small group of diggers were very carefully removing bucketfuls of sand. When they saw him coming, they downed tools and began muttering to one another in Arabic.

"You must be a fearsome employer," said Ginny, "to engender such an effect on your workers."

Amaury laughed. "It's not that. They're a superstitious bunch, you see, and believe the tomb to be cursed. I'm the one who cracked the seal, the first one to have gone inside, and so now they are waiting for me to succumb to the curse and drop dead at their feet. The longer I live, the better for them, as the curse will spread to any and all associated with the dig."

"Well, now I'm thinking twice about going inside," said Ginny.

"Oh, it's too late for that," said Amaury. "Your card's been marked. You're here at the dig."

"Ah, well then, I suppose I've nothing to lose."

"That's the spirit," said Amaury. "The entrance is just over here. I hope you're not claustrophobic…"

He led her down into the excavation pit, taking her hand and guiding her across a wooden gangplank that had been tenuously balanced across two blocks of stone. When he reached the other side, he dropped into a crouch, indicating a small cavity in the side of the trench.

It was no taller than three foot high, and about the same width, but she could see sandstone blocks were supporting it. "In *there*?" she said.

"Yes. We need to wriggle in on our stomachs," said

Amaury. "The seal has been broken, and there's a small drop into the tomb on the other side. You can stand up in there, once you're in."

"And how do we get back out again?" Ginny could hear the tremulousness in her own voice. She hadn't expected to go crawling about underground. The idea didn't immediately appeal to her.

"The same way," said Amaury. "Don't worry. One of the workers will help us back up. I've done this plenty of times."

"Why haven't you fully excavated the entrance?" said Ginny.

"These things take time. They have to be done slowly. If we haven't shored it all up properly, the sand will just spill back into the tomb." He put a hand on her shoulder. "Trust me, Ginny. You'll be fine."

"All right," she said. She tried not to think of Landsworth's bizarre warning. "You go first, I'll follow behind you."

Amaury nodded. He dropped down onto his front, reached into the opening, and pulled himself through. A moment later she heard him land on the other side, and after a moment of scrabbling about, his voice echoed through the hole. "Come on. I'll catch you."

"Here goes nothing," muttered Ginny, lowering herself onto the warm sand and wriggling forward like a snake.

No sooner had her fingertips reached the edge of the lip than she felt Amaury's hands take her wrists, sliding her forward. She couldn't make out much in the darkness, and for a moment, panic threatened to overcome her. What on earth was she doing here, in the middle of the Egyptian desert, climbing into a dark tomb with a Frenchman she barely knew?

Then she was falling, tumbling head first into the void on the other side of the hole, and Amaury was catching her, gathering her up and preventing her from hitting the floor.

"It's all right. I've got you."

She righted herself with a gasp, smoothing the sand from the front of her blouse. The only light in the tomb was leaching in through the small hole she'd just entered by, and she could make out nothing beyond the silhouette of Amaury, standing close by.

"Are you okay?" he said.

"Yes, yes. I'm fine," said Ginny, a little hastily. "But it's so dark in here. Aren't you going to light a torch?"

"I was waiting for you," said Amaury. "The effect is quite spectacular." He took a matchbook from his pocket and struck one, the flare momentarily under-lighting his face and giving him a sinister aspect. He stooped and collected a wooden torch from a pile just by the door, and put the flame to it. A moment later, the stench of burning pitch filled her nostrils.

As the flame began to take, however, she soon forgot her discomfort; the light from the torch seemed to stir the room to life, as if summoning it from the depths of time.

The walls were covered in gold; more gold than she'd ever seen, or could have possibly imagined. It had been beaten into sheets and affixed to the walls of the tomb, then engraved with row upon intricate row of hieroglyphs. It seemed to absorb the light, taking on a warm, radiant glow. Amaury held the torch aloft, stepping further into the room. Even the ceiling had been paneled in the stuff.

Ginny was breathless, unable to speak. She realized she had raised both hands to her mouth in shock. "It's... oh, *thank you*, Jacques," she managed to stammer. "It's magnificent."

"I knew you'd love it." He laughed. "Better than the pyramids, no?"

"Oh yes," agreed Ginny.

"No one has walked in this tomb for over three thousand years," he said, "aside from you, Landsworth, Fabrice and I."

"I don't know what to say," said Ginny. "What does it all mean?"

"It's the story of Sekhmet," said Amaury. "She is the daughter of the sun, and a goddess of war and might." He pointed to a large image of a lion-headed woman on the far wall. Her arms were outstretched, and she was basking in the rays of the sun. "That's her, there."

"So the person who's buried here is paying tribute to Sekhmet?"

"The person buried here *is* Sekhmet," said Amaury. He met Ginny's gaze. "At least according to local legend. Her astral form still walks in the underworld, of course, but her avatar was buried here, to rest in the sands for eternity."

"And you believe that?" said Ginny.

Amaury shrugged. "I believe it's the find of a lifetime," he said. He pointed with the torch to a small opening in the wall. "There's more, through there."

Ginny stepped aside to allow him to pass.

The adjoining chamber was not lined in gold, but was brimming with funeral goods: a glorious chariot, so well preserved that it looked as if it might still be ridden into war;

neat rows of Canopic jars; effigies of Horus and Osiris; a bed, a chair; a box overflowing with jewelry and tributes. The walls here, too, were covered in hieroglyphs, painted this time, and beginning to flake away. She could see they charted the journey of a soul through the afterlife, as it passed through the physical world and onwards into the fields of the dead.

A passageway stemmed from here, leading deeper underground, and Amaury seemed anxious to show her. Ginny had to duck her head beneath the lintel of the doorway, and hunch over as the passage narrowed and dipped.

"It's a bit of a squeeze," said Amaury, from up ahead, "but it's worth it." She could hear his ragged breath in the confined space, and the stench of the burning pitch was almost overpowering. Nevertheless, she pressed on, anxious not to miss anything.

The passage opened out a moment later into a third chamber, and once again, Amaury was proved right. Here, a statue of the lion-faced Sekhmet presided over what could only be described as a stone table—although the top of it was concaved, like a large dish, and adorned with a headrest. The statue had its hands spread above the table, as if bestowing some absent figure with its blessing.

"This is as far as we've excavated so far," said Amaury. "There are more rooms branching off from that passageway. We'll open them up soon."

"It's fascinating," said Ginny. "Is this where they prepared the body?" She crossed to the table, running her hands over it. It had been chiseled from stone, but was exquisitely smooth and cool beneath her fingertips.

"We're not entirely sure," said Amaury. "We believe it's where the Egyptians thought Sekhmet would raise a new avatar. The layout of the tomb is unlike anything we've ever seen. It's almost as if it's been built to a specific plan, as if they thought the alignment might somehow bring her power."

"And the body," said Ginny. "Where's that? I didn't see a coffin."

"We haven't found one yet," said Amaury. "It may be behind one of those walls in the other chambers. Yet I have a suspicion we're not going to find a body here."

"You don't honestly believe that a goddess was buried here, do you?"

"Christians believe that Jesus, the son of Yahweh, was buried in a cave, only to rise again and transcend to the heavens," said Amaury, as if that explained everything.

"So what you said, about waking the gods...?"

"Perhaps," said Amaury. "Or maybe I'm just taken with the romanticism of it all. I am French, after all, and it's a nice story."

Ginny laughed, but the room had suddenly grown cold. "Thank you, Amaury, but I think I need some fresh air now. It's a little stale down here."

"Of course, of course," he said. He smiled hopefully. "But it was worth it? You canceled your plans to be here. I hope you found what you were hoping for?"

"Oh, without a doubt," said Ginny. "You have my gratitude. It's been quite the experience."

"Indeed it has," said Amaury. "Now, if you'll follow me, we'll get you out of here and find somewhere where you can shelter from the sun while we finish up our work."

He turned and dipped into the tunnel, leaving Ginny momentarily standing in the shadow of Sekhmet, an envelope of darkness closing in around her. She looked up at the implacable face, and shivered, then turned and hurried after Amaury, anxious to return to the light.

TEN

"Now look here—it's quarter past eight in the morning and I haven't even had breakfast yet. This is no time to be answering questions."

"I would say I understand, Mr. Landsworth, but I've been up since three dealing with *yet another* brutalized corpse, and so you'll have to forgive me. This won't wait, even for you." Donovan flicked ash on the hotel carpet, and took a swig of his coffee to underline his point. He was standing on the threshold of Landsworth's hotel room, while the rather rotund Englishman tried his best to finish doing up the buttons on the front of his shirt. At least, Donovan considered, he'd put his pants on before opening the door.

"Yes, well, I suppose you'd better come in, then," he said, finally relenting and throwing the door wide for them to enter.

"*Thank* you," said Donovan. He tried hard to keep the sarcasm out of his voice, and failed. He ushered Mullins through, and followed after.

He was feeling rather worse for wear. What he'd told Landsworth wasn't *strictly* true—it was closer to half three when the call came through, but at that time in the morning, Donovan tended only to look at the short hand of the clock. *Eggs is eggs*, as his old mom used to say.

Uniform had turned up another body, this time a male, found in a trash cart down in the Village. The third in as many days, and this one had been cut up too, although it didn't seem to bear any resemblance to what had happened to Autumn Allen. This was a simple cut and run job.

As best as Donovan could tell, his attackers had cornered him in the mouth of the alley and sliced him up with a couple of short blades. Vettel—happy as ever to be dragged from her bed—had counted fifty-two wounds on the scene, and judging by the state of his clothes, Donovan thought that number would probably double by the time the autopsy was over. Many of them had been to the hands and forearms as he'd tried to fight them off, and his best guess at the moment was that there'd been two killers, working in concert.

The dead man's name had been George Alexander, a Cypriot, and whoever had done for him had left his wallet and all his effects untouched, just like in the Autumn Allen case. There was another similarity, too—Alexander had a tattoo, a small one on the underside of his left wrist, depicting an Egyptian cartouche. The very same cartouche that had been carved into Autumn Allen's back just a couple of nights before, and the same cartouche that Donovan was there to question Landsworth about. He needed answers, and he was determined that Landsworth was going to give them to him.

It was Mullins who'd tracked the Englishman down, going through the museum to trace the manager of the exhibition. It seemed he'd arrived in town aboard the *Centurion*, along with his exhibits and a small army of assistants, who'd already been set to work assembling the displays for the grand opening.

He really didn't seem pleased to see Donovan, and that had Donovan wondering if there was more to it than his hurry to get to breakfast.

"So tell me, Inspector—what is this all about? I've only been in town for a couple of days, so you'll have to forgive me if I'm not quite up to speed on all the local news." He rubbed a hand over his jowls.

"Murder," said Donovan, already beginning to lose patience with the man. "I've got two bodies, both connected by an Ancient Egyptian symbol. I want you to take a look at it, is all, and tell me if it's familiar."

Landsworth gave a visible sigh of relief. "Oh, is that all? You could have had one of the team at the museum do *that*."

"No," said Donovan. "I said that I wanted *you* to take a look at it, Mr. Landsworth." He placed his coffee cup down on the sideboard and crossed to where Landsworth was perching on the end of his bed. "Here." He handed him a photograph.

Landsworth blanched at the sight of Allen's carved flesh. "Oh dear," he said, redundantly. "How awful."

"Yes, we're aware it doesn't make for tasteful viewing, Mr. Landsworth," said Mullins, much to Donovan's surprise, "but if you could tell us whether you recognize the marking?"

"Well yes, of course. I wouldn't be much of a scholar if I didn't. It says 'Thoth'."

"As in the deity?" said Mullins.

"Yes, officer, precisely." Landsworth beamed. "You know, it's good to meet a young man who's been educated in the classics. Too few these days show an interest in our early history."

"Yes, yes," said Donovan, making it clear he was directing

his frustration at Landsworth, and not Mullins. "So why would anyone carve the name of an Ancient Egyptian god into the back of a dead woman?"

"Well how should I know?" said Landsworth defensively. "*I* didn't do it, if that's what you're thinking?"

"Not at all, Mr. Landsworth," said Mullins. He eyed Donovan, just making sure that he wasn't stepping out of line by interceding. Donovan nodded, and reached for his cigarettes. "The thing is, this wasn't the only mark left on the woman's body that night. The men who did this to her pinned her down and used the tip of a sharp knife to cut these Ancient Egyptian symbols into her skin. Then, once she'd finished screaming, they throttled her to death and left her for us to find, hours later, in the gutter." He rubbed his chin. "So you see, we're very anxious to find the men responsible."

"I can imagine so," said Landsworth.

"Then this morning, as the Inspector has already intimated, another body turns up, this time in a trash cart down in Greenwich Village. At last count the dead man had suffered fifty-two separate knife wounds. He'd bled all over the floor. And what do we discover? He has a tattoo on his wrist. A tattoo of this same symbol." Mullins tapped the photograph, still clutched firmly in Landsworth's grip.

"I really can't see what this has to do with me?" said Landsworth. He looked shaken, but was feigning confidence. Mullins had him on the run.

Donovan was impressed. He'd never seen Mullins so riled.

"It seems like an awful coincidence that a new exhibition arrives in town at just the same time that bodies start to turn up, marked with these Ancient Egyptian symbols," said Mullins. "Wouldn't you say?"

"Well, yes, I suppose so," said Landsworth. "But coincidence is all it is. I can't see how I, or any of my associates, could be in any way connected. I've been in Egypt for months, as I explained, and only entered the country a couple of days ago. This man with the tattoo, for example—I presume it wasn't a recent embellishment? He'd had the marking for some time?"

Mullins frowned, glancing at Donovan.

"Yet to be established," said Donovan. He decided to try a different approach. "Your new exhibition? Does it feature any exhibits pertaining to Thoth?"

"Well, yes, as a matter of fact, the whole thing is pretty much dedicated to him. Him and Sekhmet, anyway. That's what we were excavating out there, in Egypt. A temple dedicated to Thoth."

"We?" said Donovan.

"Well, yes, one doesn't undertake such endeavors alone, Inspector. I have a partner, an archaeologist called Jacques Amaury."

"And where is this Amaury?" said Mullins.

"Luxor, I'm afraid. He doesn't much go in for this end of things. Much prefers to be in the thick of it all with his trowel."

There *had* to be a connection. It was too much of a coincidence. Donovan was sure the man was hiding something.

"Do people still worship Thoth?" said Mullins. It was another unexpected question, but a good one, considered Donovan. He made a mental note to congratulate Mullins when they were done.

"Not so far as I'm aware," said Landsworth, "but it's not inconceivable."

"Then the man with the tattoo might have belonged to some sort of revivalist cult?"

"I wouldn't know," said Landsworth. "It makes for a fine story, detective, but I'm not aware of any so-called 'revivalist cults', or what business they would have murdering young ladies in New York City." He looked at Donovan. "Now, if you're finished with your questions, I really must be getting along. I have a great deal to do before the exhibition opens."

"Yes, of course, Mr. Landsworth," said Donovan. He dropped the butt of his cigarette into his coffee cup, drowning it in the dregs. "Just one more question?"

"Yes, what is it?"

"What can you tell me about a woman called Ginny Gray?"

He watched Landsworth's face drain of color. "I... well... nothing at all, Inspector. I've never heard of a woman by that name. Who is she?"

"Just someone we're looking into," said Donovan.

Landsworth gave an affected shrug.

"Thank you for your time, Mr. Landsworth. We may yet have cause to call on you again."

"At a more reasonable hour, one should hope," said Landsworth. "You'll probably find me at the museum."

Donovan stepped out into the hallway and pulled the door shut behind him. "That's one lying bastard," he said to Mullins, as they walked down the hall. "Put a tail on him, night and day. He's in this up to his neck."

"And then what, sir?"

"Get some rest. I need you in good shape for later. You did good work in there, Mullins."

"Thank you, sir."

"Oh, and call the precinct, tell them I won't be coming in."

"You're heading home too, sir?"

"No. I have to pay a visit to a friend."

ELEVEN

"If you don't hurry up and open this godforsaken door, I'm shooting off the lock and coming in regardless. I know you're in there."

Gabriel rolled over and groaned. The pounding in his head seemed to be keeping perfect time with the thumping on the apartment door. He'd already tried burying his head under the pillow, but that didn't seem to be doing much to keep the noise at bay.

"All right, all right!" he called, finally deciding that Donovan wasn't going to be dissuaded. He glanced at the clock. He'd only been in bed for three hours, and he ached *all over*.

He rolled out of bed, nearly tripped blearily over his boots—which he'd abandoned in the bedroom doorway the night before—and stumbled over to the door, just as Donovan started beating on it again. He yanked it open, and Donovan almost tumbled inside.

"Good God, you look dreadful," he said, when he'd righted himself.

Gabriel glanced down at himself. He was still wearing his trousers, but had ripped his shirt off before getting into bed, and now, in the light of day, could see the streaks of dried blood, open wounds, and massive purple bruises that had formed across his chest. Even looking at them hurt.

"Rough night?" said Donovan, pushing the door shut and crossing to the drinks cabinet.

"Something like that," said Gabriel.

"Mind if I…?" Donovan held up the whisky decanter.

Gabriel nodded. "Bit early for you, isn't it?"

"I haven't really been to bed," said Donovan. He dropped into one of the chairs by the window, threw back his head and downed the drink. He placed the glass on the windowsill with a *clink*. He looked at Gabriel, and then wrinkled his nose. "You might want to think about giving this place a bit of an airing."

Gabriel laughed, wincing as it set off a series of wracking pains in his chest. "Yeah, maybe next week, when I've got a bit more time on my hands."

Donovan smiled. "Tell me."

Gabriel shook his head. "No, you first. You're the one dragging me out of bed at such an ungodly hour."

"Funny, you're the second person to complain about that this morning."

"Then maybe you should pay attention," said Gabriel. "Perhaps the universe is trying to tell you something."

Donovan offered him a withering look. "We've found another body," he said. He scratched at his beard absently. "Different this time. A man. All slashed up and dumped in a trash cart."

"And you think it's connected?"

"I *know* it's connected. He had a tattoo, on the underside of his wrist. The same cartouche we found cut into the back of Autumn Allen. Mullins thinks it might be a reprisal killing."

"From the mob?" said Gabriel. "That would make sense, I suppose."

Donovan nodded. "It would have to be the Reaper's boys. He's the only real game in town these days. Although we still haven't got anything concrete to link him to the dead woman."

"I'm planning to put in an appearance at the Café Deluxe this evening," said Gabriel. "I thought it sounded like just the sort of place that Gabriel Cross might like. I'll ask a few gentle questions, listen to the chatter, see if I can't pick up on anything that might help."

"Be careful," said Donovan. "In a place like that you'll be surrounded. They'll have all the exits covered, and there's no way I could even get close. There won't be any cavalry riding in to bail you out if something goes down."

"As if I've ever needed that," said Gabriel.

"Hmmm," was Donovan's only response.

Gabriel lit a smoke and threw his cigarette tin to Donovan. "Anyway, the ship. Things happened there last night, Felix. Things I can't quite explain. There's something very wrong with that exhibition."

He outlined the previous night's events for Donovan, including his encounter with the statues, and the fact he'd found evidence not only of the symbol, but that a woman had been transported, possibly against her will, inside the crate.

"Of course, you realize I can't do anything with that information," said Donovan, "at least not officially. But I *knew* that bastard was lying."

"Your other early riser?" said Gabriel.

Donovan nodded. "Robert Landsworth. An Englishman.

He's in charge of the exhibition, and was partners on the dig with another man, Amaury, who's still out in Egypt. Mullins and I gave Landsworth a bit of a rough time this morning, and I got the sense he was hiding something. Now I'm sure of it. He *knew* what was on that ship. He probably put it there."

"He can't be behind the murders though, can he? At least, not the woman. He was still on the ship."

"I know. And I don't think he'd be capable of it, either. Physically, I mean. But it's a ruddy great coincidence that his exhibition is linked to Thoth, and so are these murders." Donovan pulled the ignition patch on his cigarette, and leaned back, taking an appreciative draw.

"Thoth?" said Gabriel.

"He told us that's what the symbol meant. The cartouche. It's the name of an Ancient Egyptian god. Mullins seemed to know all about it. Turns out he's a bit of a history buff."

"Thoth was the god of knowledge," said Gabriel, "responsible for keeping the heavens in check. That's about as much as I remember."

"Well, whoever he was, he's got a lot to answer for," said Donovan. "Mullins wondered if it was a cult of some kind, a revivalist sect, trying to bring the old religion back."

"He's a smart kid. You should listen to him."

"What do you think I'm doing here, reciting it all to you?"

Gabriel laughed, and then, wincing, decided to get up and search for some painkillers. He found them in a bureau drawer, and, after spilling a heap of unopened mail onto the carpet, took six, swallowing them dry. He left the landslide of post where it had fallen.

"Keep on like that and the medication will get you faster than the injuries," said Donovan.

"It's not as if I have any other options," said Gabriel, "except to strap it up and keep going. We've got work to do. These murders might be the key to bringing down the Reaper, if we can prove there's a connection. It's the best shot we've had in months." He walked over to the sink and poured himself a glass of water. "And then there's Ginny. I'm determined to make sure she's all right, Felix, even if she doesn't want to see me."

"About that," said Donovan. "When I mentioned her name to Landsworth, he went as white as a sheet. Denied all knowledge, of course, claimed he'd never heard of her, but there was something there, a spark of recognition."

Gabriel placed his empty glass on the counter. "Sounds as if I should pay him a visit."

"Not yet. I know you're anxious to find her, but give me a couple of days before you go roughhousing. I've got a tail on him. If he so much as twitches, I'll know about it. At the moment he's the best lead we've got. I can't risk scaring him off."

"All right," said Gabriel. "A couple of days. The first sign you get that she's here in New York, though, you let me know."

"Of course. I want her back as much as you do," said Donovan. "She's the only one who knows how to keep you in check."

Gabriel smiled. "Two days. Then I'm going after him."

"If you're in any fit state. You need to *rest*."

"And you need a vacation. Neither of us is very good at getting what he wants."

Donovan pulled himself up out of his chair. "Isn't that the truth." He took another cigarette from Gabriel's tin, before walking to the door. "Take care of yourself, Gabriel. And maybe take a shower."

"You cut down on the cigarettes, and I'll think about it," said Gabriel.

He heard Donovan chuckling as he pulled the door shut behind him.

The Café Deluxe was pleasant enough, considered Gabriel, except that it reminded him of every other jazz club in every other city he'd ever visited. The lighting was low, the music was loud and the morals were loose. He supposed there was a time when that would have seemed like a draw, but now, it just left him feeling hollow. There was nothing to connect him to these people and their empty lives, their days filled with drinking and fucking and drinking some more.

Not that his own life was particularly exemplary. He couldn't really argue that putting on a mask and flying around the rooftops brawling with mobsters was any better than what these people were doing—in fact, in the eyes of the law it was worse—but at least he felt he was doing something with his life. After returning from the war he'd soon fallen back into his old ways, playing host to the infinite party, blotting out the world and all its madness with booze, and girls, and anything at all that didn't remind him of France, and the blood-spattered faces of his comrades, and the thing he'd seen out there in the farmhouse.

The Ghost made him better. It gave him a purpose, a means of fighting back against the horror. That had to make it better than this, didn't it?

Gabriel placed his empty glass on a nearby table, and decided to take a walk to the bar, cutting across the main lounge.

It was as ostentatious as only the very rich can palate: cut-glass chandeliers dripped from the ceiling, dark wood paneling lined the walls, and sweeping balustrades separated the main seating area from the dance floor.

On stage, a jazz quartet played a swaying, bluesy lament, fronted by a dark-haired woman who clutched the microphone stand tightly with both hands, as if it were her only anchor to the real world. Her voice floated above the smoky chatter, stirring feelings of loss within Gabriel.

Mob men—clearly identifiable by their attitude, if not their attire—swilled expensive drinks, smoked pungent cigars, and generally treated the women in their company with the utmost contempt, ignoring them for the most part, except to grab at them inappropriately or send them to fetch more drinks.

Gabriel tried not to watch, for fear he'd feel moved to intercede. It was the arrogance that grated on Gabriel—the sense of assumed ownership over another person. He could never claim to have behaved well toward the women in his life— he had always kept too much from them, for a start—but he had always shown them respect.

This particular brand of ill behavior, however, seemed reserved for men who believed themselves to be in control, or else saw it as a casual means to assert that they were; men who thought themselves invincible, above the law—the sort of men who worked for the Reaper.

Gabriel found a quiet spot toward the end of the long bar and pulled out a stool, placing himself within earshot of a large table of mobsters. He called the barman over and ordered a whisky sour, then settled in to eavesdrop.

It wasn't the most riveting discourse, but the men seemed to be discussing the recent reports of the floating apparition, and how a number of their colleagues had been attacked by the specter in the midst of carrying out one of their "jobs".

He listened for a while to their speculation, most of it wild, claiming that it was the spirit of the Reaper's dead girlfriend, come to avenge them for her untimely death, or else it was an Angel of the Lord, unleashed from heaven to bring judgment down upon the unworthy. One of them, a quieter, brooding man with a stick-thin physique and harelip, even claimed to have seen it himself, floating above Fifth Avenue, trailing ghostly bandages behind it as if caught in an unearthly gale.

Gabriel took their wild claims with the pinch of salt they deserved, although the reference to the Reaper's dead girlfriend was interesting—Donovan had been looking for something that linked Autumn Allen to the mob, and perhaps this was it. He'd said the woman was carrying a hefty weight in diamonds, and that they'd clearly been gifts from a prosperous admirer. Perhaps she wasn't just connected to the mob, but to the Reaper himself? That would certainly explain why no one had come forward to help with the police enquiries.

He made a mental note to follow it up with Donovan.

Talk had moved on now to sport and women, and Gabriel knew that he wasn't going to get anything else useful out of the people here. They were low-level mobsters at best, nothing more than goons, and if the Café Deluxe itself was a front for the Reaper, it was only as a place to launder money and allow his men to wind down. He couldn't see any evidence of anything more clandestine going on here, aside from the usual sort of gambling and drinking one found in venues such as this.

He downed his whisky and placed a handful of dollars under the glass on the bar. Then, rising from his seat, he saw her standing there at the other end of the bar.

Ginny.

She looked resplendent in a red and white dress, and she was wearing a red feather in her hair, which had grown since he'd last seen her, now falling around her shoulders in luxurious blonde curls. She was looking straight at him, holding her glass out before her in a salute, her familiar coquettish grin on her painted red lips.

For a moment, Gabriel didn't know what to do. His head was suddenly full of questions. What was she doing here, in a mob bar, dressed like that? How had he missed her at the docks?

He supposed there would be time to answer all of that later. He grabbed his jacket from the back of his stool, and turned to beckon her over, but a large group of men, who had arrived only moments before, had suddenly swarmed around the bar, obscuring his view.

Frustrated, he pushed his way through them, eliciting a series of curses and threats. When he arrived at the other end of the bar, however, she was nowhere to be seen.

Confused, Gabriel turned on the spot, trying to catch a glimpse of her red and white dress. She couldn't have gone far. He'd only been a moment.

There was a man sitting close to where she'd been standing. He was hunched over the bar, staring into his drink. He was a swarthy-looking fellow, with a tanned, healthy complexion and a thick black beard. He was wearing his collar open, and his tan jacket seemed somewhat out of place amongst all the formal black suits around him.

"Excuse me," said Gabriel, "but there was a woman here, just a moment ago. She was wearing a red and white dress, with a feather in her hair. Could you tell me which way she went?"

The man peered at him, as if weighing him up. "There was no woman here," he said. He had a soft, Gallic lilt to his accent.

"You must be mistaken," said Gabriel. "She was just here, only a moment ago. I came straight over. A blonde, pretty, about so tall." He tapped his shoulder, indicating her approximate height.

"No," said the man. "I'd have remembered a woman like that." He picked up his drink and took a swig, turning his back on Gabriel.

Frowning, Gabriel left the man to his drink. The barman was down the other end of the bar, now embroiled in fixing drinks for all the new arrivals. Even if Gabriel were able to get a word in edgewise, it was unlikely he'd have seen where she went.

He decided to try the dance floor, just in case she was in one of her playful moods. Here, a group of women were dancing to a jazzy, upbeat number, kicking their heels high and waving their hands about, laughing breathlessly, their tasseled skirts swishing about their knees. A handful of men stood around the edges, watching them hungrily. He watched for a moment, scanning the faces, but there was no sign of her here, either.

For a moment, he wondered whether he'd imagined it all, whether it was the booze, or the painkillers, or the god-awful weariness finally catching up with him. She'd seemed so vivid, though, so real. Yet the man at the bar had been so insistent…

Nevertheless, he had to trust his gut. She'd *been* there. He was sure of it.

He left the dance floor and walked the rest of the bar, checking every face, every dress, every shadowy nook—but there was no sign of her. He stepped outside and smoked a cigarette in the street, watching people filing out to their cars or hailing cabs to take them home. Then, after a while, he went back inside and ordered another drink, taking a seat at the bar, close to where he'd seen her. The Frenchman had moved on, his empty glass still sitting there with a handful of crumpled notes underneath it.

He nursed the drink for another hour, scanning the crowds, but it was clear that she had gone.

After a while, the barman asked him if he wanted another, but he shook his head and tossed a few bills on the bar. Then, having never felt quite so alone, he left, hoping the balmy summer night would help to clear his mind as he strolled home.

A few hours later, the Ghost cut the ignition to his boosters and lowered himself slowly onto a fire escape. The iron frame creaked as he set down on the platform, grasping hold of the railing to steady himself.

He stood for a moment, surveying the street. It was late, and the streetlights glowed with a soft sheen, as if they'd somehow stored up the final vestiges of daylight and were now breathing them back out into the streets, sprinkling light upon the city.

There was no one around. The little café had closed up some hours earlier, and the lights in the apartment windows were now beginning to wink off, as one day transitioned into another, and sleep drew people to their beds.

He waited a while, watching Ginny's apartment from his vantage point on the other side of the street. There were no lights on inside, and no signs of movement. If she'd returned here after visiting Café Deluxe, she'd already turned in for the night.

When he was sure that he wasn't going to be observed, he swung down from the fire escape, dropping the few feet to the sidewalk. He landed silently in a crouch, cringing as he felt the wound in his back open up with the motion. He was going to have to get it seen to, he realized—he could feel the blood running freely again, despite his best attempts to clean and dress it after his bath earlier that day. At least the dressing would mean he didn't leave a trail of blood behind him as he worked.

He crossed the street, keeping low, and took the steps down into Ginny's lobby two at a time, keen to remain out of sight.

A quick scan of the heaped trash told him that someone had been here since his last visit—the leaves had been swept to one side by the opening and closing of the door. The wedged-in mail had been removed from the letterbox, too.

For a moment he hesitated, unsure what to do. Perhaps he should have come as Gabriel, after all? Then, with a shrug, he rapped three times on the door, and stood back to see if anyone would answer.

He half expected the light to blink on, the door to swing

open, and Ginny's laughing face to be peering out at him, berating him for taking so long to follow her here. The moment stretched, however, and there was no response, and no sound of movement from inside.

He tried again, one last time, but again it proved fruitless, and no one came to the door.

Someone had been here, though. It made logical sense that it was Ginny. He'd hoped she'd come straight back to him, maybe heading out to Long Island to stay at the house, but if she had returned to New York with no intention of seeing him, then this was where she would come. Only, the look on her face in the club earlier suggested things weren't over between them.

He tried the handle, but the door was still locked. Seeing no other option, he threw his shoulder against it, once, twice... and on the third time the lock burst and it yawned open with a bang.

Cautiously, he stepped inside, pushing it shut behind him. It would be an easy enough job to repair the lock, and at least this way he could put his mind at rest...

Or so he thought, until he saw the devastation that had been wreaked across the entire apartment. The place had been burgled, or certainly ransacked—the furniture had been overturned, the drawers pulled out and upended on the floor. The cushions had been slashed, and the bookcase had been emptied, all of Ginny's precious history books rifled through and discarded in an unceremonious heap.

Someone had been very thorough.

"Ginny?" He dashed through to the bedroom, hoping

beyond hope that he wasn't about to find her there on the bed, her throat slit.

It was empty. He heaved a sigh of relief. The sheets had been dragged from the mattress and thrown in a heap on the floor, and the wardrobe had been emptied of all her dresses. Her jewelry boxes, too, had been upturned and then discarded in the corner. Rings, brooches and earrings had spilled across the floorboards like marbles, colorful stones and pearls all trodden on in the culprit's haste. Whatever this was then, the Ghost realized, it wasn't a robbery.

Even the bathroom had been overturned, the cistern opened, the light fittings unscrewed. The kitchen was the same. The entire place had been gutted.

What secret could Ginny possibly have that was worth all of this? And what did it have to do with her mysterious disappearance? Had the culprit found what they were looking for? It was impossible to tell.

He wondered once again whether he'd really seen her that night, or whether it had been some form of mirage, his mind playing tricks on him. It certainly wouldn't have been the first time, but he still couldn't shake the nagging feeling that there'd been something more to it. If she wasn't really there, someone had wanted him to *think* that she was.

He felt his hackles rise. Could that mean it was a trap? Was someone trying to lure him out? Perhaps they'd seen the devastation he'd caused on the boat, and were out for revenge. He decided he'd better get out of there, just in case. A small basement apartment was not the sort of place he wanted to find himself cornered in.

One thing was certain, though—whoever *was* responsible for this mess had let themselves into the apartment with a key. That meant that Ginny was either back in New York, or the key had been taken from her aboard the *Centurion*. Either way, he didn't like the inference.

The Ghost pulled a length of twine from inside his coat and secured the broken door. He'd drop an anonymous tip to the police, alerting them to a burglary at this address. They'd probably assume the door had been smashed during the break in. At least that way, Donovan would realize something was up, and his men would properly secure the building.

For now, though, he needed to retreat to his apartment, to mull things over and tend his wounds. Donovan had been right—he did need some rest. He was doubtful he'd get much sleep, but he was no good to anyone—especially Ginny—beat up the way he was.

The next day he would visit Arthur at the museum, see if he couldn't find out a bit more about Landsworth. If the man knew something about what had happened to Ginny, then Gabriel was damn well going to get to the bottom of it. He'd given Donovan two days to make his move, but that didn't mean he couldn't help things along a little in the meantime, particularly if he remained in his civilian guise.

As he climbed the steps to street level, he couldn't shake the feeling he was being observed. A quick scan of the street told him it was still deserted, however, and so he fired up his boosters and took off into the night sky, leaving a streaming trail of light behind him.

TWELVE

Donovan watched smoke curl from the smoldering tip of his cigarette, twisting through the air like a twirling ribbon, before slowly dispersing on the breeze from the open window.

"I thought we could take a trip today, Felix." He felt Flora stir on the bed beside him. She stretched luxuriously, like a cat in the sunlight. "Maybe even take a drive to Brooklyn, or Philly, pick up some of those egg rolls you like."

"Mmm hmm," murmured Donovan, rolling the cigarette between his lips.

Flora sighed. "You're working, aren't you?"

Donovan plucked the cigarette from his lips, spilling ash across his naked chest. "No. *No.* I'm here, in bed with you. It's my day off."

"I know that look, Felix."

"What look?"

"That distant expression. You might well be lying there, smoking a cigarette and pretending to listen—"

Donovan held his hand up in self-defense. "Hold on a moment, Flora. I said—"

"No. It's all right, Felix," she said, speaking over the top of him until he relented. "I married you. I knew what I was getting into. You're a million miles away. Your mind is someplace else entirely, and it's *okay*. That's the job. That's *you*."

Donovan eyed her warily, wondering if this was some kind of obscure test. "So you're not mad? About your trip?"

Flora smiled. "If I were going to leave you for being an absent husband, I'd have done it years ago." She gave him a playful shove. "Now go on, haul your ass out of bed and go and save the world, or whatever it is you do."

Donovan laughed. He leaned closer, gathering her up in his arms, bringing her lips closer to his. God, she smelled good. "Saving the world can wait just a little while longer," he said, running his fingers down the curve of her back.

"Well," said Flora, laughing, "when you put it like that…"

Donovan sat for a while in his favorite armchair, sipping at a coffee that had gone cold some time earlier, and chain-smoking cigarettes. He'd been running things over in his mind, trying to find an angle on Landsworth.

He was certain the man was involved somehow, and that the exhibition—or at least the ship that had brought it in—was tied in some way to the two murders. He couldn't yet figure out what Landsworth had to gain from it all, though. Why would a man who'd spent the last few months in Egypt—an archaeologist, for God's sake—have any reason to go up against the mob? It made no sense. Coupled with that, he'd got the sense from Landsworth that he was scared of something. Maybe he'd found himself in uncomfortably deep waters, and wasn't quite sure which way to turn. He certainly wasn't the ringleader. He lacked the arrogance and the confidence for that.

Donovan decided he'd have another go at him tomorrow, maybe bring him into the station. He didn't seem like the sort of man who'd take long to crack under pressure. Probably just holding him in a cell for a couple of hours would be enough to get him talking.

He glanced up at the sound of the holotube trilling on the sideboard, and, with a groan, jumped up from his chair, sighing as the cat immediately hopped up and took his place. He glared at it as he crossed to the sideboard, but its only response was to yawn, and then curl up in a ball.

"Donovan," he said into the receiver, as he waited for the image to resolve.

"Mullins here, sir." The image began to form as he spoke, seemingly crystallizing from the hazy blue light. Mullins was leaning right into the terminal, so only his face was visible. The lips were moving, but they weren't yet in time with the sound. "I'm sorry, sir, I know you're taking the day off, but you told me to let you know of any developments."

"It's all right, Mullins. It's not like I can think of anything else, not with all of this going on. What's new?"

"I think I've found the connection you've been looking for, sir. Between Autumn Allen and the Reaper."

"Go on."

"I've been going through the boxes of personal effects the boys brought back from her house, and there's a locket. No one seemed to think much of it, of course, but my sister's got one just like it. It's worthless, really, sentimental old junk, but there's a hidden catch. It opens both ways." Mullins's lips had finally caught up with his words.

"And?" prompted Donovan.

"The front compartment contains a picture of her mother. The rear contains a photograph of her with Paul Abbadelli, the Reaper. He has his hand around her waist."

"Got him!" said Donovan. This was the breakthrough they'd been waiting for, something definite to link the woman to the mob. Not just the mob, either, but the Reaper himself. He couldn't have wished for a better opportunity.

"Well done, Mullins. At the very least, you've given us reason to interview him, and a clear connection to the dead woman. Now if we can just find a way to prove the other death was a reprisal killing…" He stubbed his cigarette out in an ashtray on the sideboard. "But let's not get ahead of ourselves. First things first. Fancy a ride out?"

"Where to?" said Mullins.

"Well, here first, to pick me up. Then I think it's time we paid Mr. Abbadelli a visit."

"To his *house*, sir?"

"No, to his bloody boat in the Pacific Ocean. Yes, to his house. We can't be scared of these people, Mullins. Otherwise they've won."

"All right. I'll be over shortly," said Mullins, and he clicked off the receiver.

Donovan replaced the handset and grinned. That was one part of the puzzle finally falling into place. Now he just needed to get to the bottom of the Egyptian business, and see if he could find out what had happened to Ginny Gray.

* * *

"It feels a bit like walking into the lion's den, sir," said Mullins.

"It's exactly like walking into the lion's den, Mullins," said Donovan. He watched as two men approached the car. He could see the bulge of handguns in the line of their suits. They were burly types, too. No doubt handy in a fight. "Try to see that as a good thing."

"I'm not sure *how*, exactly."

"I'm sure you'll figure it out." He reached for the window release, and began to wind it down. "When you do, be sure to let me know."

He looked up at the goon staring in through the car window. "Hello," he said. "We're here for a little chat with Mr. Abbadelli."

They were parked outside the gates to the Reaper's mansion. It was surprisingly tasteful, unlike some of the more ostentatious houses they'd passed on the drive over. Modern, but built in a classic, timeless style, with sweeping lawns to the front, and a long gravel driveway leading up to the porch. It reminded him of Gabriel's place in Long Island.

"Mr. Abbadelli regrets he's not seeing anyone today," said the goon. He put his hand on the car roof and leaned in. Donovan saw his jacket flutter open and the butt of the handgun jutting out from its leather holster. It was clearly intended to intimidate him.

"Oh, he'll want to see us," said Donovan. "I think you should open the gates before you upset him."

The goon frowned for a moment and glanced at his colleague, clearly not used to receiving backchat. "And you are?" he said, after a moment. Donovan could hear the hint of hesitation in his voice now. He'd learned long ago how to deal with this sort of bull-headed idiot—to show him you had bigger balls.

"Inspector Donovan and Sergeant Mullins from the New York Police Department." Donovan opened his own jacket, flashing his badge, and ensuring that the goon caught an eyeful of his weapon, too.

"Wait here. Turn your engine off," said the goon.

"It's already off," said Donovan, before winding up the window.

They watched through the windshield as the two goons held a brief conference, and then one of them—the one who'd been talking to Donovan—opened the side gate and marched off up to the house.

Mullins finally let out his breath with a long whistle. "I'm impressed, sir. The way you handled him then. You didn't bat an eyelid."

"I'll let you in on a little secret, Mullins. I was bloody terrified. I learned a long time ago, though, that people like that, they're just putting on an act. Beneath all that bullshit they're just as scared and insecure as the rest of us. Probably more so." He paused to light a cigarette. "So the only thing to do is put up your own front. Pretend like you're the bigger animal. Puff up your chest and don't back down. Sadly, it seems to be the only thing they respect."

"I'll remember that," said Mullins.

"See that you do," said Donovan. "It'll save your life, one day." He waved his cigarette in the direction of the gate. "Seems like it worked, too. He's waving us through."

The second goon, at a signal from the house, was opening the main gates and beckoning them to drive through. Mullins fired the ignition, and the engine rumbled, the furnace belching thick black soot into the atmosphere behind them. He teased the accelerator, and they purred through the gates, churning the gravel as they rode on up to the house.

The first goon was waiting for them at the top. Mullins pulled the car to a stop, and opened his door, clambering out. The goon put his hand out for the keys. "Here. I'll park it for you."

"No need," said Donovan. "We won't be staying long." He slammed the car door and pointed up at the house. The main entrance was open, the door ajar at the foot of a small flight of stone steps. "In there?"

The goon nodded, and Mullins slipped the keys into his pocket.

"Remember," whispered Donovan, as the two of them walked up into the house, the goon behind them, "don't let them separate us. Stick together, and we'll be fine."

Mullins nodded.

The hallway was spacious, but with a minimalist, understated look. The walls were white and pristine, save for a large, gilt-framed mirror on the left, and a small portrait on the right, depicting a man—Abbadelli, suspected Donovan—standing in the grounds of his house, posing with an elderly pair, who must have been his parents. The floors had been laid in glistening white marble, and Donovan noted that the stone was shot through with traceries of deep red veins. They looked to him like tributaries of spilled blood that someone had tried, and failed, to remove.

There wasn't much furniture to speak of—a small holotube table beneath the mirror, a potted aspidistra, and a hat stand, bearing only a single trilby. At the end of the hall, a carpeted staircase led directly up to the second floor, while a series of doorways on the right and the left led deeper into the opposing wings of the house.

"Wait here," said the goon. He crossed the hall and rapped precisely on one of the doors. Donovan heard a muffled voice call out from the other side, and the goon opened the door, stepped inside, and closed it behind him. Moments later he emerged, and with a look that could only be described as distaste, walked directly past Donovan and Mullins, and out of the main entrance again.

"Someone's not happy," said Mullins quietly.

Left to his own devices, Donovan decided to make himself at home. He shrugged off his overcoat, folding it over his arm, and then crossed to the holotube table. The place seemed almost too clean—somewhat clinical—and the lack of personal effects told a story of its own. There were no photographs, no heaps of unopened letters, nothing to suggest that a person really *lived* here. Everything seemed so cold and clean, even the sole family portrait; as if the Reaper ran his life in the same way he ran his organization—with a cruel efficiency.

Donovan turned at the sound of footsteps on the marble. A man had emerged from the same doorway as the goon. He was dressed in a sharp gray suit, his collar open casually at the neck. He had a tanned complexion, a prominent nose, and a thick head of oily black curls. He was clean-shaven, and shorter than Donovan had expected, perhaps only reaching as high as Donovan's shoulder. He was wearing a broad grin.

"Inspector Donovan! *Felix*, if I may?"

Donovan didn't dignify that with a response. It was a good opening salvo, however—the man had clearly done his research. Abbadelli was letting him know that he understood precisely who Donovan was, and probably that he knew all about his family, his colleagues, and his personal habits, too.

"And Sergeant Mullins. It's a real pleasure to see you." Abbadelli crossed the hallway with his hand outstretched in greeting. Donovan took it, feeling as if he was somehow betraying himself just by accepting the clammy embrace. This, he decided, must be what it would feel like to do a deal with the Devil.

"Now listen, you've driven all the way out here to see me. Let me have one of the guys fix you a drink."

"Thank you, Mr. Abbadelli, but there's really no need. We won't be keeping you for long," said Donovan.

"No, no, it's the least I can do. I absolutely insist. Hell, if I'd known you were coming I'd have laid out a spread. Now, what'll you have?"

The man painted a good picture of the gregarious host, but the vaguely threatening undercurrent was hard to miss. Donovan decided he'd better have a drink. He had every intention of nailing this bastard to the wall, just as soon as he got the chance, but for now, it would be easier to cooperate, to play along. "I'll take a whisky," he said. "Straight."

"And you, Sergeant?"

Mullins glanced at Donovan, who inclined his head. "The

same," he said. "Thank you." Donovan thought it would do the poor guy some good, maybe steady his nerves a bit. Hell, he could do with it himself.

"Carlos, see to that," said Abbadelli, snapping out an order to a young valet, who stood at the foot of the stairs, clearly awaiting their order. Donovan hadn't even noticed him there. He must have sneaked up behind Abbadelli as soon as he heard the man's voice. He scuttled off in a hurry with his orders.

"Through here, Felix. Come and talk to me in my study." Abbadelli pushed on the door and strolled back into the room. "Carlos will have those drinks for us in just a moment."

Donovan followed him through, trying to keep his wits about him.

The study was just like the hallway, devoid of anything resembling a real life. It was well appointed—the fixtures and fittings were all tastefully arranged, and had probably cost the earth—a leather-topped desk, rows of walnut bookcases, a Turkish rug. The books looked unread, however, and again, it lacked the personal touches. This was a room where business was done.

"Please, take a seat," said Abbadelli, indicating two chairs before his desk. He walked around behind it and dropped into his own. It was set higher than the others, allowing him to maintain eye contact on a level with Donovan.

"Now, tell me how I can be of assistance. I do so much like assisting the New York Police Department. I have so many friends in the force, I feel like I'm part of the family." He grinned, but there was no humor in his eyes.

Donovan tried not to rise to the bait. The thing was, the man was telling the truth. He'd already bought off half the police force, especially in the outlying precincts, and Donovan and Mullins were probably the only two homicide detectives who hadn't already had one of these "meetings" with the man to discuss their fee. It occurred to Donovan that Abbadelli might have even thought that was the reason for their visit. It would certainly explain why he was so keen to play the illustrious host.

"A woman's been murdered," said Donovan. "We'd like to ask you some questions."

Abbadelli frowned. "I'm very sorry to hear this," he said. "But it puzzles me you'd bring this to my door. I am, as you know, a simple businessman."

Donovan had expected this. Abbadelli was going to claim ignorance, attempt to whitewash the whole thing. Well, Donovan wasn't going to let him get away with that. He decided to play it hard and straight. "Do you mind if I smoke?" he said, reaching inside his jacket pocket.

"Be my guest," said Abbadelli, amused. He pushed a cut-glass ashtray across the desk toward Donovan.

Donovan withdrew his packet of cigarettes, along with the locket, which he'd secreted there earlier. He placed it on the desk beside the ashtray while he lit his cigarette. "Do you recognize this?" he said a moment later.

Abbadelli shrugged. "It's a woman's locket. I must have seen hundreds of them in my time."

"This particular one," said Donovan. "Does it mean anything to you?" He expelled smoke from the corner of his mouth.

"I can't say that it does," said Abbadelli, clearly growing impatient.

It was a dangerous game Donovan was playing, agitating the man in this way, but it was the only way he could see of getting past the smooth, implacable façade. He pushed the locket across the desk with his forefinger. "Take a closer look."

Abbadelli picked it up, turned it over in his palm, and then clicked the release. The door hinged open, revealing a picture of Autumn Allen's mother. He held it up, so that both Donovan and Mullins could see. "I've never met this woman in my life," he said, snapping it shut.

"The other side," said Donovan, twirling his finger in the air. "It's got two catches."

With a sigh, Abbadelli did as Donovan directed. The other door popped open. He stared at the photograph for a moment in silence.

"That is you, isn't it, Mr. Abbadelli, with your arm around the woman?"

Abbadelli closed the locket and handed it back to Donovan. He slipped it back into his pocket. "Yes, that's me," he said. "I must have met her at a party, something like that. I can't say I knew her well. What was her name?"

"Autumn," said Donovan. "Autumn Allen." He took another draw on his cigarette. "The thing is, Mr. Abbadelli, she obviously knew you. She kept a picture of you in her locket, along with one of her mother. I can't imagine she'd have done that for a passing acquaintance."

"You can imagine what you like," said Abbadelli. He looked up as Carlos rapped on the door, and beckoned him in. The valet set the drinks down before them—including a brandy for

Abbadelli—and then made a swift exit, pulling the door closed behind him.

"She was wearing a lot of diamonds, this woman, when we found her," said Donovan. "Hundreds of dollars' worth. I'm sure if Mullins here had our uniformed boys visit all of the local jewelers we'd be able to turn up some receipts."

"Is that a threat, *Felix*?" said Abbadelli.

Donovan tried to keep his cool. "Not at all. I work for the police department, Mr. Abbadelli. We're not interested in threats. Only in establishing the truth. Let me tell you a little story."

"If you must," said Abbadelli, leaning back in his chair.

"You see, this woman," said Donovan, "she died in the most brutal way possible. The men who did this to her, they took their time. They held her still, her face pressed against the wet sidewalk, while they carefully selected each and every spot, running their hands over her body like artists preparing a canvas. Then, taking a sharp ceremonial knife, they used the tip of the blade to—very slowly and precisely—slice icons into her flesh." He leaned forward in his chair. "Can you imagine how that must have felt? That poor woman, lying there, whimpering, crying out for help, calling for her loved ones, as these men slowly cut her flesh to ribbons, all for the glorification of some ancient god."

He could see Abbadelli's hands had become bunched fists on his desk. His jaw was working back and forth as he ground his teeth.

"It was a hell of an end to a young life. She'd been out for dinner, eaten pasta and drunk fine wine. She'd enjoyed a tumble between the sheets with her male admirer, and she was probably floating on cloud nine as she made her way home. Maybe if she'd had one fewer glass of wine, she'd have heard them coming, been able to get away. But she didn't. They *did* catch her, and they *did* torture her, with no one coming to her aid."

Donovan crushed the butt of his cigarette in the ashtray, then dusted his fingers. "After they'd finished, they choked her to death like an unwanted puppy, carved a final symbol on her back, and abandoned her there on the street. A pair of drunks, stumbling home from a jazz club, found her a few hours later when they nearly tripped over her body. They probably thought about leaving her there, but in the end their consciences got the better of them, and they called it through to the precinct. Not until they'd already got home, mind. They weren't in that much of a hurry. After all, she was already dead."

Abbadelli's fist suddenly struck the top of his desk. "All right! That's *enough*."

He gave his drink a violent shove, and the glass tumbled off the edge of the desk, smashing on the floor before Donovan. He watched the amber liquid ooze across the tiles, and carefully adjusted his posture, moving his boots out of the way.

"Enough," said Abbadelli, again.

"You see, all I'm looking for here is justice, Mr. Abbadelli," said Donovan. "Justice for Autumn Allen. I'm sure you can appreciate that. I want to know who carved those symbols into her body, and I want to know why."

Abbadelli had risen from his chair and was pacing the room now, tapping his finger against his chin, clearly wrestling with something. He stopped after a moment, seeming to make up his mind. "Say that I *did* know her. What would that mean?"

"It would simply mean that you were able to help us with our enquiries," said Donovan. He reached for his cigarette packet and withdrew another, offering one to Abbadelli, who took it with an appreciative nod.

"You'd keep me out of it?"

"That depends," said Donovan. "Did *you* kill her?"

"Of course I didn't kill her!" snapped Abbadelli.

"Then in this matter, yes, I see no reason for you to concern yourself with talk of courts, or trials, or anything of that nature. So I'll ask you again—in what capacity did you know Autumn Allen?"

"She was my lover," said Abbadelli. "I intended for her to become my wife."

"You loved her, then," said Donovan.

Abbadelli nodded. For the first time since they'd met, the mob boss looked vulnerable. Whoever killed this woman had struck a very hard blow against a very powerful enemy.

"And what I said, about the events that night—I was right? You had dinner, you made love, and then she left for home by herself?"

Abbadelli slumped back into his chair, and Mullins slid his untouched whisky across to him. Abbadelli eyed him appreciatively, and then downed it in one. "I was asleep. I'd never have let her walk the streets alone at night. It's too dangerous. You know that. Especially to... to..."

"I think we understand," said Donovan. "To someone so connected to a *businessman* like you."

"What we *don't* understand is *why*," said Mullins, finally plucking up the courage to chip in. "Someone was trying to send you a message, weren't they? That's what those Ancient Egyptian symbols were all about. They wanted you to know who was responsible."

"The Circle of Thoth," said Abbadelli. He practically spat the words.

Donovan glanced at Mullins. Now they were finally getting somewhere. "Some silly little cult. That's all they are. Fools who think their old gods are going to protect them."

"Protect them from what, Mr. Abbadelli?" said Donovan.

"It's just some crackpot religion. Who knows what they believe? Look, they're the ones who killed Autumn. That's what those marks were all about. They were placing a curse on her, or some kind of curse on me. That's the last thing they said to me. That I'd be cursed for what I'd done to them."

"And what had you done to them?"

"Nothing! Not really. Look, there's a scrap of land on the Upper East Side. It's been sitting derelict for years. Land is a precious commodity on Manhattan; you know that, so does everyone. I wanted to buy it, that's all. Build a new hotel, maybe a bar. I did a bit of digging, found out who owned it. Turned out to be this 'Circle of Thoth'. I thought it would be an easy transaction—take a bit of useless land off their hands, fill their coffers."

"But they didn't want to sell," said Mullins.

Abbadelli nodded. "I might have leaned on them a little too hard. I tried to persuade them into letting it go. It was nothing more than that—just a little pressure in the right places. Or so I thought." He ran a hand through his hair. "It was after that they started talking about all this apocalyptic stuff. The End of Days, how the earth would soon resemble the heavens, and how my soul was going to be cursed through all eternity for the things I'd done."

He realized his cigarette had burned down to his fingers while he'd been talking, and he dropped it in the ashtray. "I thought that was it, some ridiculous magic spell, a 'curse upon my soul'. Then people started turning up dead."

"*People*?" said Donovan. "Not just Ms. Allen?"

Abbadelli realized he'd said too much. Donovan could see it in his eyes. He ignored the question. "They killed her over a scrap of land," he said. "And you know what, I wasn't even that bothered about it. I saw a chance to make a few quick bucks, that's all. And now those bastards have gone and done this."

"You should have come to us," said Donovan.

Abbadelli smiled. "A man like me? Not so much."

"Where can we find them?" said Mullins. "The Circle of Thoth. Do they have an office, a church, someplace where you always met?"

"They did," said Abbadelli, "but I hear it burned down in a terrible accident." He stared at Donovan, willing him to defy him.

Donovan decided to play it cool. "And you've no idea where they've moved on to since? This scrap of land you mentioned?"

"There's nothing there. It's just a patch of wasteland. The hotel that once stood there was demolished years ago. There's nowhere for them to go."

"This exhibition that's coming to the Met," said Donovan. "The one that's opening tomorrow. Has that got anything to do with this 'Circle of Thoth'?"

"I couldn't tell you," said Abbadelli.

"All right," said Donovan. "I think we've got enough to be getting along with." He grabbed his whisky off the desk and drained the glass. It hit the back of his throat with a welcome burn. "Thank you for your time."

Abbadelli came around from the other side of the desk, and clasped Donovan by the hand again. "No, thank *you*, Felix. I appreciate your discretion. I really do. Everything you're doing to find Autumn's killers—it won't go unnoticed. You should come to dinner one night. Maybe bring Flora, eh?"

Donovan swallowed. "Maybe once this is all taken care of," he said, as diplomatically as possible.

"Yes, of course, of course," said Abbadelli. He patted Mullins on the shoulder. "Don't let him work you too hard, Sergeant," he said. He walked them to the door. "I trust you can find your own way out?"

"We'll be in touch," said Donovan.

"I'll be waiting," came the ominous reply.

THIRTEEN

"You always manage to pick the worst possible moments. It's as if you're *trying* to make my life difficult."

"Only trying?" said Gabriel. "I must admit, I thought I was doing better than that."

"Oh, you know what I mean," said Arthur, heaving an affected sigh. "Remind me what it is that you want again? I tuned out on the holophone after you said the words 'urgent', 'must meet', and 'today'."

Gabriel laughed. Arthur Wolfe was one of his most trusted acquaintances—a curator at the Metropolitan Museum of Art. They'd been through a lot together, and Arthur never allowed him to forget it. Not that he was genuinely put out—it was just another of his English affectations.

He was a scrawny man, tall and angular, with a thick mop of mousy hair. His wire-framed spectacles always seemed to be sliding down his nose, and he wore pullovers under his jacket, even in the summer. Lately, he'd started to develop a slight mid-Atlantic twang, and he hated it when Gabriel pointed it out.

Gabriel supposed it *was* a fairly one-way relationship. He only ever came to visit Arthur when he needed something, and although he'd been clear that it would always work the other way around, too, he supposed a museum curator didn't have a lot of call for the help of an illegal vigilante. If he was honest with himself, Gabriel was surprised how often he found himself calling on Arthur's help during the course of his investigations. Maybe, once this business with Ginny was over with, he would make a bit more of an effort, invite the guy over for dinner or something. He didn't seem like the type to enjoy one of the parties. It was another reason why Gabriel liked him.

"I was hoping for a bit of a preview," said Gabriel. "I thought maybe we could take a walk through the new exhibit?" They were sitting on a park bench across the street from the museum entrance. The building cast a long shadow over the park. Pigeons flapped about their boots, searching for non-existent crumbs.

"It's not finished yet," said Arthur. "Thus my admonishing tone. We're opening tomorrow, and I could really do with being on hand to help with the final preparations."

"I know," said Gabriel, "and I'm sorry. It's just—look, Ginny has gone missing."

"*Missing*?" said Arthur. "Didn't she head off to Egypt to see the sights?"

Gabriel nodded. "Yes. And she was supposed to come back on that ship, the *Centurion*."

"The same one that brought the exhibits?"

"Exactly. Only she didn't make it. Or rather, she did, but something happened to her onboard. Something that Felix thinks might be linked to the exhibition and Robert Landsworth."

Arthur rolled his eyes. "Why is it always *my* museum? Tell me that."

"There's more, I'm afraid," said Gabriel. "There've been a

couple of murders, too, and the victims have both carried certain... marks. One a tattooed cartouche of the name 'Thoth', the other... well, let's just say it was similar, and leave it at that."

"And with the timing and nature of the exhibition, you're drawing a parallel," said Arthur. "Well, I guess that's understandable. Although I'm not sure what I can do to help."

"Well, you can start by telling me if you've seen anything untoward going on, from Landsworth, or anyone else who's got a hand in the exhibit?"

Arthur thought for a moment, and then shook his head. "Not that I can think of. They're just a bunch of academics, like me. Landsworth's a bit of an old fop, really, a bit ineffectual. He likes to stomp around, giving everyone orders, and then when his back is turned they all get on with doing what really needs to be done. I have a hard time imagining him as a killer, or masterminding some sort of evil plot."

"All right," said Gabriel. "What about Thoth?"

"What about him?"

"Anyone shown a bit too much of an interest lately? Have you heard anything about a revivalist religion, a cult, anything like that?"

"No, definitely not. I mean, everyone's *interested*. The exhibition is basically a recreation of part of a temple to Thoth, from a previously undiscovered complex at Karnak. We've got visiting academics here to write papers, university students, that sort of thing." Arthur paused while he shooed a pigeon away with the edge of his boot. "There's a big buzz about it all, actually. The relationship between the temple and a nearby tomb suggest a hitherto unexplored connection between Thoth and Sekhmet, and the manner in which they were worshipped."

"Sekhmet?" said Gabriel. "Remind me, it's been some years."

"Daughter of the sun god Ra. She was a warrior goddess, who often took the aspect of a lion."

"Ah… now that makes sense," said Gabriel.

"It does?"

"This is going to seem like a strange question, Arthur, but have you ever heard of any Egyptian statues… coming to life?"

"Only in cheap dime novels and story papers," said Arthur. "Why?"

"It doesn't matter," said Gabriel. "It was just a passing thought. Are you going to let me take a look, then? I promise to be on my best behavior."

"I suppose so," said Arthur. "We can take a quick walk around. If anyone asks, you're a patron of the museum, all right?"

"I *am* a patron of the museum," said Gabriel.

"I think, after all of the things you destroyed last year, you're still operating at a deficit," said Arthur.

Gabriel laughed. "Come on, I know you're busy." He stood, scattering pigeons, his face creasing in pain. He was going to see Astrid after this, in the hope that she could fix him up a bit, as well as shed some light on the more unconventional aspects of the case.

"Are you all right?" said Arthur as he crossed the road.

"Nothing to worry about," said Gabriel. "Just one too many of those dime novels you mentioned."

* * *

Given that the exhibition was meant to be opening the next morning, everything behind the scenes appeared to be in rather a state of disarray. This, Arthur told him, was down to Landsworth, interfering at the last moment to make changes to the planned layout. It hadn't gone down well with the setup crew.

"He's here?" said Gabriel.

"Somewhere about," said Arthur. "Probably making a nuisance of himself." He hitched up the edge of a heavy red drape, which hung over the entrance to the temporary wing where the exhibition was being assembled. "Through here. And remember—a *quick* look."

He'd expected the exhibition to resemble every other gallery of antiquities he'd ever seen—broken pots, rusted tools and grave goods displayed inside glass cabinets, rows of statues mounted on plinths, the occasional tour guide to ensure you weren't touching anything you weren't supposed to, or to offer a dry, onerous commentary on the nature of each exhibit and those who had made it.

Here, though, things were a little different. They'd taken the whole business of recreating the temple to heart. The exhibits were arranged in the manner they'd been discovered, or at least in the way they'd been intended; the toppled statues had been righted and the columns had been propped upright with scaffolds, carefully painted in the same hues as the stone.

They'd partially rebuilt a colonnade, as well as reassembling a small building, its outer walls decorated in worn, but still visible, friezes. Sand had been scattered underfoot to add to the effect, and Gabriel half expected to feel the hot desert wind on his face as he followed Arthur along the colonnade, feeling dwarfed by the enormity of it all. He wondered if there was anything left at the original site. The museum must have paid a small fortune to the Egyptian government to gain permission to ship it all across the water.

Arthur stopped at the end of the colonnade, in the shadow of the building. Here, scores of men buzzed around carrying hand tools, while others were up ladders, still splashing sand-colored paint onto the walls, or hanging small printed signs beside the exhibits. Two of them were even manhandling an ancient statue into place inside an alcove, and Gabriel bristled at the sight of it.

"I have to admit, Arthur, the effect is quite striking."

"Isn't it just? Whatever Landsworth's faults, he's really delivered the goods," said Arthur. He scratched his nose, a little sheepish. "Of course, it's not exactly *accurate*. They've shortened the length of the colonnade, and the tomb was much further away and buried under the sand. But I think people will appreciate the effort."

"And all of this is dedicated to Thoth?"

"Yes. It's a small part of a much larger temple complex. Over there, for example," he pointed to the other end of the colonnade, "they found the upper body of a colossal statue with the head of an ibis, and beneath it was a pretty substantial network of tunnels and chambers."

"And mummies, presumably? You mentioned a tomb?"

"Ah, now that's the fascinating thing. They still haven't turned up any bodies. Even in the tomb, they didn't find a coffin, just a statue of Sekhmet presiding over a stone table or altar. We think it might have been used as a preparation area for the dead. In fact, it might not even be a tomb at all, but a different sort of temple altogether, of a sort we've never seen before. That's what's so exciting about it."

"Arthur? Arthur?" They both turned at the sound of another Englishman, to see a large man in a gray suit stomping over the sand toward them.

"Ah, hello, Mr. Landsworth," said Arthur. He sounded less than enthused.

"Listen, we've got a terrible problem back there with the signage. How are people going to know which way they're supposed to flow around the exhibits?"

"They probably haven't had chance to put the signs out yet. I'll look into it," said Arthur. He glanced at Gabriel. "Please, allow me to introduce my friend. He's a patron of the museum."

Landsworth stuck his hand out, and Gabriel took it. "Sorry, old chap. I'm afraid we're feeling the pressure a bit today, what? Grand opening tomorrow and all that."

"I understand," said Gabriel. "Nevertheless, it's a pleasure to meet you, Mr. Landsworth. I must compliment you on the exhibition. What a find! And so interesting..." He continued to pump Landsworth's hand enthusiastically, drawing an uncomfortable frown from the man.

"Yes, well, I fear I can't take all the credit," said Landsworth, brimming with false modesty.

"That's right," said Gabriel. "You had a partner back in Egypt, didn't you? I forget his name now..."

"Amaury," said Landsworth, "but how did you...?"

Gabriel, still holding the other man's hand, gently rotated his arm, revealing a small black cartouche on the underside of his wrist. He'd drawn it there with a fine black pen earlier that morning, carefully copying the symbols from the photographs Donovan had given him, hoping it wasn't going to smudge. "I believe we have a mutual friend," he said. "Miss Ginny Gray?"

Landsworth's reaction was quite startling. He practically yanked his hand free of Gabriel's, as if suddenly the recipient of an electric shock. "Well, I… I'm not really sure I recognize the name," he said, full of bluster. "But then, there are so many people associated with an archaeological dig of this scale, Mr…?"

"Oh, I'm sure you remember her! A blonde woman, a native New Yorker? You wouldn't have been able to miss the accent. She wrote me from Egypt, told me she'd got involved with your expedition. It sounded as if she was having a whale of a time. She mentioned you by name, Mr. Landsworth! She only had good things to say."

"Oh, well, yes, perhaps now you come to mention it, maybe I did meet her on one or two occasions." He took a handkerchief from his jacket pocket and mopped his brow. "I'm afraid I didn't catch your name?"

"Well, of course, I'll be sure to remember you to her," said Gabriel. "I'm seeing her later for dinner. In fact—you'd be more than welcome to join us?"

The lack of comprehension on Landsworth's face told Gabriel everything he needed to know.

"Oh, no, thank you, but I fear duty calls," said Landsworth. He glanced at his watch. "Speaking of which, I really must be getting back to the exhibition. There's still so much to be done before tomorrow's grand opening." He held out his hand again. "It's been a pleasure, Mr…?"

Gabriel shook it a little too vigorously. "No, no, the pleasure is all mine. Thank you for your time. And good luck with the exhibition." He released Landsworth's hand and turned on the spot, taking Arthur by the arm and leading him in the opposite direction.

He heard Landsworth make an odd little sound, somewhere between a sigh and an *mmph!*, but didn't look back, despite the fact he could feel Arthur tugging rather frantically on his sleeve.

"Well, that wasn't suspicious at *all*," said Arthur, when Gabriel finally allowed him to stop in the shelter of a doorway. They were standing in one of the Greco-Roman galleries, adjacent to the Egyptian wing. It was looking sadly depleted. Gabriel decided not to mention the fact to Arthur, imagining it was still something of a sore point.

"You know I don't go in for subtlety," said Gabriel.

Arthur gave him the sort of disapproving look that only an English public schoolboy could achieve. "Yes, and now he's going think *I'm* mixed up in whatever's going on, too. What am I going to say when he asks for your name?"

"Oh, tell him. I was only trying to spook him a bit. It worked, too. Did you see his face when I mentioned Ginny?"

Arthur nodded. "Unfortunately, I did. What do you think is really going on?"

"I have no idea yet," said Gabriel, "but I intend to find out. I'm going to call on Astrid. She might be able to shed some light on the more… metaphysical aspects of it all."

"All right. I'll keep my ear to the ground here," said Arthur.

"Well be careful. We don't know who or what we're dealing with yet," said Gabriel. "And stay away from those statues."

"What is it with you and statues today?"

"Trust me. You never know what they're thinking."

"You're a strange man, Gabriel Cross," said Arthur. "Oh, and will we be seeing you for the parade tomorrow?"

"A parade?"

"To open the exhibit. They're closing Fifth Avenue. Floats, candy floss, the lot."

"Yes, all right. I'll be there," said Gabriel. "Now get back to work, before Landsworth comes looking for you. Otherwise no one will know which way to flow around the exhibits tomorrow."

"I hate you," said Arthur. "I really, really do."

FOURTEEN

Astrid Lunn was an unconventional woman, both in terms of her beauty—which was exceptional—and her general outlook on life. She was intensely feminine, yet often wore men's clothes, and didn't mix well with others, typically preferring the company of books to people.

She referred to herself as an "occult detective", although Gabriel thought what she really meant to say was "soothsayer" or "witch", or whatever the modern equivalent might be. He presumed her to be independently wealthy, although it was entirely possible that she was, indeed, operating a private detective agency out of the back of her premises, specializing in a very particular sort of case. She certainly had the wherewithal.

She lived in an abandoned church in Greenwich Village, a venerable, crumbling old building that had been boarded up for years, while modern, commercial buildings had sprouted all around it, hemming it in, diminishing its place in the world.

Now, people simply drifted past on their way to and from their offices or clubs, failing to even cast a glance at the old place, an arrangement which suited Astrid just fine. Gabriel often wondered if she'd somehow cast a glamour over the place to make it seem invisible, but the truth was most likely far more mundane—that familiarity bred ignorance, and that people often ignored the beautiful things on their doorsteps, particularly if those things had no immediate bearing on their lives.

Gabriel, meanwhile, had developed a real fondness for the place. To him, it felt safe, in a strange, primal sort of way—a sanctuary, nestled in the heart of the city, protected by a legion of leering gargoyles. It wasn't the religious connotations, or even Astrid's reassuring presence, but the sense that it was the only place in Manhattan that wasn't coveted by other people.

Arthur had introduced him to Astrid some months earlier, during the events leading up to the Shadarach affair, and he'd found her an invaluable ally ever since. She didn't ask too many of the wrong sort of questions, she was highly intelligent, and she had an insight into the more mystical side of life that, as far as he was concerned, was unparalleled in all New York.

There was one catch—she'd only ever known him as the Ghost, and today, visiting for the first time in daylight hours, he'd come in his civilian guise. He wasn't yet sure how she was going to take it. He'd considered waiting for nightfall, but time was pressing, and besides—it was high time she knew the truth.

He loitered on the street corner for a short time, enjoying the mingling scents of the restaurant opposite, looking for an opportunity to sneak in unobserved. After a while, watching people drift past in a constant stream, each of them lost in their own little worlds, he realized there really was no point, and walked up to the front door, popped the hidden catch, and stepped inside.

The church hall was gloomy, filled with the musty odor of rotting wood. With the windows boarded over the only light that filtered through came from the holes in the roof; golden rays that seemed to have an almost physical texture in the gloaming, pooling on the flagstones by his feet. He stepped around them as he crossed to the far end of the hall, passing a heap of crumbling pews. He didn't know when the church had last seen a Christian service, but if the degeneration was anything to go by, it had been some years. It felt to him like a metaphor for his own lapsed spirituality.

He found the inner door that led to the former vestry, now given over to Astrid's workshop and living space, and rapped on the door.

"Hello? Anyone at home?"

Footsteps followed, and then the door creaked open and Astrid's smiling face peered out, blinking into the gloom. Her long dark hair was tied up in a ponytail, hanging loose over one shoulder and revealing her soft white neck. She had a button nose and full pink lips, and striking eyebrows that were now raised in a look of surprised greeting.

"Hello, Gabriel, come in," she said, in her cheery, singsong voice. "It's nice to see you without your mask."

He was about to argue that he never wore a mask, but then realized that was *exactly* what he did. He laughed. Well, at least the whole identity thing wasn't going to be an issue.

"I… *thank you*," he said, finally. "It's good to see you, too."

Her living quarters were as unique as she was; the walls were plastered with pages torn from books, maps, sketches, newspaper articles, photographs. At first, he'd taken them to be related somehow to an ongoing case, but he'd since realized that the walls were a sort of extension of everything in her head, and she papered them here, like random memories, stored away for later recall. Whenever she needed to refer to something, she always seemed to know exactly where it was.

A long workbench had been affixed to the far wall, running the length of the room. It was perhaps the most orderly work area that Gabriel had ever seen, even taking into account his days in the army; neat drawers and cupboards had been arranged underneath it, each of them labelled and containing everything from electrical components, to hand tools, to sprigs of holly. In the far corner, the carcasses of old, abandoned books—from which she'd already removed the pages she was interested in— formed a sorry, moldering heap.

A battered leather armchair served as her sole comfort in the whole place, and he presumed that was where she slept, too; the only other rooms were an adjoining chamber where she kept her clothes and toiletries, and a small bathroom stemming from that.

"I wondered how long it would be before you came to see me," she said. "I presume you're here about the apparition?"

Gabriel frowned. The apparition. He'd nearly forgotten about that. The mobsters had mentioned it again the previous night, at the Café Deluxe, but in his haste to pursue Ginny, he'd forgotten all about it. "Well, actually, that's not why I'm here."

Astrid frowned, peering up at him. She seemed to be weighing him up. "There's something wrong," she said. The concern was evident in her eyes. "Come on, sit down, tell me." She led him over to the armchair in the corner. He sat, and she dropped into a crouch before him, taking his hand. He wasn't entirely sure how to react.

"I took a bit of a beating. I have a wound on my back—I

know it's an imposition, but I wondered if you might take a look. I didn't really have anyone else to go to."

"No, not that." She frowned. "I mean, of course, I'll take a look. But that's not what I meant. I mean there's something *wrong*."

"Ah," he said. He supposed he shouldn't have been surprised by her perceptiveness. "In that case, it's rather a long story."

She smiled, standing. "Well, I'd better put the kettle on, then."

Over hot tea, he told her of Ginny, Landsworth, and the murders. Most particularly, he told her about what he'd found on the *Centurion*, and his encounter with the living statues.

"I hoped you might be able to tell me I'm not going crazy," he said afterwards, while she prepared a bowl of steaming water and some towels.

"Far from me to be the judge of that," she said, with a laugh. "Now take off your shirt and let me see to this wound."

Gabriel did as she said, removing his jacket and carefully unbuttoning his shirt. He watched her expression as she appraised him, setting the bowl down on the ground.

"You should be in a hospital," she said, running her fingers over his back. They felt cool and soft. "These bruises—you took more than just a beating. You must know that your ribs are broken, too. You're lucky to be alive."

"I know," said Gabriel. "Believe me, I know."

"Is this what those statues did to you?"

"They didn't help," said Gabriel, conjuring as much levity

as he could. "But most of it was the night before. I went up against one of the Reaper's new 'Enforcers'."

"The man-machines," said Astrid, nodding. "I've heard about them."

"They're virtually indestructible."

"Whereas *you're* not. You should know your limits. Decide when to get out." She was using wads of cotton wool soaked in the steaming water to clean away the fresh blood that was still seeping from the wound on his back. He tried not to react, but his muscles twitched as the hot liquid worked its way into the puckered groove. She put her hand on his hip, steadying him.

"This is a mess," she said. "What did this to you? I'm no expert, but I can see it wasn't a blade."

"A stone ankh," he said, "and it damn well hurt."

"I'm going to have to stitch it," she said. "You realize that?"

He nodded, then realized she was standing behind him. "Yes, do what needs to be done. And thank you."

"You're welcome," she said. "I might yet need you to return the favor, one day."

"I do hope not," he said, "but only for your sake."

She crossed to her workbench, pulled open a drawer, and sought out a needle and thread. "This is going to hurt," she said.

"More than having my ribs shattered by a machine with a wrecking-ball fist?"

"Probably." She laughed. "But I'll make it quick."

When she'd finished, she took a roll of bandages and strapped his chest, winding it up and round his shoulder. He felt constricted, but immediately better.

"You're not to go out fighting again until this is healed," she said, as he crossed to the kettle and filled it up for a second pot of tea. "Doctor's orders."

"If only," said Gabriel. "Things are rarely that simple, and the bad guys don't tend to wait around for me."

"Oh, so you're one of the good guys, are you?" she said, with a crooked smile. "I hadn't realized."

He laughed. "Well, aren't *you*?"

"I haven't quite decided yet." She dropped into the armchair, but not before dragging out a stool for Gabriel to sit on, too. "But let me have another look at those photographs, and I'll see what I can tell you."

He handed her the sheaf that Donovan had given him a couple of days before. "This one says 'Thoth'," she said, tapping the picture, "but I'm guessing you already knew that?"

He nodded.

"And the rest are just cosmetic. But this one is interesting." She was holding the mark that consisted of a series of nested shapes. "It's a Hermetic symbol. It's different from the others, but connected."

"Go on."

"Well, Hermeticism is a complex subject, but it's essentially based on three elements: the trinity of alchemy, astrology and theurgy. You could consider these the study of the physical world, the stars, and the gods, if you liked."

"A religion?" asked Gabriel.

"In a sense. But that's only part of it. It's a system of philosophy and magic, of attempting to comprehend the mysteries of the universe. The scientific method evolved from the Hermetic approach, the desire to test and explore and push boundaries." Gabriel held out a mug of tea and she took it gratefully, clutching it to her chest. "But yes, religion is at the core of it. More than that, though, there's a core belief about the microcosm representing the macrocosm, and vice versa."

"You've lost me," said Gabriel, propping himself on the stool.

"'As above, so below'," said Astrid. "It's one of the tenets of the Hermetic tradition. The physical world represents the heavens, and the heavens represent the physical world. They mirror each other. What happens here, on earth, is a direct reflection of what's going on in the other realm. In this one, one might influence the gods, or be influenced by the gods."

"All right," said Gabriel, "but I'm failing to grasp what this has to do with Thoth and the Ancient Egyptians."

"Thoth was the god of knowledge, responsible for the calculations that kept the heavens in order. In Greek and Roman times he became associated with Hermes, and then later, with the origins of the Hermetic tradition. Thoth is the start of it all."

"So you think the people behind all of this are followers of this Hermetic tradition?"

"More than followers, if your living statues are anything to go by. More like practitioners. If they're able to turn ancient statues into living idols, I'd say they're pretty adept at the alchemical art of transmutation, wouldn't you?"

Gabriel shrugged. "I'd say that it hurts when one of them stabs you in the back with an ankh."

Astrid sipped her tea, but he could see she was grinning.

"So, whatever they're doing, it's some sort of plan to influence the gods?"

"Maybe," she said, with a shrug. "It's difficult to know. They could just be a bunch of crackpots with a taste for the esoteric."

"Well that's a very useful perspective," he said, laughing. He placed his empty mug on the floor by his feet. "But one I'll take under advisement."

"See that you do."

"So, about this apparition. You really think there's something in it? Should I be concerned?"

Astrid laughed. "Oh, Gabriel. You don't see it, do you? It's all connected. The apparition is part of the answer. Get to the bottom of that and you'll find what you're looking for."

He frowned. "What do you mean?"

"I mean it's no coincidence that a floating apparition appears over the streets of New York at precisely the same time as a ship arrives from Egypt carrying ancient treasures with a habit of coming to life, and a woman turns up dead, covered in ritual markings. They're all part of the same story."

Gabriel got to his feet. His mind was suddenly buzzing. He'd been a fool. "And Ginny?"

Astrid met his gaze. "Who can say? But if she's mixed up in all of this, the same path will lead you to the answer you're looking for."

He crossed to Astrid, leaned over, and kissed her on the cheek. "Thank you," he said. "For everything." Their eyes met for a moment, and then he straightened up, and crossed to the door.

"Don't be a stranger," she said. "If you need anything, I'll be here."

"That's more reassuring than you could possibly know," he said.

"Oh, and next time," she called after him, "bring pastries. You *never* bring pastries!"

Laughing, he pulled the door shut behind him.

FIFTEEN

Finally, the temperature had dropped.

Ginny sat on the terrace in a light flower-print dress, sipping a cool glass of water and staring up at the stars. They were so vivid here, and so plentiful. It looked as if someone had taken a paintbrush and speckled the sky. The sight of them made her feel small and insignificant; not in a diminishing way—just that it reminded her of her place in the universe, the cosmic scale of things. Being here, too, surrounded by the wreckage of eons—it made her troubles seem distant. The last few nights, she'd slept better than she had in months. She was feeling ready now to make the journey home, to rekindle her relationship with Gabriel, and to face whatever challenges came her way.

Tomorrow, she would take the train to Cairo, where she would visit the museum and arrange the short trek out to see the pyramids the following day. Then, soon after, she would take a steamship home to New York. She'd booked a ticket aboard the *Centurion*, and had already sent a telegram ahead to Gabriel, telling him to expect her. The time had come. It felt right.

"Now, here is a lady who has properly acclimatized to a life in the desert." She looked round to see Amaury standing by her table, smiling down at her. "A far cry from when we first met, just a short time ago." He took her hand, and kissed it. "You look radiant, Mademoiselle."

Ginny felt her cheeks flush. She was going to have to find a way to let him down gently. "Thank you," she said. "It's nice to see you again."

"Indeed. Have you enjoyed your time in Luxor?" He pulled out a chair to join her. They'd arranged to have dinner here together on the terrace, to celebrate her final night. She watched him take a cigarette from a small silver case and light it with a match. Smoke wreathed his head.

"It's been eye-opening," she said. "I'll say that much."

"Not what you expected, then?" he said.

"So much *more*. I mean I knew there'd be ruins—that's why I came. But it's more than that, isn't it? Like the Egyptian empire never really went away. It permeates everything. You can see the threads of culture stretching right back, all the way to ancient times. I hadn't expected that."

"You're an intelligent woman, Miss Gray. You see things as they really are, and not how the guidebooks would have you believe." He leaned forward, placing his hand on top of hers. "I shall miss your delightful company very much."

Ginny swallowed, carefully extracting her hand. "Listen, Jacques. I need to be straightforward with you about something. You're a delightful man, you really are, and you've been such a sport, taking me under your wing, showing me the sights, trusting me with the trip to your dig. I'll never forget it. Really I won't. It's just…"

"You have someone waiting for you back in New York," he said.

Ginny breathed a short sigh of relief. "Yes. It's complicated, but that's about the size of it." She reached over and touched his arm. "Are you terribly angry with me?"

Amaury smiled. "How could I be? You've given me no promises, no cause to hope. I admire you very much," he said, "and it does not surprise me to hear your heart is already given to another."

"Well, that's a relief," said Ginny. She sat back in her chair. "Now, what will you have to drink? It's a lovely evening, and I'll be damned if we're wasting it talking about things that will never be."

Amaury laughed. "Are all women from New York so direct?"

"Only if they know what's good for them," said Ginny. She beckoned the waiter over and ordered two gin and tonics.

"Now," said Amaury, "before you object, I want to give you something, and I want you to accept it without a fuss."

"Oh, really," said Ginny. "There's no need. You've done far too much for me already. I shouldn't like to take advantage."

Amaury rolled his eyes. "I like that you are not very good at doing what you are told," he said.

Ginny laughed. She could see he was going to be offended if she refused. "Oh, all right then, what is it?"

Amaury took a little leather purse from his pocket and placed it on the table between them. It was small, and decorated with an amateurish painting of the Eye of Horus. She'd seen hundreds like it at the tourist markets all over the city. She stifled a frown. All that fuss over something that wouldn't even fetch a couple of cents back home?

"It's... well... it's..." she stammered, unsure what to say.

"Well open it!" said Amaury.

She picked it up, cursing herself for being so foolish. There was something small inside, and so she undid the leather strap and tipped it out into her palm. It was a small golden ring, its face inlaid with lapis lazuli and marked with a symbol that she recognized from the site of the dig—nested triangles, squares, and circles. It was beautiful, and she had the sense that it was very, very old.

"I can't accept this," she said, wide-eyed. "It's an antique. It belongs in a museum."

Amaury grinned. "Do you like it?"

"Very much."

"Then it belongs on the finger of someone who might treasure it," he said. "It is a ring, and rings are made to be worn, not to sit in display cases in dusty museums in the far corners of the world." He shrugged. "Besides, Landsworth has already filled his pockets until they overflow. His greed seems to know no bounds. It is obscene to watch. His exhibition will be the talk of the world. Let him show off all the trinkets he does not understand, while you take something of meaning from all our efforts."

"Where's it from?"

"The tomb of Sekhmet, where we ventured together into the dark. Let it be a memento of your trip."

"Well, if you're certain?" said Ginny.

He nodded.

"Then I shall treasure it," she said.

She moved to slip it back into the leather purse, and he sat forward, holding out his hand for her to stop. "Oh no," he said, "please, try it on. I should like to see you wear it."

"Very well," said Ginny. She slid it carefully onto the little finger of her right hand. It was snug, and she held it up so he could admire it.

"Perfect," he said. "Just perfect."

"I shall have to treat it with great care," she said. "Tell me, what does the symbol mean? I saw it at the site, too, in the large courtyard area. It doesn't look terribly Egyptian."

The waiter had arrived with their drinks, and she lowered her hand, a little self-conscious. Amaury waited until he had deposited their drinks and left.

"It is a symbol that is very dear to me," he said, "a reference to the interconnectivity of all things. When Thoth calculated the heavens, he observed that the heavens resembled the domain of men. What occurred above, amongst the gods, was mirrored below. Thoth conspired for things to remain that way, for the benefit of mankind. If the lands of men might always resemble the realm of the gods, then mankind might always be happy, and the gods always in control." Amaury took a swig of his drink.

"Over the years, however, mankind disrupted those plans, as the great pharaohs believed themselves worthy of divinity. Mankind forgot its place, and the realms of gods and men drifted apart. Over thousands of years, mankind forgot about the gods, and the gods fell into a long and restful slumber. There they wait, dreaming of a time when they might be awoken in order to realign the heavens and the realm of men."

"So, when you spoke of waking the gods, it was this you were referring to?" said Ginny.

Amaury waved a dismissive hand. "Oh, no, merely that in excavating the ancient monuments, we might once again show them to the world. It is a good story though, is it not?"

"It's marvelous," said Ginny. "Thank you, Amaury." She sipped at her gin, enjoying the cool, crisp taste of it on her palate. "I shall write to you from the *Centurion*, and again when I reach New York."

"The *Centurion*?" said Amaury, surprised.

"Yes, I booked my ticket this morning. I leave from Cairo in a few days."

"Then you shall have a traveling companion, for that is the vessel Landsworth has arranged to transport the antiquities to New York."

Ginny tried not to look too dismayed. "Wonderful," she said, painting on a smile.

Amaury chuckled. "Come now, Miss Gray. There is no need to be coy. I see that Mr. Landsworth has not made the best impression. It is a particular skill of his to alienate people. Let me guess—he issued you with a 'warning' in the desert, telling you to keep away, and that you should never have agreed to come along to the dig?"

Ginny frowned. "Well, something like that," she said.

"Ah," said Amaury. "He told you I was not to be trusted."

Ginny swallowed. She was starting to feel a little uncomfortable. "I'd prefer to put it all behind me," she said. "Let's just say that I shall not be sharing a table with him during our crossing, and leave it at that."

"Very well," said Amaury, amused. "But I fear for Mr. Landsworth's safety if he inadvertently crosses your path."

Ginny couldn't help but laugh. "Well, perhaps you should offer *him* a warning of his own."

"I might just do that," he said, raising his glass. "Come now, let us toast your final night in Luxor. Here's to you, and whatever the future might bring."

"To the future," said Ginny, clinking her glass against his. She leaned back, looking out across the desert at the distant stars. Only this time, she couldn't shake the feeling that they were looking back.

SIXTEEN

"You know, I'm starting to get the impression you can't keep away, Inspector Donovan. And here's me thinking you had a distaste for corpses."

"I do," growled Donovan, chewing on the end of his unlit cigarette. He was back in Vettel's laboratory, staring at the milky-white corpse of an overweight mobster. This one had been in the morgue for well over a week, chilling in one of the storage cabinets, and the flesh had taken on a pale, sickly hue. The man was going blue around the lips, and his eyelids were shut tight and rimed with frost. Donovan could see the little ice crystals, resting on the tips of his eyelashes. There was a six-inch gash in his throat, yawning open to expose the muscles and arteries inside.

"I have to hand it to you," she said. "You hide it well."

"Very droll," said Donovan. He bit down too hard on the cigarette and it split, flooding his mouth with dry tobacco. He plucked it out and tossed it in the trash, trying to hide his distaste.

"Whoever tipped you off was really on to something, Felix. Take a look at this." She crossed to the corpse and lifted the man's arm, presenting his wrist.

Donovan frowned.

"Come on, he won't bite," said Vettel. "But I might if you

don't get over here and let me show off a bit. I've been putting in the hours to help you out with this one."

"I know, I know," said Donovan. "And I appreciate it. I really do." He went to join her.

"Here," she said. She pointed to a small, puckered mark in the flesh.

"What is it? Looks like he was wounded in the fight. It's just a ragged tear."

"Look again," said Vettel. "In light of Autumn Allen."

With a sigh, Donovan leaned closer, peering at the wound. She was right—the scabrous line traced the faint shape of an ibis. It was simple, and the perpetrator clearly hadn't taken care in the same way they had with Autumn Allen, but there was no doubt—it was derived from a similar ancient design. "An ibis," he said. "I see it."

"Indeed. And do you remember who this man was?"

"Howard Fuseli, a mobster working for the Reaper," said Donovan. "They were marking the corpse, making sure the Reaper knew who was responsible. Good God, I wonder how far back this goes."

"I can give you some idea," said Vettel. "But first, the throat. Look at the gash."

"I'd rather not."

She ignored him, running her index finger back and forth, just above the wound. "He was slashed from left to right by someone employing a large, curved blade. It was sharp, but see how it's basically ripped his larynx out? It's a particularly brutal way to go. Judging by the lack of other wounds on the body, I'd say this was definitely an execution, rather than a brawl.

Someone probably held his hands behind his back, maybe pulled his head back a little, while another slashed him once across the throat."

"At least it was over quickly," said Donovan, "which is more than he deserved."

Vettel drew a cotton sheet over the corpse. "This was the only one I still had in storage, but I've got scans of the others."

"Others, as in plural?" said Donovan.

"I wouldn't have said it otherwise." She walked over to her holograph terminal and flicked it on. The lamp emitted its familiar hum as it warmed.

"No Sergeant Mullins today?" said Vettel. "I thought you two were inseparable these days."

Donovan decided not to take the bait. "I told him to wait in the car."

"Saving him from the corpses?"

"Saving him from *you*. I think he finds you a little intimidating."

"Me?" said Vettel. "But I'm a pussycat!"

"You're a damn good doctor and you don't take any shit," said Donovan. "That's what he's not used to. None of them are. When you've been in this job as long as I have, you've seen plenty of people come and go. We've had our fair share of surgeons, and you're the first who's ever really given a damn. That counts for a lot in my book, but it scares the hell out of the lads at the precinct. They don't know how to act around you. They're used to tossing the police surgeon a body and getting a perfunctory report. You, on the other hand, ask a lot of questions. Difficult questions. Some of them think you're making their job harder, that you're just breaking their balls because you can. They haven't cottoned on yet that it's actually because you're good at your job."

Vettel smiled. "I knew I liked you for a reason," she said. The holograph blinked on behind her, and she turned and inserted a series of glass plates from a stack she'd pre-prepared on the counter.

"Right, here we go," she said, as the image of a body shimmered to life in the mirrored cavity. "Joey Malone. Killed three weeks ago in what we all assumed was a mob battle."

With the Reaper going around assuming control of most of the smaller outfits, there'd been a lot of this over the course of the last few months. No one was talking, of course, and it was almost impossible to prosecute, even when the police knew who was responsible. Consequently, a lot of the deaths were written off, chalked up as statistics and forgotten about. It was wrong, of course, they all knew that, but small-time gangsters taking each other off the streets had never seemed like a priority.

"But it wasn't?" said Donovan.

"I'm beginning to think not," said Vettel. "At least, not in the way we thought. Look at the gash in his throat."

Donovan leaned closer. The hologram was startlingly realistic, and the kid's face—he couldn't have been more than eighteen years old—was set in a horrible, rictus snarl. There was no denying that the slash in his throat was a close match to the one that had put an end to Fuseli, however.

"And a mark on the wrist?"

"Not in this instance," said Vettel. "The killer must have been in too much of a hurry, but here's another." She hurriedly switched out the slides, and a moment or two later, Donovan was looking at a third corpse. This was an older man, around forty years, who he recognized as Albert Harness, a well-known pickpocket and snitch. Once again, his throat had been cut in exactly the same way.

Vettel switched the slides, offering Donovan a view from the reverse. She pointed to Harness's wrist. "Here," she said. "We missed it the first time, for the same reason we missed the one on Fuseli—it's crude, and it's been done in a hurry. The hallmarks are all there, though. It's the same killer, or killers."

"Any more?" said Donovan. He could see where this was going.

"Another five that all fit the same pattern, in one way or another. They all died within the last month. You want to see?"

"No, that's enough. But I do have another question. Have you had anyone in from a recent fire, probably on the Upper East Side? It'll be within the same time period, possibly more recent. It might not have been a criminal investigation, but I'm looking at a number of victims."

She shook her head. "No, sorry, nothing."

"All right, thanks." He'd have to get Mullins to check with the fire department.

"What do you think we're looking at?" said Vettel.

"Gang war on a scale we haven't seen for years," said Donovan. "The cult who did this," he jabbed at the flickering hologram, "they're known as the Circle of Thoth, and they're going up against the Reaper. I thought it all started with Autumn Allen, but I was wrong. What you've shown me today proves that it's already out of hand. If we don't put it down quickly, we're going to see all of Manhattan caught in the crossfire." He scratched at his beard. "And what's more—I think the Circle of Thoth have just brought in a LOT of reinforcements."

"What can I do?" said Vettel.

"You know what we're looking for," said Donovan, "so keep your eyes peeled. Anything comes in that looks like it's connected, call me."

"Of course," said Vettel.

"Listen, I've got to run. I need to make a call. Thank you," said Donovan. He didn't wait for her response before running out of the door.

"I'm sorry, Inspector, but Mr. Cross is away in the city at the moment. I'm not sure precisely when he'll be back, but I'm not expecting him any time soon. Would you like me to take a message?"

"No, thank you. Maybe when you speak to him just let him know that I called."

"Certainly, sir. Goodbye."

Donovan hung up the receiver on Gabriel's valet, and cursed. He'd already tried the apartment, first on the holotube, and then in person, but the man was nowhere to be seen. Donovan was half concerned that his injured body had finally given up on him someplace in town, and that he'd turn up in a hospital somewhere, too broken to be any help.

That, though, was just his frustration talking. More likely he was out visiting an ally, trying to find out more about the cultists and what they were up to, or chasing down Landsworth in search of Ginny.

Whatever the case, Donovan needed to talk to him, and soon. Things were about to spiral out of control. He could see it coming. If the Reaper sent his Enforcers up against whatever godforsaken voodoo the cult had just shipped in from Egypt, then all hell would break loose. There was no way the police department was equipped to handle the fallout.

He needed the Ghost, and he needed him *now*.

SEVENTEEN

t was a balmy night, and the Ghost, drifting high above the rooftops of Fifth Avenue, wished he were at home, sipping a margarita and listening to a lazy jazz record on the Victrola. He needed to rest, to find a moment of respite. If Ginny were there she would have forced the issue, regardless of everything else going on—she'd have whisked him back to Long Island, and they'd have spent the night together, sitting on the veranda and looking up at the stars.

Only Ginny wasn't there, and that was why he couldn't stop.

He felt as if he were caught in an endless cycle of days and nights, Gabriel and the Ghost, unable to halt his progress as he careened into whatever was coming next. He risked losing perspective; he knew that. There was no time, though—he could sense something building, like a fever slowly taking hold of the city. Soon it was going to break, and he needed to be ready to act, whatever the risk to his own wellbeing.

He circled over the rooftops, keeping low. His chest still burned with every breath, although the pain had subsided considerably since Astrid had worked her magic, particularly when he flexed his lower back. He had no intention of getting mixed up in any brawls that night; even if Astrid hadn't warned him off, he knew he couldn't withstand any more beatings. Not yet. His reactions were dulled, his body lethargic. Another fight like the two he'd already faced this week would probably see the end of him.

Tonight, his sole ambition was to catch a glimpse of the mysterious floating apparition, to put Astrid's theory to the test.

He hovered in the shadow of a water tower for a moment, before cutting the power to his boosters and lowering himself to the roof of his own apartment building. His boots crunched on the gravel as he set down.

The apparition had been seen around these parts, according to the news reports, and he hoped it was just a matter of time before it put in another appearance. He'd been circling for over an hour, covering around a square mile of the city, but so far he'd seen no indication of anything untoward. In fact, the city seemed unusually quiet, as if it were holding its breath for tomorrow's parade.

He crossed to the corner, hopping up onto the low wall. Below, even at this hour, people were still flowing about the maze of streets like blood cells coursing through the veins and arteries of the city.

Elsewhere, Manhattan was dreaming. At least, that's how it seemed to him—all the brilliant neon and fizzing electric lights, the holographic statues glowing sharp and blue in the darkness, police blimps bobbing beneath the canopy of cotton wool clouds, picked out by the tails of their own search beams. It all seemed like a distant dream, conjured up by the collective imagination of the citizens, sleeping now in their beds.

Maybe it was the painkillers talking. Or perhaps it was

what Astrid had said, about the earth reflecting the heavens and the design of ancient gods. If those gods had been supplanted, what had replaced them? Mankind itself? Did that mean they had now assumed the power to manipulate the heavens, too?

He heard a thud from somewhere behind him, and turned, half expecting to see the apparition there, watching him. There was nothing.

He crossed to the other side of the rooftop, scanning the streets as he walked. There it was again, a distant thud, like the rumble of brewing thunder. It had come from ground level, though, a couple of streets away. He boosted across to the building on the other side of the cross street, and ran across the narrow roof, avoiding a large skylight.

He peered down into the gloom, his night-vision goggles casting everything in a faint red glow.

His heart sank.

An Enforcer was down there, bearing down on an unarmed man. The sound had been its fist, pummeling the concrete as it attempted to crush him; he could see the tide of broken slabs it had left in its wake.

The Ghost sighed. To get involved now would be fraught with danger. He still hadn't come up with a practical way of stopping the Enforcers, and he doubted he'd be able to pull the same trick again, tempting it up the side of a building. He couldn't withstand the beating necessary to lure it in, for a start.

Still, he couldn't leave an unarmed man to be murdered by the thing in cold blood. He was going to have to try a snatch and grab—lift the man out of there as quickly as possible, and try not to get hit in the process.

He didn't have time to consider—he pulled the cord and dived off the building, bringing his arms around before him like a swimmer making a swan dive. The air rushed past his face, cool and invigorating, as he hurtled toward the flagstones below.

His boosters kicked in about halfway down, shooting him forward, and he angled his body, swooping down low, twisting in front of the Enforcer and grabbing for the man, grappling him around the waist.

He hoisted him up into the air and they shot across the ground. The Ghost's arms burned as he tried to cling to his payload, and the man, suddenly realizing what was happening to him, started to beat down upon the Ghost's back with both fists, yelling curses and shouting to be set down.

"All right! All right!" The Ghost twisted, sending them careening down an alleyway, and, unable to reach inside his coat to cut the power, used a nearby trash cart as the next best thing to a soft landing.

"What do you think you're doing?" bellowed the man, as he picked himself up, dusting off a filthy banana peel from his clothes. In his haste, the Ghost hadn't noticed what the man was wearing, but now he could see that he was dressed in flowing black robes, and had a scarf wrapped around his head, so that only his eyes were exposed.

"Getting you away from that thing," said the Ghost. "It was about to pulverize you."

"I was luring it into a trap, you bloody fool!" He reached behind him, pulling a curved blade from his belt. He tossed it from one hand to the other, and it caught the light, glinting menacingly. "I should kill you now for your interference, but you haven't left me the time."

He hopped down from the heap of overturned trash, and ran for the mouth of the alleyway.

"Well, I wasn't expecting that," said the Ghost. "A simple thanks would have been enough."

He ran after the man, his feet stirring puddles of effluvia from the bins. Trap or not, the man had no chance of taking the Enforcer down with a sword. He was going to get himself killed, and whoever he was, the Ghost was going to stop him. He hadn't had the opportunity to check the man's wrist for a tattoo, but the suspicion had already bloomed that he might be involved in whatever was going on with Ginny, and the reciprocal killings between the cultists and the mob, and the Ghost wanted answers. If keeping him alive was the only way to do it, so be it.

He burst from the mouth of the alleyway into the street, skidding to a halt. The man hadn't been joking about the trap. There were five, six, seven other men in the street now, all similarly attired, all wielding the same curved blades. They surrounded the Enforcer, dancing forward to jab at the pilot with their swords, drawing streaks of dark blood, as the Enforcer swung its arms in a wild, uncoordinated fashion, smashing up the sidewalk and attempting to keep them at bay.

The Ghost watched as it lumbered over to a parked car, wrenching the driver's door off and holding it up like a shield, battering away their attacks as they ducked in, swords flashing. It was impressive to watch, the way they harried it, driving it back. They were goading it toward the mouth of a different alleyway, he realized, trying to corner it, like lion tamers maneuvering an errant beast back into its cage.

The Enforcer caught one of them upside the head with the edge of the car door and he went down, blood spraying across the pavement. It took the opportunity to finish him off, lurching forward and crushing him beneath its massive foot. The Ghost cringed at the sound of cracking bones.

Another one went down, too, as it swiped its fist in a low arc, taking out his legs, knee joints exploding. He screamed as he hit the ground, but was silenced seconds later by another blow from its fist. The police surgeon was going to have a difficult time telling him apart from the concrete in the morning.

The Ghost considered his options. If he got involved now, he risked death at the hands of both factions. The idea wasn't particularly appealing. He felt entirely helpless, standing there watching the battle unfold, but there was little else to be done. His best option was to swoop in when and if they brought the Enforcer down, try to disarm one of the men and get them somewhere else where he could question them. It wouldn't be easy, but it might give him the answers he was looking for.

He hugged the shadows in the mouth of the alleyway, remaining on guard.

The men had now managed to drive the Enforcer back into the alley opening, and were holding it in check with their hit-and-run tactics, jabbing at the pilot then pulling back, trying to keep out of the way of its fists.

The Ghost adjusted his goggles, straining to see. As he watched, the shadows around the Enforcer suddenly seemed to spring to life, tumbling out of the alley mouth to reveal another six men. These, too, were dressed in flowing black robes, although they were armed with blowpipes, rather than swords.

They flowed around the Enforcer like pooling oil, their blowpipes raised. While their sword-wielding companions kept the thing occupied, they raised their blowpipes to their lips and issued a synchronous volley of darts, which struck the pilot in a meticulous line, forming a necklace of feathered darts around his throat.

The men fell back, moving outwards in a widening circle around the Enforcer, as, enraged, it hurled the car door into their midst, lifting another man from his feet and sending him careening back into a building. He struck the wall with a crunch, and slid unconscious to the ground.

The Enforcer took an unsteady step forward, and then seemed to pivot on its left foot, almost toppling. It slammed its fist into the ground to steady itself, and hung there for a moment, still and silent. Then the pilot began to seize up inside his harness, muscles twitching, spittle frothing at his mouth. His eyes rolled back in their sockets, and the Enforcer suit began to shake, mirroring his uncoordinated gestures, thrashing at the ground and sending plumes of tarmac into the air.

It toppled onto its back, still twitching as the poison ran its course, chewing up the road as it clawed unknowingly at the ground.

Within moments, the pilot was dead. The suit froze, caught in a bizarre, ungainly pose as the poison constricted the pilot's muscles, and his curling limbs caused the machine to hug itself until the pistons popped with a hissing release of gas.

The Ghost—who had been fixated on the spectacle of the Enforcer's demise—glanced around, searching for a likely target amongst the men.

They were all gone—every single one of them. They hadn't even waited around to see their work completed, but had simply melted away, running off into the night. He'd been a fool. He'd waited too long for the fight to play out.

Cursing, the Ghost stepped out of the alley mouth, wondering if any of the dead men might yet provide any clues. He twitched as he felt a prick of something sharp in his neck, and raised his hand, suddenly panicked, to find a feather dart protruding from the soft flesh behind his ear.

He could already feel the tranquilizer numbing his senses, spreading like a cold compress being held against his skin. He had seconds before he went out. If he collapsed here, the cult would have him. He couldn't imagine they would let him live, and dead, he was no use to Ginny.

He pulled the dart from his neck, having the foresight to shove it in his pocket, and then, wavering, fired up his booster jets and shot up into the sky.

The cool breeze helped to keep him sensate long enough to clear a few blocks, hopefully putting enough distance between himself and the cultists that they wouldn't be able to find him.

Blackness lined his vision. He dipped his head, targeting a nearby rooftop, and dropped like a stone, landing heavily and breaking into a roll. He came to rest in the shadow of a potted fern tree, his body already too numb to feel the pain.

Woozily, he tried to prop himself up, but the drug was already taking effect.

His last, bizarre impression was of a baboon, sitting on the low wall across the rooftop, observing him with a single, glowing eye.

EIGHTEEN

The parade had been due to start at ten o'clock, and Gabriel was running late. It was already close to eleven.

He'd woken on the rooftop around nine, the sun stinging his eyes, a pigeon pecking obtrusively at his sleeve. He'd staggered to his feet, ignoring the ache of fresh bruises, and boosted across the rooftops to his apartment building, where he'd let himself in, showered, and swallowed three cups of strong coffee in an attempt to bring himself round.

Even now, as he hurried through the park on his way to the museum, he felt tired and sluggish, as if he were wading through molasses. He'd chosen not to dose himself up on painkillers, fearing they would further impair his senses, and now, with a debilitating headache stirring, he cursed himself for not bringing them along. Still, at least he'd remembered his sunglasses; a habit acquired after years of insobriety. He was thankful for small mercies.

New Yorkers had emerged in their droves to witness the promised spectacle, and the police had deployed in equal measure, lining the avenue with metal barriers to hold back the thronging masses. Little stalls selling candied nuts, hot dogs and ice cream had set up along the route, and were on course to make a bundle, as the carnival spirit set in and people made the most of the clement weather. The noise was tremendous, filled with excited babble, honking horns and the distant rumble of drums, as a marching band led the floats along the avenue, past the cheering crowds.

The parade, he gathered, had started in Washington Square Park, and would end upon arrival at the museum. The Mayor would then declare the exhibition formally open, and no doubt Arthur and his colleagues would spend the rest of the day turning people away as they fought over the few remaining tickets for the afternoon.

Gabriel was surprised by the sudden surge of interest in the exhibition, but then, he supposed the ancient dead had always had a powerful draw—particularly to a nation like his, whose roots were still shallow when compared to some of the ancient civilizations of Africa and Europe. He doubted the city would make such a fuss over the visit of a *living* monarch, but then again—they'd probably shelled out a great deal to secure the opportunity to debut the exhibition at the Met, and so any interest they drummed up amongst potential visitors would help to soften the blow.

The area around the museum itself was dense with milling people, so Gabriel backtracked a little way, until he could find a quieter spot, closer to the railing. He propped himself against it, hunching low, his head throbbing and his mouth dry. He'd get the dart to Donovan later; see if one of the police surgeons couldn't run a comparison on the tranquilizer the cult had used to sedate him.

What had they wanted with him? Had they simply thought to incapacitate him so he couldn't follow them? If they'd meant to kill him, he'd have been dead and cold by now. And what of the baboon he'd seen, the one with the mysterious glowing eye? Perhaps he'd been rendered delirious by the drug. That was certainly the most reasonable explanation.

Then again, nothing seemed reasonable where it related to the present case; compared to living statues, ancient cults and floating specters, a baboon seemed a relatively modest proposition.

Absently he wondered if Donovan was in the crowd somewhere, and how his investigation was progressing. He decided to stop by the precinct building later that night, before continuing his search for the apparition. It was time they compared notes again, to see if either of them could fill in any of the other's blanks.

Around him, the crowd had started cheering, and he glanced up to see the parade was drawing near. The lead float comprised the head and torso of a colossal statue, rendered in papier mâché and painted to look like sandstone. It had the head of an ibis; its long, sweeping beak resembled the curve of the cultist's swords, and the sight of it caused a shudder of recognition in Gabriel.

Thoth.

The cult was taunting the Reaper. The entire parade—the whole exhibition, in fact—was a celebration of their core beliefs. They were uniting the whole of New York in a carnival to welcome Thoth to the city, right under the noses of the mob. Every time the Reaper looked at a newspaper, a street sign, a member of the public waving a souvenir flag, all he was going to see was his dead girlfriend. The audacity of it was breathtaking, but there was one thing that Gabriel was certain of—the Reaper was not going to stand for it. There was trouble in the air.

The float was being pulled along by four horses, and flanked by an army of waving men and women, many of them sporting faux Egyptian headdresses and wearing tunics and sandals. He saw others with curved wooden swords and heavy black eyeliner, and amongst them, men dressed in black robes, wearing headscarves that covered their faces.

So, it seemed the cult were expecting a fight, too.

Gabriel scanned the crowd, looking for any faces he recognized. If the cultists were here, it was likely the mob was here, too, and they'd find it easy to move amongst the crowds without being spotted by the police. If they started something now, then a whole host of innocent civilians were likely to get hurt.

The first float slid by, followed in quick succession by the marching band. Gabriel winced, the bass drum setting off tremulous detonations of pain in his head.

The next float was a pyramid, surrounded by gleeful schoolchildren, most of whom seemed to be enjoying the attention, calling out to the crowd and waving furiously at everyone they passed. They, too, were steeped in fancy dress, from pharaohs to tiny Cleopatras, complete with an ominous rubber asp.

The third float was a massive sphinx. It sat like a statuesque cat upon an enormous trailer, towed along by a motorcar. It had a man's face, complete with gaudy headdress and ceremonial beard, and sitting astride its back was a woman, waving down to the heaving crowds. People were pointing up at her and waving back, cheering her on.

Gabriel recognized her immediately. It was Ginny.

He stared up at her as the float sailed by, mouth agape. Her clothes and makeup had been designed to resemble an Egyptian queen, and she carried a golden staff in her left hand, topped with an orb. She was wearing a black wig, cut in severe bangs that framed her pretty face.

There was no doubt in his mind—this time, he wasn't seeing things. It was Ginny up there.

"Ginny!" he bellowed, cupping his hands around his mouth. "Ginny!" He broke down into a wracking cough, a white star of pain flaring in his lung.

If she heard him above the adoring crowd, she didn't acknowledge it. The man behind him was leaning in, pressing him up against the barrier, and so Gabriel shoved him out of the way and ran after the float, trying to keep pace, waving his hands to get Ginny's attention. From up there, though, he must have seemed like any other person in the crowd, calling out and gesticulating.

There was nothing for it. He was going to have to get closer.

Men in costume, all dressed in the white rags of Egyptian slaves, surrounded the float. He had no way of telling whether they were affiliated with the cult, or simply people who'd been brought in to support the celebrations. Either way, he'd have to fight his way through—whoever they were they weren't going to like him getting close.

He saw a break in the crowd, and he took it, pushing his way past a man holding a young boy, and swinging up and over the barricade. He saw people pointing and shouting, but ignored them, running up alongside the float. It must have been twenty feet high, and he couldn't see a means to scale its smooth exterior. There was probably a hidden ladder inside, but he didn't have time to waste looking for it. "Ginny! Down here!"

She glanced down at him, and their eyes met. A confused expression crossed her face, as if she doubted the evidence of her own eyes.

"Ginny, it's me, Gabriel," he called. Someone tried to block his path, but he shoved him aside, still maintaining eye contact with Ginny, running along beside the trailer.

"Gabriel?" she called. She was echoing his words as a question, as if still unsure who he was or what he was doing here, shouting up at her like this.

"Jump down! Come on, get down from there, right now! It's time to go home."

She frowned, as if his words had suddenly struck a chord.

"Come *on*!"

But then the first blow struck him in the gut, and he doubled over, gasping for breath. He tried to right himself, to push past the men who were swarming in around him, but there were too many of them, and the float was already receding into the distance.

It was like fighting against the tide. There must have been ten or more of them, surrounding him, channeling him back to the barrier. He railed against them, but they pinned his arms, pushing him back. They weren't going to do anything here, not in front of all these people, but nor were they going to allow him to get close to her.

He felt his back strike the barricade, and then he was up and over, sprawling to the ground amongst the booted feet of the onlookers as the crowd of men dispersed again.

He dragged himself to his feet, dusting himself down. His damaged ribs flared with pain. Another band was passing now, trumpets blaring, and up ahead he could see only the tail end of the sphinx, disappearing into the distance.

He was about to go after it again, when the shooting started. Around him, everyone started to scream.

"Get down! Everybody, onto the floor!" The people nearby did as he said, starting a wave that dropped like dominoes; parents sheltering their children, husbands their wives.

Gabriel tried to see where the shooting had come from, but it was no good—there were still too many people and the gunmen were already lost in the panicked crowd. Uniformed police officers were moving in, pushing everybody back, telling the crowd to disperse. The bands had stopped playing, and the only sound now was people screaming as they ran for cover, trying desperately to get away from whoever had a gun, and the terrible thing they'd done.

Three men lay dead in the road at the foot of their float, splayed across the surface. They were riddled with bullet holes, which—judging by the pattern of the wounds—had clearly come from multiple directions.

Gabriel had no doubt they were cultists, targeted specifically by the Reaper to disrupt the parade. This wasn't an attempt to strike a real blow at the enemy—at least not in terms of show of force—but to reclaim the parade, to undermine the celebration. Now, when people talked about the exhibition, it would be with the solemn knowledge of what had happened, when three unarmed men had been callously murdered in the street in front of hundreds of children. For New Yorkers, any talk of Thoth for years to come would be marred with bloodshed.

Gabriel decided he could let the police deal with this particular crisis—the reprisals would come later that night, when he'd be better equipped to make a difference. Now, he would go after Ginny.

He broke into a run, weaving in and out of the fleeing crowd, hurrying after the float.

He found it abandoned just a few hundred yards up the road, all sign of Ginny and the cultists gone. He turned on the spot, trying to see which way they'd fled, but there were hundreds of people in the immediate area, many of them wearing fancy dress, and it was impossible to tell. They'd probably bundled her off in the car as soon as the shooting started.

Furious with himself, he punched the side of the sphinx, his fist passing right through the papier mâché exterior and snapping a wooden support beam inside.

He knew they had her now, and that they'd done something to her, probably drugging her to make her suggestible, or to keep her disorientated and compliant.

Most importantly, though, he knew she was still alive. This cult—whoever they were—had kidnapped her for a reason, and he was going to do everything in his power to get her back.

NINETEEN

"I saw her, Felix. I was *this close* to getting her back, and I screwed it up." He was pacing back and forth across the precinct roof, his hands balled into fists. "She looked right at me, as if she didn't recognize me anymore."

"These people, Gabriel, they're dangerous. Did you hear what I said about Vettel and the dead mobsters?"

"Yes, of course I heard you," snapped the Ghost. He wheeled around to face Donovan. "I *know* they're dangerous. I've seen what they can do. Last night I watched them put down an Enforcer like it was nothing but a stray dog. They nearly put me down, too. But *listen* to me. They've got Ginny. I've seen it now with my own eyes. I have to get her back."

"We're going to get her back," said Donovan. "Okay? We'll do it together. We'll bring these bastards down. But not like this. If you go out there tonight, by yourself, half dead from existing wounds and so angry that you're not thinking straight, you're just going to get yourself killed." Donovan took out his packet of cigarettes. "So sit down, shut up for a minute, and smoke one of these." He held out the packet, extending one of the cigarettes.

The Ghost glowered at him for a moment, and then took it. He pulled the ignition tab, watched the tip flare, and took a long, steady draw. He turned his back on Donovan, staring out across the glimmering rooftops.

He knew that Donovan was right—he just felt so *helpless*. Ginny was out there, alone, and he couldn't do anything about it. He wasn't good at biding his time. He'd never been a patient man at the best of times, and now—well, if only he knew whom to hit, he'd at least feel like he had a plan of some kind.

"I'm sorry," he said, after a while.

"There's no need," said Donovan. "I understand. If it were Flora… well, I can only imagine." He walked over to join him at the edge of the roof. The wind whipped up his coat and ruffled his hair. "But you have to trust me. We'll do this the right way. We'll nail them both, the Reaper and this Circle of Thoth."

"What about Landsworth?" said the Ghost. "Is he our way in? He admitted he'd met Ginny."

"You spoke to him? I thought we'd agreed th—"

"Hold on," said the Ghost, cutting him off. "There was no roughhousing, just as we agreed. I happened to bump into him at the museum yesterday while I was talking with Arthur. I tested the water, is all—told him we had a mutual acquaintance, and surreptitiously showed him a tattoo of a cartouche on my wrist."

"You did what?"

"Don't worry—I drew it there that morning, on the off-chance."

"The off-chance, eh?" Donovan sighed. "How did he take it?"

"He panicked. He didn't know what to say. I think he's scared, Felix. In too deep with no way of getting out, but not particularly happy about what's going on."

"I'm going to bring him in. Let him sweat it out in a cell for a while and see if he'll talk. I would have done it this morning, but what with everything that happened at the parade…"

"There's going to be a war," said the Ghost. "And we're going to be caught in the middle. There'll be more death in the streets before it's done. We need to be ready."

"Easier said than done," said Donovan. "We've both fought in a war before. Nothing could have prepared us for that."

"This is different," said the Ghost. "This is New York. This is *our* town. I'm damned if I'm going to let them take it from us, not after everything we've done to protect it."

Donovan nodded. Smoke plumed from his nostrils, but he didn't say anything.

The Ghost scanned the nearby rooftops, searching for any sign of the baboon. The thought had occurred to him that the cult might be using it to spy on people, its glowing eye a form of transmitter, but he could see nothing amongst the darkened recesses of the other buildings. "Astrid thinks the apparition is connected," he said.

"The one in the news reports?"

"Yes. She's convinced it's got something to do with the cult. She laughed when I told her we'd ignored it."

"What *isn't* connected," said Donovan. "That feels like a more pertinent question. I feel like I can't see the wood for the bloody trees."

"It seemed simple when it was just the Reaper," said the Ghost. "I knew what I was up against, then."

"He's a tough cookie," said Donovan. "Not to be

underestimated. He wants to have Flora and me over for dinner."

"He *what*?" The Ghost tossed the stub of his cigarette on the ground at Donovan's feet. "Please don't tell me you're considering it?"

"Of course not. *No*. It's just… he knows about Flora. He looked me right in the eye and told me h—"

"He looked you right in the eye? Felix, is there something you haven't told me?"

"Mullins and I paid him a little visit. That's all. Asked him a few questions about his dead girlfriend. How do you think I got the name of the cult? He gave us a location for them, too—a place he'd already burned to the ground. Mullins checked it out. It was derelict."

"You don't want to find yourself in his debt, Felix. That's how these things start," said the Ghost. "Don't let him think he's done you a favor."

"He *knows*," said Felix. "He knows I'm out to get him. That's what the dinner invitation was all about. It was a threat, not a gesture. He was warning me that he knows about my family. That he could come after them at any time." Donovan's shoulders slumped. "I tried to send Flora away again, but she won't hear of it."

"Then we have to move fast," said the Ghost. "We have to figure out our next move."

Donovan suddenly stumbled, and the Ghost flicked out a hand, grabbing him by the front of his jacket to stop him tumbling over the lip of the building. He eased him back to his feet.

"What the hell was that?"

There was a thud, and the ground beneath them trembled again. The Ghost heard voices from down below, calling out in alarm.

There was another thud, and then a third, followed by a steady succession.

"Are you armed, Felix?" he said, ratcheting up his flechette gun.

Donovan pulled his handgun from its holster. "And ready."

"Make them count." He leaned over the edge of the precinct building, peering down. "There are two of them, headed this way. I'll try to draw them off while you make a run for it."

"Two *what*?"

"Enforcers," said the Ghost. "It seems like the Reaper *really* wants you to make that dinner date." He watched as the two man-machines methodically scaled the side of the building, their fists taking chunks out of the wall as they bashed handholds, hauling themselves up.

Below, armed police officers had spilled out of the building and were taking potshots, their bullets ricocheting off the metal ribs of the Enforcers' exoskeletons, sparking bright and sharp in the darkness.

Donovan was peering over the edge now, too, his weapon ready.

"Bullets aren't going to do much good," said the Ghost. "Whatever the Reaper's pumped into the pilots seems to make them impervious to pain. Maybe a shot to the head, but hit them in the chest and they'll just keep coming."

"All right," said Donovan. "Head it is." He glanced over his shoulder at a clanging sound from behind him, followed by metal scraping against stone. "Umm, I don't think they've come alone," he said, backing up.

The Ghost followed his gaze to see a grappling hook had landed on the roof and snagged against the lip. The attached rope was pulled taut, disappearing over the edge.

Someone was scaling the building from the alleyway at the side. He ran over to take a look. At least five cultists were running up the wall, swords tucked in their belts and blowpipes clasped between their teeth. There were more in the alleyway below, stirring the shadows.

"You know that war we were talking about?" he called to Donovan. "It's starting now."

He backed up toward the door. "Get inside, and get out," he said. Below, the sound of gunfire had become a cacophony as more and more police officers came running out of the building, targeting their attackers. The men below had no idea that Donovan and the Ghost were on the roof, of course—they'd always kept their conferences private, to avoid Donovan having to face any awkward questions. As far as everyone else knew, he just liked to take in the view while he smoked.

"Not likely," said Donovan. "Like you said, this is *our* city, and they've brought the war to my patch."

The first of the Enforcers had almost reached the roof, its arm smashing down through the wall, sending hunks of masonry crashing to the street below. Its massive hand sunk into the gravel, digging deep into the fabric of the roof itself, searching for purchase. Its other hand came over the top a moment later, and it hauled itself up, climbing to its feet.

"Good God," said Donovan, taking it in properly for the first time. "Look at it."

"It's not a person anymore. It's a machine."

"I don't care what it is," said Donovan. "It doesn't belong on my roof." He raised his gun and fired, but the bullet pinged off the frame, whistling away into the night.

The Ghost flexed his neck, trying to loosen his shoulders.

This was going to hurt. A *lot*.

He dropped into a crouch, and then ran at the Enforcer, triggering his boosters as he leapt at it, grabbing for its head guard. If he could overbalance it, catch it by surprise while it was still standing precariously on the very edge of the roof, he thought maybe he could carry it over, dropping it to the street below.

The Enforcer was too fast, however, and swung its arm up, catching the Ghost in the shoulder and battering him out of the way. Unable to stop himself, his arms wheeling, he went over the edge, plummeting toward the sidewalk.

He fought to take a breath, gulping at the rushing air. His heart was thrumming, pounding in his ears. His eyes were trying to close, and blackness beckoned. Fighting with everything he had left, the Ghost forced his arms flat by his sides, bringing his legs together as he fell into the dive.

Police officers, failing to understand he was trying to help, opened fire, guns barking. One of them clipped his thigh, scoring a hot, painful gash, but he had no time to consider it. The ground was coming up too fast.

He arced his back, forcing his head up and his legs down. The pressure was incredible, and his ears felt as if they were about to burst. The sidewalk was only yards away...

And then the boosters seemed to catch, and he was shooting upwards again, wavering as he tried to steady his course. He crested the top of the building, shots still ringing out all around him.

Donovan was up there alone, firing into the face of the first Enforcer as the second was dragging itself over the ledge.

The Ghost flung himself into another dive, arms extended, flechette gun spraying. He knew it wouldn't do much to dissuade the Enforcer that was bearing down on Donovan, but it might distract it long enough for him to make a break.

His flechettes chewed a fist-sized gouge in the pilot's chest as he concentrated his fire, swooping away at the last minute to avoid another swipe from its fist. Donovan had taken his cue, ducking out of the way and running around behind it, but the other one was now nearly on top of them, and the black-clad cultists had also started to spread out onto the roof.

He could see Donovan wavering, unsure which of them to aim his weapon at.

He dropped onto the roof, tumbling into a roll and springing back to his feet close to Donovan. His broken ribs felt as though they were on fire. He put a hand on the other man's arm, lowering his gun. "Let's just see what happens next," he said.

The two of them fell back as the cultists surged in, more and more of them spilling over the lip of the roof. They divided, circling both Enforcers, blades drawn.

Once again, the cultists appeared to be deploying the same tactics—harrying the Enforcers, goading them with their blades while maneuvering them into a more desirable position—in this instance, the very edge of the rooftop.

The second Enforcer—the one which had only just clawed its way onto the roof—took a swipe with its fist, pivoting on one foot in order to widen the arc. Three of the cultists went tumbling off the edge of the building, screaming to their deaths, while another was tossed across the rooftop, crumpling into a bloody heap on the gravel.

The others closed ranks, maintaining the circle, still darting forward to slash at the pilot then falling back, keeping the Enforcer pinned in place.

The Ghost heard another scream, and turned to see more of the cultists fall, while the first Enforcer had two of them pinned beneath its foot and was slowly pressing them into the roof, squeezing the life out of them with its immense bulk.

He thought that maybe he could try again, while the cultists had it distracted—charge it with his boosters on full thrust and send it plummeting from the roof. He couldn't see any other option. He steeled himself.

And then, with no apparent warning, the cultists suddenly fell back, lowering their swords and bowing their heads.

Confused, the Ghost glanced at Donovan, who seemed just as nonplussed as he was. The first Enforcer took a step forward, as if tentatively testing the water, waiting to see how the cultists would react. They remained perfectly still.

Something stirred above them, like a change in the currents of the wind.

The Ghost felt sunlight on his face, and looked up, almost dazzled by the sudden glow. It wasn't sunlight at all; in fact, it wasn't even the glow of the womanly apparition that had drifted into view above the rooftop—it was a hot desert wind; a warm breath against his throat; the exhalation of a goddess.

She hung there in the sky like a whispering phantasm, her arms trailing by her sides, her head thrown back, calling upon the stars. She was wreathed in bandages that seemed to unravel about her arms and legs, billowing in an unearthly wind. She carried an ankh in her left hand, and behind her head was the glowing form of a sun disk, bright and pure. He found it hard to discern her features from down on the rooftop, but he could see that her hair was whipping about her face, mussed by the same supernatural breeze, and her eyes shone with light so intense that it caused an afterglow to stain his retina, even through the lenses of his goggles.

She hovered for a moment, regarding the scene that had been unfolding on the rooftop. Even the Enforcers had stopped in their tracks, their slack-jawed faces upturned toward this ancient specter.

She raised her hands, and the light around her seemed to coalesce, curling into impressionistic shapes. They grew in intensity, their outlines becoming slowly more defined, until the Ghost could see the head and shoulders of twin lions, stirring at her feet. They had the same quality as the woman herself—ghostly, ethereal, unreal. Yet when they roared, he could feel their power, awakening a primal, ancient fear, deep in his gut. The apparition flicked her wrists, and the lions rushed forward, charging the Enforcers.

The Ghost watched, awed, as the phantoms seemed to pass *through* the Enforcers, bursting through their chests, only to dissolve into nothingness as they erupted through the other side, like billowing smoke made from the purest light, dispersing on the breeze.

The effect on the Enforcers, however, was uncanny. The life seemed to simply blink out of them. One moment it was there—the final vestiges of humanity, the spark of life that drove the machines—the next it had gone, as if the lions had simply consumed it. As one, the Enforcers seized up, toppling backwards over the lip of the precinct building.

Donovan rushed to the edge as they fell, peering over, calling to the men below to get out of the way, and seconds later the Ghost heard the crunch of their exoskeletons hitting the sidewalk, smashing craters into the road.

He stared up at the apparition, utterly lost for words. It was beautiful, and deadly—a thing not of this world. He found it difficult to focus on it properly, as if it were not entirely there, as if this was light that was never meant to be witnessed by human eyes.

Boots crunched on gravel. The Ghost tore his eyes away from the apparition. The remaining cultists were gathering, retreating to their ropes. Close by, Donovan raised his gun. "Stay where you are," he called. "Or I'll shoot."

One of the cultists stopped, while the others continued to the other side of the roof. "We came for the Enforcers," he said, "but we will not hesitate to kill you, too. Follow us, and you die."

He turned and ran after the others, who were now taking to their ropes, disappearing steadily over the lip of the building.

Above, the apparition was already drifting away, its ethereal light fading as it was slowly swallowed by the darkness.

Donovan was readying himself for a shot.

"Felix, no!" called the Ghost. "Remember what you said? Now's not the time. We'd be dead in minutes. We'll have our chance."

Donovan lowered his weapon. The frown on his face said more than words ever could. They stood, watching as the last of the surviving cultists disappeared over the edge.

"This is going to take some explaining," said Donovan, after a moment. The rooftop was utterly devastated, with chunks taken out of the walls, holes punched into the floor, and dead bodies strewn about haphazardly, blood pooling and mingling with the gravel.

"The war has begun," said the Ghost. "And it seems the Circle of Thoth has a secret weapon."

"At least we know Astrid was right," said Donovan. "The apparition is involved."

The Ghost nodded. He could hear footsteps in the stairwell behind them as an army of police officers came hurtling up toward the roof.

Nearby, someone groaned. It was one of the cultists, the one who'd been tossed across the roof by the Enforcer. He was still alive—his leg snapped at the knee, blood trickling from the corner of his mouth—but he was dragging himself across the rooftop by his fingertips, heading for the rope.

"Go," said Donovan. "Don't let them catch you here. I'll see to *him*." He nodded at the cultist. "Maybe now we'll get some answers."

The Ghost ran, leaping over the side of the building and powering his boosters, sailing off into the night, just as the policemen spilled out behind Donovan, guns blazing.

TWENTY

"I'm not going to say I told you so," said Astrid. She was standing by her workbench, her hand on her hip and the hint of a smile twitching the corner of her mouth. "But I told you so."

Gabriel stood in the doorway. He'd come straight over that morning after a quick stop at the bakery to collect pastries. He'd spent another hour the previous night, searching the rooftops for any sign of the apparition, but it had vanished, along with the cultists.

"We're not there yet," he said. "You *were* right, though—the apparition is definitely a part of whatever the cult is doing. I was hoping you might be able to help us to identify it?" He looked sheepish. "And by that, I mean if I tell you what it looked like, can you tell me what you think it is?"

"I can do one better than that, I think," she said. "But let's start there." She fixed him with a disapproving stare. "Now are you coming in, or are you going to stand there in the doorway all morning?"

Grinning, Gabriel fetched the stool from under the workbench and pulled up a seat, leaving the armchair free for Astrid.

"Coffee, today," she said. "It's too early for anything else."

"I'd always taken you for an early riser," said Gabriel.

"More of a night owl," she said. "That's when all the interesting stuff happens."

Gabriel laughed. "I can't disagree with you there."

She dropped into her chair while the coffee brewed on the stove, folding her legs up beneath her. She was wearing a pale-cream blouse, the top three buttons open at the neck, and a pair of loose-fitting gray culottes. A pendant hung from her neck, a small silver vial of some sort, and she was wearing a brace of rings on the fingers of her left hand. Her hair was pinned up casually, as if she hadn't quite had time to see to it yet. "Describe it to me," she said. "Try not to miss anything out."

Gabriel outlined everything he had seen the night before on the rooftop, from the ankh, to the lions, to the sun disk and the strange, ethereal wind.

"Sekhmet," said Astrid, without a moment's hesitation. "The warrior goddess, daughter of the sun god Ra. It's an avatar, a manifestation. Whatever they've done, they've brought her back."

"The tomb," said Gabriel. "That's what they found during the dig—the tomb of Sekhmet, close to the temple of Thoth. They've brought it here, recreating it at the museum. Arthur said it was just ceremonial, that they'd never found a body. Could this be why?"

Astrid seemed to consider this for a moment. "It's unlikely a three-thousand-year-old corpse could be reinvigorated in the way you describe," said Astrid, "and really, that's not how all of this works. At least, I don't think so. This is new ground for me, too." She hopped off her seat as the coffee pot started to boil over, hurriedly removing it from the stove. She poured them two mugs, and the steaming scent of it made Gabriel's stomach lurch.

"The way I see it, the ancient gods were not bound to physical forms in the way that we are. They were more transient than that, everlasting. At least within their own realm, which mirrored the realm of men, as we've already discussed. Whenever they wished to traverse our realm, they would take an avatar, inhabiting the form of a human for a short time. When they later returned to their celestial form, their business here concluded, they would leave no trace of their passing."

"So you think that's what's happened here?" said Gabriel. "That they've somehow found a way to wake Sekhmet?"

"It would make sense," said Astrid. "The shape and form of the tomb might help to provide a clue. If there was no body, though, it might be nothing but a ceremonial tomb, as Arthur suggests, designed to mark the passing of an avatar once Sekhmet had returned to the heavens. It might even have been a device designed to aid in the forging of another."

"A device?"

Astrid nodded. "Buildings can have power too, Gabriel. They can channel energy, provide an anchor with the heavens. If the chambers in the tomb mirror the resting place of Sekhmet in her own realm, it might be how they woke her."

Gabriel swallowed. So now they weren't just contending with a phantom. They were dealing with the avatar of a living god. The week really was going from strength to strength.

"What do they want?" said Gabriel. It was a rhetorical question, but Astrid drummed her fingers on the arm of her chair as she considered her words.

"Isn't it always about power? About proving you know best, that your ideology is superior to that of others? Isn't that always what these people want? Awakening ancient gods, harnessing the power of inter-dimensional entities, even just beating down on the kids from the next neighborhood—it's always about power, about proving you're right by making sure someone else is *wrong*."

"I know you're right, Astrid, but I need to figure out *how*. How are they trying to do it? What's their next move? If I've any hope of stopping them, I need to understand."

She placed her coffee on the floor by her chair, and stood, holding out her hands. "Come on, the pastries will have to wait. I've something to show you."

He took her hands and she heaved him up, leading him through to the antechamber where she kept her personal belongings. A large wooden wardrobe stood against one wall, although most of her clothes seemed to be hanging from freestanding rails, or folded away on shelves. She crossed to the wardrobe and opened both doors.

"Astrid, what's this all about? I'm not here to give fashion advice."

"Shhh," she admonished. "You'll spoil the effect." He watched as she stepped *into* the wardrobe. There was a click, and then the sound of creaking hinges as a panel in the back of the wardrobe opened, revealing a small void behind. Astrid ducked her head and stepped through, waving for him to follow.

Curious, Gabriel did as she indicated, following her through the strange portal.

He found her standing in a small chamber on the other side.

It smelled damp, and the air was frigid. There were no windows, and the only light came from a single electric bulb, hanging on a cable that dangled from the rafters. The walls had once been painted white, but were now streaked with grime and decay, and he could see that mice had left their spoor in the corner, dashing in and out of a tiny hole in the outer wall for shelter.

In the centre of the room was a chair, covered by a gray woolen blanket. He could tell from the shape and form that someone—or some*thing*—was sitting in it.

"What's going on?" said Gabriel.

"I'm about to show you something, and I need to know that you're going to keep it to yourself. Can I trust you?" She looked more intense than he'd ever seen her.

"You can trust me, Astrid. I've trusted you, haven't I?"

"All right then," she said, and grabbed hold of the blanket, sweeping it off the chair with a flourish. She dropped it to the floor by her feet. "Meet 'the Seer'."

Gabriel stared at the thing in the chair. It was an automaton, of sorts—or at least that was what it looked like—a mannequin in the approximation of a man, plated in ancient, tarnished brass, and carefully wired with tiny wheels and pulleys. Its face was a blank, staring mask, its mouth an open slit—whoever designed it had forgotten to paint in its face. It had a strange, box-shaped object bolted to its chest, and its arms were resting upon its lap. It was moldering—there was no doubt about it— the small leather patches on the inside of its elbows and the back of its knees were dry and cracked, and there were stains where it had sat against the rotting chair for too long.

Gabriel knelt before it, marveling at the workmanship. He'd

seen music boxes before, filled with the most intricate mechanisms designed to make a tiny simulacra of a bird twitch and sing, but this was beyond anything he could have imagined. The closer he got, the more he could see the labyrinthine workings between every plate, at every joint. It was a marvel of the watchmaker's art, writ large. It belonged in a museum, not here, rotting away in a derelict old church.

He straightened up, rubbing his palm across his jaw. "It's remarkable," he said. "But what is it?"

"I told you," said Astrid, grinning mischievously. "It's the Seer." She patted its head affectionately. "It was built in 1771 for George the Third, King of England, by a secret cabal of watchmakers, alchemists and Hermeticists. It's designed to predict the future, and it works, too—within reason."

Gabriel raised an eyebrow. "How the hell did you get your hands on it?"

"When it was discovered the King was suffering from an ailment of the mind, it was deemed too risky for the device to remain in England, and so it was hidden away, transported to Holland. When its keeper was murdered in a chance robbery, it was abandoned, left hidden for years inside a secret cavity in a Dutch wall." She rubbed her hands together, staving off the chill. "There were rumors, of course, people had heard of its existence, and it became one of the most desired occult objects of the early nineteenth century. Bonaparte wanted it, as he thought it might help him defeat the English at Waterloo. William Godwin coveted it, and it's thought his late-night talk of the object might have, in part, inspired his daughter to write *Frankenstein*."

"Go on," said Gabriel, intrigued.

"It wasn't discovered until nearly a hundred years later, at the turn of this century, still walled up inside the crumbling old house in Amsterdam. Workmen were brought in to do repairs, and there it was, peering out at them from inside."

"It was smuggled out of Holland by a pair of British agents. They wanted to keep it out of the hands of the Queen, who would have employed it in extending her Empire even further across the globe. These agents sent it with a trusted ally to Gibraltar, where it remained for over twenty years. It finally made its way here two years ago, when Queen Alberta reignited the search for it, and a friend entrusted it to me for safekeeping."

"I see why you were so keen for it to remain a secret," said Gabriel. "That's quite a tale. But does it even work anymore? I mean... look at it."

"No one has tried to operate it since the British agents in 1903," she said. "But I'm game if you are?" She grinned.

"What, *now*?" said Gabriel.

"There's no time like the present," she said. "What's the worst that can happen? It doesn't work, and we go back to drinking coffee, eating pastries, and trying to fathom what the cult is up to. On the other hand, if it works, you might find the answers you're looking for."

Gabriel stared at the thing for a moment. It seemed like madness. Surely it was nothing but an old parlor trick, like that chess-playing Turk that had caused such a sensation in its time, but had turned out to be concealing a human operative all along. Then again, he trusted Astrid implicitly, and he supposed he didn't have anything to lose. After all, he'd just been convinced that the thing he'd seen on the rooftop the previous night was an avatar of an ancient god. There wasn't much skepticism left in him after that.

"Okay," he said. "What do we have to do?"

"Take off your shirt," said Astrid.

"What, really?"

She laughed and shook her head. "No. But it was worth a try. I need to go and fetch some things from the workshop. Wait here. I'll be back in a minute."

"It operates on a similar principle to those living statues you encountered," said Astrid, as she laid out a small cotton sheet on the floor, and assembled her paraphernalia. She was reading from an old, yellowed manuscript as she worked, selecting a strange assortment of icons, herbs, pickled rodent parts and vials containing what appeared to be congealed blood.

"You mean it's going to come to life and try to kill me?" he said.

"I mean it has no obvious power source," said Astrid, "save for the contents of the box in its chest."

"Which are?"

"Everything I'm about to put in it," she said. She finished laying everything out according to the pattern in the book. She'd previously marked the sheet with lines of dusty chalk, drawing the familiar hermetic pattern of nested shapes, into which she'd laid the components of her ritual in precise order.

"Right, open the compartment for me," she said.

Gabriel did as instructed, carefully undoing the latch and

opening the panel. It was stiff, and creaked, and he was worried it was going to come away in his hand at any moment.

Inside, the compartment was blackened with ancient ash.

Astrid had moved round to join him, and he watched, fascinated, as she took the components one at a time, laying them carefully within the machine's chest, following a very specific order laid out in the manuscript. Then, when she had finished, she rolled up the cloth, found a strip of matches, and struck one.

"Would you like the honor?" she said, holding it out to him.

"I'd sooner leave it to the expert," he said, "if it's all the same."

Astrid nodded and stepped forward. She gently laid the match inside the compartment, and then closed the door. "There," she said. "Now we wait."

She stepped back, coming to stand beside Gabriel.

For a moment, nothing happened. Gabriel could smell dried lavender smoldering inside the thing's chest. Black smoke was curling out from the edges of the compartment door, and, disturbingly, from the open slit of its mouth, as if it were exhaling.

"I think all we've managed to do is hasten the thing's demise," said Gabriel.

Astrid shook her head, holding her forefinger up to his lips to silence him. It was still covered in chalk dust. She was watching the Seer intently. He could see the hope in her eyes; she needed this to work. For her, it was some sort of validation, proof of her methods, her way of contributing to the investigation. He had no idea what he'd tell Donovan if they did get anything useful out of it. He'd gone along with talk of living statues—an eighteenth-century automaton that could predict the future was another thing entirely.

Within moments, the whole room was beginning to swim with filthy smoke, and Gabriel was close to running for cover. He could feel it tickling his sore lung, and he spluttered, raising his hand to his mouth.

He heard Astrid say something, but didn't quite make it out because of his coughing fit. "I'm sorry, what did you say?" he asked, once he'd recovered. The smoke was stinging his eyes now, too.

"Not me," said Astrid, from beside him. She had an excited gleam in her eyes. "*Him.*" She pointed at the automaton.

Gabriel stepped closer, lurching back in surprise when the Seer lifted its head with a jerky, sudden gesture, turning to look right at him. He could hear the gears and levers clicking and whirring inside of it.

"As above, so below," it said, its voice a strange mechanical burr, as if it were being generated by the turning of the cogs themselves. "So below, as above."

"What does it mean?" said Gabriel, looking to Astrid.

"Just *listen*," said Astrid.

"The ancient ones once more walk the realm of men. The Empire of Greed shall be refashioned to their purpose. The heavens shall soon align, and the world shall know the wrath of Thoth." Its head jerked suddenly to the left, and it made a sound like a long and heartfelt sigh, smoke pluming from its mouth.

"Come on," said Astrid, wafting her arm before her face, "let's get out of this smoke." She led him back through the wardrobe, closing the panel behind her.

"I'm not really sure how to follow that," she said. She looked dazed, her face covered in streaks of soot.

"I'm not sure you could," said Gabriel. He wiped his eyes, which were still watering from the smoke. "Pastry?"

Astrid looked at him, and burst out in rapturous laughter.

"Well, it worked," said Gabriel. "In a manner of speaking. We almost burned the place down."

"Wasn't it magnificent?" said Astrid. "To think, a device built a hundred and fifty years ago can still do *that*. Do you see now how those statues must have been brought to life?" She was pacing up and down in her workshop, buzzing with excitement. "The alchemical principle is exactly the same."

Gabriel found himself grinning, despite everything. Her enthusiasm was infectious. "Yes, I see it," he said. "But the things it said—what did they mean? They sounded pretty ominous."

"As above, so below," said Astrid. "It was referring to the hermetic principle I told you about. But then it repeated the maxim backwards: so below, as above. It's a warning, especially when it's coupled with what it said about the 'Empire of Greed' being 'refashioned' to suit the purpose of the gods."

"The Empire of Greed—that's Manhattan, right?"

"I can't think of a better description," said Astrid. "That's what we've been building here, isn't it—the capitalist utopia, the land of possibility."

"And by 'refashioned'…?"

"So below, as above," repeated Astrid. "The Circle of Thoth

intend to reshape parts of Manhattan to reflect the heavens. 'The heavens shall soon align, and the world shall know the wrath', etcetera, etcetera. Think about it. They're trying to bring back the ancient gods by mirroring the architecture of the heavens. They've already succeeded with Sekhmet—it sounds as though Thoth is next."

"And then we shall know his wrath," said Gabriel. "That doesn't sound like a whole bunch of fun."

"Not if he intends to level Manhattan and rebuild it as his new domain on Earth, it doesn't," said Astrid. "There must be a structure somewhere, a place where they intend to channel Thoth's power into another vessel. The museum?"

"Possibly," said Gabriel, "although I didn't see anything fitting that bill. There's a colonnade, some statues, and the tomb of Sekhmet."

"It must be somewhere else, then. That's the key. Find that, and we have a chance of disrupting their plans before they manifest Thoth."

"And Sekhmet?"

Astrid smiled. "This time I really *do* need you to take off your shirt."

TWENTY-ONE

"So, he's still alive, then?" said Donovan. He was flicking ash into the dregs of his cold coffee, in lieu of the ashtray, which was overflowing and had started to present something of a fire risk. He'd have emptied it, if it hadn't been for the storm of chaos that had erupted in the aftermath of the previous night's attack. Or, he supposed, maybe he wouldn't have. It was a good excuse, though.

It was long past lunch, but he hadn't managed to eat yet, and he was starting to get grouchy. It had been weeks since he'd last managed to head to *Joe's* for his favorite pastrami sandwich. When this was over, it was the first thing he was going to do, and damn the waistline.

He ditched the end of the cigarette and immediately lit another, hoping it would help to suppress his burgeoning appetite.

"Barely," said Mullins, who was sitting on the other side of the desk, also smoking a cigarette. He'd been trying to cut down, but recent events seemed to have somewhat interfered with his plan. "The doctor says he won't survive another night. Too much internal bleeding, apparently. Half his organs were ruptured when that Enforcer hit him."

"Right," said Donovan. "We'd better get down there, then. I've got some questions I want to put to him before he shuffles off this mortal coil."

"You're not likely to get much out of him," said Mullins. "He's dosed up on morphine, and he doesn't seem to be in the mood for talking."

"We'll see about that," said Donovan. He wasn't a particular fan of strong-arm tactics, but the cultist wasn't to know that. A well-placed threat had loosened just as many tongues for him over the years as a sharp fist to the gut.

"Hospital, then?" he said, getting to his feet. He tossed Mullins the car keys. "Here, you're driving."

They left the bustling office, traversed a couple of flights of stairs, and quit the precinct building via the main entrance, where workmen were hurriedly erecting wooden scaffolds in order to repair the damage. The roads were going to take longer to repair, and for now, traffic was being rerouted around the block. Donovan could still see patches of sawdust clinging to the asphalt were the cultists had landed, bursting like water balloons filled with blood and bones. The memory of it made him shudder. Maybe he'd have to pick a new spot for his meetings with Gabriel; the roof wasn't going to feel the same again after what had come to pass.

The car was parked a little way up the street—thankfully avoiding the destruction of the previous night—and Donovan walked round, climbing into the passenger seat. Mullins fired up the engine, and they purred away, trailing a column of thick black smoke.

He was hoping for some good news. So far, it hadn't been a day for it.

He'd sent Parkhurst and another of the uniformed boys out to pick up Landsworth, but they'd returned empty-handed, claiming he wasn't to be found at his hotel, or at the museum, and that the curator had claimed he'd not shown his face since the shooting at the parade the previous day.

The wheedling bastard was on the run. Donovan knew it. Their visit to the hotel had spooked him, and whatever Gabriel had said to him at the museum had only made matters worse. The shooting must have been the final straw, and he'd upped and made a run for it. He'd had Parkhurst alert all the ports, but in a city like this, if someone really didn't want to be found, they could go to ground for months. Especially if they had powerful friends, and Donovan was certain that Landsworth was well connected to the Circle of Thoth.

He couldn't blame Gabriel, not really. If it was Flora who was missing, he doubted he could have been so restrained. All the same, he cursed himself for not getting to the man earlier. His gut had warned him soon enough, and he'd played it cool, rather than trusting his instincts.

Nevertheless, the cultist in the hospital presented an opportunity. He'd had multiple guards posted on him all night and all morning, and they'd been careful to ensure there was nothing in the ward that he could employ as a weapon, against either the police or himself.

They purred through the bustling streets in silence. It was unlike Mullins to be so reflective. "What is it, Sergeant? Something's on your mind."

Mullins glanced at him, and then returned his eyes to the road. "I was going over what happened last night, sir, is all."

"And?"

"And what, sir?"

"And what were your conclusions?"

Mullins looked uncomfortable. "Not so much conclusions, sir, as questions. I was thinking about the Ghost. You know I've had my concerns about him in the past."

"I do."

"And then, after what he did to help Florence Wu—I can see why you think what you do of him, sir."

"And what's that, Sergeant?" said Donovan.

"You respect him, sir. And so do I. His tactics might be anathema, but he gets the job done, and he's on the side of the angels."

"I'm sensing a 'but'."

"All I was wondering was… would we have so much trouble if he wasn't around? I mean, does he attract them, the lunatics and psychopaths and supernatural stuff? Would the Reaper and those cultists have even attacked the precinct last night if he hadn't been there?"

"He arrived afterwards, Mullins. Once the fighting had already started. I was up there on the roof having a smoke."

Mullins glanced across at him. "Yes, sir. If you say so, sir."

Donovan sighed. "You're a clever sod, I'll give you that, Mullins. Maybe a little lacking in diplomacy, but you're turning into a damn fine detective."

"Thank you, sir."

"And the answer is 'maybe'," said Donovan, lighting another cigarette and tossing his empty packet on the back seat. "Maybe he does attract them. Maybe the precinct wouldn't have come under fire if he'd been somewhere else last night. But I look at it like this—he doesn't create those madmen, or those things that lurk in the darkness. They're already out there, drawing their plans. If it weren't him, it would be someone else—maybe someplace else, true, but then someone has to deal with them. It might as well be us. He took a long draw on his cigarette. "And you're right, his tactics sometimes leave something to be desired, but if we engage with him, if we *work* with him, then he can do things we can't, get to the places we can't go. There's incredible value in that. Having someone we can trust on the outside, it brings perspective."

"So you're saying he's worth it? He's worth the risk?"

"I think I am, Sergeant, yes. I'm saying the city's better off with him than without him."

Mullins pulled the car to a stop. They'd reached the hospital. "That's all right then, sir. Just so that I understand." He turned the key in the ignition, and the engine died. "Let's go find us some answers, then."

The sight of the cultist in his hospital bed did little to alleviate Donovan's notion that he was having a bad day. If he'd hoped to get much of any coherence from the man, he was going to be bitterly disappointed—the dying cultist was hooked up to an intravenous drip, strapped to the bed to stop him thrashing, and presently in a state that resembled a drug-induced delirium. He was rolling his head from side to side on the pillow and mumbling. His eyelids were fluttering, his hands squeezed so tight into fists that the nails had dug into his palms and blood was trickling down his wrists.

"See what I mean, sir?" said Mullins apologetically. "He

doesn't seem to be doing so well."

"Nor would you if one of those things had tossed you across the rooftop," said Donovan, and immediately regretted it. He altered his tone. "All right, but we're going to have to try something. Fetch one of the nurses, would you?"

Mullins went out into the corridor and told one of the uniformed men they had on guard to track down a nurse. She appeared in the doorway a few moments later, looking flustered. "Look, this isn't the only patient I have to deal with, you know," she said haughtily.

"No, but I bet he's the only one who might have information on the whereabouts of a kidnapped woman," said Donovan. "So if you don't mind, we'd appreciate your help in trying to save her life."

The nurse looked suitably taken aback. "Well, yes, of course," she said. "What do you need?"

"I need to bring him round."

"He's dying... Inspector?" He nodded. "He's in excruciating pain, even with the medication. If we turn off the drip, he's going to suffer."

"Remember what I said—there's an innocent woman's life at stake. This man—he's a killer. A cold-blooded murderer. Now, I know you have a job to do, and no one should have to die in pain, but we just need a minute to question him, that's all. Then as far as I'm concerned you can pump him full of whatever you like."

"Lead, preferably," muttered Mullins.

The nurse nodded. She walked over to the drip and turned a little red tap. "There. I'll be back in five minutes to turn it back on. He'll probably start screaming in two." She glanced at her watch, and left.

Donovan watched the cultist writhing on the bed, lost in the throes of his opiate dream. Whatever the drugs were doing for him, they didn't appear to be offering much comfort.

"Did we pull a name for him?" said Donovan.

"John Doe," said Mullins. "The boys are working on it, but his prints don't seem to be on record, and obviously no one's coming forward."

Donovan nodded. He'd expected as much.

The cultist had stopped writhing now, and his face had creased in a confused frown. His fists opened, his fingers flexing, and then he suddenly sat bolt upright, thrashing against his bonds. His eyes were wide and staring, and fixed on Donovan. He opened his mouth, as if trying to scream, but nothing came out. It was one of the most horrendous things Donovan had ever seen.

"Who are you?" said Donovan, his voice level.

The man's eyes widened. He leaned forward. Then he started whimpering. His wrists thrashed against his bonds again. Donovan reached forward, grabbed him by the shoulders and shoved him back down onto the bed.

"I asked you a question," he said.

The man's eyes finally seemed to register something, flicking back and forth across Donovan's face. He made a noise that started like a rasping cough, and as Donovan watched the cultist's face crack into a pained smile, it became a dreadful, hissing laugh.

"Where is she?" said Donovan. "Where are they holding her?"

"You're too late," said the cultist. There were speckles of blood flecking his lips.

"Too late for what?" said Donovan. "The Circle is moving against the Reaper?"

"Sekhmet's army awaits her. She will rise and clear the way for Thoth. Too late..." He trailed off, still laughing. "Too late..." He started to fit beneath Donovan's grip, and Donovan released him, stepping back from the bed.

Mullins was at the door, calling for the nurse. She came running, pushing Donovan aside. She tried to clear the man's airway, but it was bubbling with blood. "I hope you got what you wanted," she said, with scorn, "because it's the last thing he'll ever say."

"Then it'll have to do," said Donovan, standing aside as an army of doctors poured into the room.

He beckoned to Mullins, and they left.

They didn't speak until they were in the car and Mullins had started the engine. "The ravings of a madman?" he said.

"I don't think so," said Donovan. "I think it's about to start. Last night was a warm-up act. Tonight they're going to show their hand."

"Then where to?"

"There's an apartment on Fifth Avenue, Mullins. I think you can imagine who lives there. We need to go and fetch him. We need to go and get the Ghost."

"Very good, sir," said Mullins. "I was hoping you were going to say that."

He turned the wheel, and they pulled away from the curb, slipping out into the mid-afternoon traffic.

TWENTY-TWO

ave for the trees, Central Park was perfectly silent and still. They whispered to one another in the breeze, sharing secrets, singing a gentle lament. The Ghost didn't know if the thought was comforting, or unsettling.

They were hunkered down amongst the boughs—he, Astrid and Donovan—watching the museum entrance, while Mullins waited around the corner with a select force of armed police officers. They'd been hand-picked by Donovan, who'd chosen only those men he thought wouldn't balk at the first sign of anything... unexpected. This time, Donovan assured him, they'd been warned not to open fire on the Ghost if he put in an appearance, but to focus their attentions on the cultists. He hoped they'd been paying attention.

Of course, they had no real idea if they were correct in their assumption about the museum—that it would form a sort of nexus point for Sekhmet's attack—but Astrid had argued that the tomb was the seat of her power, and that the "army" the dying cultist had spoken of was most likely comprised of ancient statues, shipped in from Egypt along with the exhibit and awaiting the call to arms. It made sense, and so here they were, camped out amongst the trees, waiting to see if anything would happen.

Donovan had found him at his apartment earlier that afternoon, having returned with Astrid to make preparations for the evening. He'd been in his workshop, constructing a pouch of explosive rounds for his flechette gun—the same kind he'd used against the Roman's "moss men" over a year earlier, to devastating effect. He hoped they'd make a difference if they did encounter any further statues—or Enforcers—that night.

The appearance of Mullins had been something of a surprise; for well over a year now, the Ghost had strived to keep the identity of his alter ego secret from the man. Mullins had initially taken a dim view of the Ghost and his activities—often citing him a criminal, as dangerous in his own way as the enemies he fought to protect the city against—but in recent months his attitude seemed to have softened, and he'd even come to see the Ghost as something of an ally. He'd barely batted an eye as Donovan had shown him into the Ghost's apartment and the nature of the Ghost's true identity had become apparent. He'd simply shaken Gabriel by the hand, taken one of Donovan's cigarettes, and joined in with the ensuing conference.

Their stories, of course, had dovetailed, and whilst Astrid and Gabriel had remained sketchy on the details of their morning's activity, it was clear both parties had come to the same conclusion—that the Circle of Thoth were about to escalate matters, and that the Reaper's mob were not the only target.

Following the previous night's attacks at the precinct, the police had already cracked open their vaults and gathered a number of hand grenades, which they'd issued to the armed officers, instructing them to be deployed only in the direst circumstances, and only then against enemies such as the Enforcers. The Ghost hoped they'd be enough—if Astrid's fears were realized, handguns and batons weren't going to stand any of them in much stead.

He sensed movement out of the corner of his eye, and squinted, focusing in on the museum steps. A single blue dot was wavering, skipping back and forth in a nervous fashion, like an errant fairy. He adjusted his goggles, increasing the magnification and boosting the sensitivity of the night vision. It was the baboon, scuttling about in the shadows, its electric eye gleaming.

"They're coming," he said, just as the museum doors blew out from the inside, and the blazing light of the goddess brought a false dawn to the street outside.

She slid out into the night, gliding on her ancient, mysterious winds, trailing ribbons of tattered bandages and wrapped in a halo of ethereal sunlight. She raised herself higher, arms outstretched by her sides, a warrior queen at the head of her army.

Behind her marched upwards of ten ebon statues, dragging themselves through the splintered remnants of the doors. They stormed out onto the steps, implacable faces upturned to their goddess in the sky. Black-robed cultists swarmed around them, numerous and deadly, their curved blades drawn and glinting in the reflected light.

"Ready?" said the Ghost, turning to Donovan.

"As I'll ever be."

"Then give them hell."

He leapt from the cover of the trees, barreling forward,

flechette gun erupting. The explosive rounds showered the first wave of statues as they reached the foot of the steps, detonating with a sound like machine-gun fire and flensing hunks of stone from their heads and upper torsos.

One of them hissed as it saw him coming, its jackal-shaped jaws hinging wide, before the upper half of its head exploded and it crashed to the ground, still and lifeless.

The police officers had heard the opening salvo and were now emerging from the other side of the museum, effectively pinning the cultists from behind. Their handguns barked, and black-robed men went down, showering the sidewalk with splashes of crimson blood.

Donovan, too, was striding from the tree line, weapon raised, snapping out shots at cultists, dropping them like dead weights where they stood.

A grenade went off close to the Ghost, and he boosted off the ground to avoid the shower of shrapnel caused by two more exploding statues. Flames guttered, the asphalt melting into sticky puddles.

Above, the avatar of Sekhmet watched events unfolding, her face contorted in fury. Shapes were beginning to gather in the light beneath her outstretched hands. The lions were coming.

The Ghost came down again, loosing another barrage of flechettes, one of which ricocheted off a baboon-headed statue and struck a cultist in the shoulder. He winced, his hand going to the wound just as the flechette blew, taking his head and shoulders with it.

The cultists had now dispersed, trying to close the gap with Mullins and his band of police officers. The police were holding their own, however, shots still ringing out as the cultists charged, their guns proving far more effective than the enemy's swords at this range.

The crump of a second grenade reduced another lumbering statue to a shower of dust, leaving a crater in the museum steps in the process.

Arthur was *not* going to be happy.

The Ghost looked round, searching for Astrid. She was standing beneath the cover of the trees, hurling little fragments of bone into the fray, which she'd painstakingly inscribed with runes that afternoon in his apartment. He had no idea what they were supposed to do, but they appeared to be having some sort of effect on the remaining statues, causing them to stumble unsteadily, as if dizzy or confused. He guessed they must be somehow disrupting the control being exerted over them by the goddess, but whatever the case, it was making them easier targets, and he took another two of them out with his explosive rounds.

The Ghost fell back, looking to the skies.

Sekhmet faced him, glaring down at him with burning eyes. He could feel the power radiating from her; feel the searing hate, as if the light of her was causing him to shrivel in her presence. The ghostly lions had now fully formed beneath her palms, straining against their phantasmal leash, and she flicked her wrists, setting them free. They roared, and the Ghost fought the urge to run.

He planted his feet, standing his ground as they rushed him, their jaws widening as they swooped in for the kill. Simultaneously, they burst across his chest, the force of them causing him to stagger back, dropping to one knee. He clenched his jaw, resisting the urge to cry out. The light radiated *around* him, hot and angry, as if his body itself was a shield and he was trying to hold back a gale.

After a moment, they dispersed, dissolving away into the night. He stood, trembling but alive. The runes that Astrid had scrawled across his body in her workshop that afternoon—carefully removing and replacing the strapping over his ribs—had worked, protecting him from whatever life-stealing magic the goddess had employed.

He could see now that a handful of police officers had fallen to the cultists' blades, but that they still had the upper hand, and the cultists' numbers were thinning. Only one remaining statue lumbered at the base of the museum steps, too, already missing one of its arms and a hunk of its hip.

It was time to take the fight to the goddess. Astrid had assured him that the same runes that would protect him from her magic would allow him to land a solid blow upon her ghostly form. Now was his chance to put it to the test.

He fired his boosters, surging up on a plume of flame, heading directly for Sekhmet. She saw him coming and tried to swing out of the way, but he was too fast, and he wrapped his arms around her waist, sending them both spinning skywards.

She felt warm and solid beneath his hands, despite her ghostly aspect, and as she struggled in his grip, thrashing at him with her ankh, he twisted, looking her properly in the face for the first time. Their eyes met.

A cold sensation spread through his gut. He felt bile rising, panic stirring. He froze, unable to act, surging higher and higher into the sky. The face that was now staring back at him had been etched into his mind a thousand times; he'd cupped it lovingly in the bedroom, watched its lingering smile from across the room, traced it in his dreams as he'd longed for her to return.

"Ginny?" he said, in disbelief. "*Ginny*!"

It was *her*, right there in his arms, spinning through the air, glowing with the caustic light of her possession. She'd tried to kill him only moments earlier, and even now, this close, there was no hint of recognition.

Ginny had become the vessel of Sekhmet. It explained everything, of course it did, and the realization hit him like a lead weight. If he was honest with himself, he'd suspected it from the very first moment Astrid had explained her theory, but had refused to admit it, even to himself.

He didn't know what to do. He held onto her as they spiraled lower again, on a direct collision course with the trees.

"What have they done to you?" he called over the screaming wind, but it was too late, and they hurtled into the upper branches of a tree. He let go of her as the trailing limbs struck him thick and fast, whipping his face, and the last thing he saw before unconsciousness snatched away all thought was the sight of her, drifting away again on a carpet of light, lost and out of reach.

TWENTY-THREE

Ginny...

    Ginny...

        Ginny...

            Ginny...

                Sekhmet...

Waking.

Pain.
Darkness.

Adoration.

Sekhmet.

Ginny woke with a start.
Her breath was ragged.
It was dark, and the air was cold and still. She'd been here

for some time. She could tell by the way her body ached; how the muscles in her lower back had begun to seize. She tried to move, but she felt lightheaded and nearly swooned.

She could hear voices—no, a single voice. She tried to speak, but her lips wouldn't move. Her tongue felt thick in her mouth.

The voice… it was in her head. She couldn't understand what it was saying, but it wanted her to get up. She stirred, slowly moving her legs.

"Easy, now."

This was a different voice. A familiar voice. Amaury.

"What…?" she managed to stammer, dizziness causing the entire world to spin on its axis.

"Careful," he said, coming to her aid, taking her by the shoulders. "It's just the aftereffects of the drug. You'll be fine. Better than fine! You'll feel renewed."

The voice in her head was pressing her to move again—an incessant, impatient buzzing. She ignored it.

"Where…?" she said.

She felt a cup touch her lips, and she thirstily gulped at the cool water within. A match flared. She watched it bobbing in the darkness for a moment, until it started to grow, becoming a fist-sized ball of flame. Someone had lit a torch. She recognized the stink of burning pitch.

Slowly, the room resolved around her, the shadows banished by the warm glow.

She was back in the tomb, deep beneath the ground. She tried to sit up, but the world lurched again, and she fell back, resting her head against the hard surface. Above her, she could see the hands of Sekhmet, fingers splayed. It was the idol she'd seen on her first visit here. She was lying on the concave table, deep inside the tomb.

She rolled onto her side, feeling nauseous. Amaury was standing in the doorway, holding the torch. They seemed to be alone.

"Why am I here?" she said. And then her mind slowly caught up, and she realized that it was only Amaury who could have brought her here, only Amaury who'd had the opportunity to drug her drink on the terrace. It was *him*. He'd done this. "What have you done?"

Amaury smiled. "Don't worry, Ginny. I'm not going to hurt you. In fact, no one is ever going to hurt you again." He stepped closer. "I said I had a gift for you."

"The ring."

"A mere trinket," he said. "The real gift was far greater."

Was. What did he mean?

She tried to sit up again, and winced at a sudden pain in her head.

"Shhh, be still. There's a voice inside your head, isn't there?"

"I... yes, I think so. I don't understand."

"Don't trouble yourself. You're quite safe. You see, I had to drug you to bring you here. You might have caused a fuss, and we couldn't have that. The thing is, you're so perfect, Ginny. Perfect in every way. We couldn't have asked for anyone better."

"You're not making any sense," said Ginny. This time she did sit up, swinging her legs down, and the pain in her head subsided.

"That's it," said Amaury. "Listen to it. Do what it says. It'll hurt less that way."

She frowned. The whispering voice was like a constant background droning, a murmuring in her inner ear. It was speaking in a strange, foreign tongue, but she somehow knew that it wanted her to stand. When she didn't, she felt another lancing pain, just behind her left ear. She dropped down from the table, gasping for breath, and the pain subsided again.

"You see," said Amaury, "the sooner you let her in, the sooner you'll be free."

"You bastard," she growled. "I trusted you, and this is what I get for it." She lashed out at him, her hand balled, and as she swung, she saw that her fist had begun to glow, taking on a strange, ethereal aspect. It struck Amaury in the chest and he fell back, stumbling, catching hold of the wall to stop himself going over. He righted himself, still smiling.

"I see she exerts more of an influence with every passing second," said Amaury. "This is good."

"Who?" demanded Ginny. "Tell me what you've done!"

"Sekhmet," said Amaury. "You are very privileged, Miss Ginny Gray. As the world turns and the heavens are reshaped, you shall be one of the first to walk both realms. Sekhmet lives again inside of you. When Thoth reclaims the world, you shall be the first to stand by his side, and all shall know your wrath."

"My God," said Ginny. "You really believe it, don't you? You really do think you can wake the ancient gods?"

"You are living proof," said Amaury. "Fight it if you must, but you know it to be true. You can hear her, can't you? She's there, inside of you, waiting to come out."

Ginny glanced at the idol behind her, at the table she'd been lying on. "That's what this place is, isn't it? It's not a tomb at all. It's never *been* a tomb. It's some kind of… resurrection machine. That's what you've been doing here in the desert. You must be insane!"

She doubled over as another pain shot through her head, like a hot poker, right behind her eyes. For a moment she could see nothing but speckles of white light. The voice was growing stronger, louder. She knew she wouldn't be able to fight it forever.

"The exhibition," said Ginny. "You're targeting New York."

"What better place to begin than the Empire of Greed," he said. "Where temples have been raised to the sky in worship of the false idol—money. Together, we shall tear it down and start anew."

Ginny felt a sensation building inside of her, the stirrings of something she couldn't control—excitement, fear, anticipation.

"No!" she cried, clutching at her head. "Ginny… Ginny… Ginny… Ginny…" Tears were streaming down her cheeks. She looked up at Amaury, pleading, but he only smiled indulgently, waiting for the moment to pass. She thought if only she could keep saying it, then it might remain true. "Ginny… Ginny… Ginny… *Sekhmet.*"

"There," said Amaury. "Now doesn't that feel better?"

TWENTY-FOUR

Light bloomed.

The Ghost opened his eyes. He was staring up at the ceiling. The plaster was cracked, and there were moldering patches in the corner where there'd been a leak in the apartment above and no one had ever bothered to repair it.

Home, then. Or his New York apartment, anyway.

He sat up, setting off a wave of dizzying pain in his head. He put a hand to the back of his neck, groaning. His broken ribs burned.

"Careful," said Donovan, "you're going to have quite a lump."

The Ghost looked round to see Donovan was sitting in his favorite armchair, smoking a cigarette and helping himself to the whisky.

"What am I doing on the floor?" said the Ghost, slowly getting to his feet. And then the memories flooded back, and he remembered the fight at the museum, the tree, and Ginny.

"I brought you back here once it was over. You were out cold. Astrid said she saw you fall from the sky and hit a tree."

The Ghost nodded, and then wished he hadn't. "Did she tell you about Ginny, too?"

"She said you were calling her name as you came down. And that Sekhmet got away."

"Not Sekhmet," said the Ghost. "Ginny."

"What?" said Donovan, heading over to the sideboard to pour him a drink. "I think that tree's knocked the sense out of you."

"No, *listen* to me, Felix. Sekhmet *is* Ginny. That's what they've done to her. They've turned her into the vessel. When I got close..." he trailed off. He could see from the look on Donovan's face that he didn't need to explain any more.

"Good God," said Donovan. "The vile bastards. No wonder you didn't bring her down."

"I froze, Felix," he said. "I didn't know what to do."

Donovan passed him a whisky. He downed it in one, and then pulled his goggles and hat off, tossing them on the sideboard.

"At least now we know what we have to do," said Donovan. "What it'll take to get her back."

"All that power..." said the Ghost. "We don't know what it's done to her. She didn't even recognize me. She tried to kill me."

"I saw what happened, with those... lions," said Donovan. "Where did you learn to do that? I watched them take down two Enforcers last night, but you simply got up and walked away. It was remarkable."

"Astrid," said the Ghost. "She worked her magic again."

"Quite literally, in this case," said Donovan. "She's an impressive woman, Gabriel. She didn't seem at all phased out there. Although afterwards she just... well, she upped and ran off in the middle of our conversation."

The Ghost frowned. "She must have had good reason. That's not like Astrid. She's a valuable member of the team."

"Oh, so we're a team now, are we?"

"Well—you, me, Mullins, Astrid... Ginny," he said. "What

else would you call it?" He poured himself another drink. "Mullins did well tonight."

"He lost a few men, but the Commissioner will probably award him a bloody medal for the way he took down those cultists. He deserves it, too."

There was a rap at the door. The Ghost looked at Donovan, frowning. "Mullins?" he said.

Donovan shook his head. "No. He's down at the station, sorting out the paperwork. He won't be done for hours yet."

The Ghost crossed to the door and peered through the spy hole. "Astrid?" he said, pulling it open a moment later. "What's the matter?"

She was leaning against the doorjamb, panting for breath. He let her in, closed the door behind her, and fetched a glass of water as she propped herself against the windowsill. She'd obviously run all the way there.

"I know where they're keeping her," she said, when she'd regained her composure a moment later.

"Who?" said Donovan.

"Ginny!" She took another long gulp of water. "There was this… baboon, and I followed it." She looked at Donovan. "I'm sorry for cutting out on you, leaving you to deal with… well, *him*, but I caught sight of it, and thought if I followed it, it might lead me somewhere useful."

"Astrid, I could kiss you," said the Ghost.

She smiled. "Maybe later."

"So what, you know where they're based?" said Donovan.

Astrid shook her head. "No. I don't think this is their base of operations or anything. It's far too small for that. More like a safe house. It's a rundown apartment over a shop on Twenty-Third and Fourth. I watched them take her inside. There were about five of them, and the baboon."

"Was she still... well, was she *Ginny*?" said the Ghost.

Astrid nodded. "She must have reverted to normal before I caught up with them. She looked drained or delirious. They practically had to carry her."

The Ghost looked at Donovan. "Have you got any bullets left in that gun?"

"Enough," said Donovan.

"Then we're going after her. If we strike while they're still reeling from the ambush, we might have a chance of getting her out of there."

"More to the point," said Astrid, "Ginny herself will be too weary to manifest again this soon after a battle. We'll be safe from Sekhmet."

"And what do we do with her when we've got her?" said the Ghost. "She's not herself. She didn't know who I was."

"I have some ideas on that front," said Astrid.

"All right. Then we do it—right now," said the Ghost, reaching for his goggles.

"One thing first," said Astrid.

"What's that?"

"Pour me one of those damn whiskies. I've just run all the way here."

Donovan laughed. "You know, you grow on me more every time I meet you."

* * *

The shop was actually a small bakery on the intersection of the two roads. The shelves in the window were empty, and had been for some time. Dead flies had settled in the windows, and a small handwritten sign had been posted on the door, declaring the shop "under new management".

It was late now, and only a few lonely cars hissed by, tires kissing asphalt. The temperature had dropped, and a cool breeze was blowing in off the river. The Ghost's heart was thrumming like a jackhammer as he squatted on a fire escape across the street, watching for any hint of activity from the windows. The lights were off, and the place seemed deserted. There could be scores of them holed up inside, or just a handful—they wouldn't know until they made their move.

Donovan was down below, skulking in the shadows, and Astrid was on the opposite side of the intersection. He had a mind to leave her there while they went in, but she'd asked him for a gun, and he wasn't about to start patronizing her, not after everything she'd done. Like Donovan had said, she was a remarkable woman, and she was doing this to help him get Ginny back. Who was he to tell her not to get involved for her own protection?

There was no subtlety about their plan. They weren't planning to sneak in via the roof, or try to get her out without a fight. When Astrid gave the signal, they were converging on the door to the baker's shop and forcing their way inside, then shooting anyone who came at them until there was no one left in their way. They'd try to retain the element of surprise, of course—at least until the first shot was fired. After that... well, he supposed it would depend on what resistance they met.

He saw Astrid give the signal, and grabbed the rail on the fire escape, leaping over and landing in a crouch below. He dashed across the street, Donovan coming up behind him. "Ready?"

"Ready," they both replied in concert.

He gave the door an almighty shove with his shoulder, and the lock splintered almost instantly. The shop hadn't been built with security in mind; no one would suspect an Ancient Egyptian resurrectionist cult of hiding the avatar of a reborn goddess here. He supposed that was the point.

They slipped inside, scattering to create more targets.

There was an open doorway behind the counter, and the Ghost inched round, peering around the frame. No one seemed to be coming down the stairs from the apartment above. He nodded to the others to indicate he was going up. Cautiously, they followed behind him.

He winced as his boots creaked on the old wooden stairs. Up ahead, they hit a small landing, and then doubled back on themselves, going higher. He kept to the wall, head raised, weapon arm covering the landing as he walked.

He reached another small landing. There was a door here. He frowned, unsure whether to try it, or to go higher first. Donovan was frowning at him from the stairs below.

The decision was made for him a moment later when he heard a toilet flush, and the handle on the door turned. He spun, squeezing the trigger on his weapon as the door opened. The emerging cultist caught a hailstorm of metal discs in the chest. He stumbled back, gurgling, and toppled into an empty bathtub. The Ghost heaved a sigh of relief. Then the flechettes exploded, spraying the corpse across the walls in a gory, violent eruption, and all hell broke loose.

The Ghost took the next flight of stairs three at a time, hitting the landing just as two further cultists swung out of another doorway, pistols raised. These guys, then, didn't go in for the typical sword and blowpipe affair. The Ghost cursed, diving into a roll. Their guns snapped out a series of shots, leaving pockmarks in the wall where he'd been standing. He came up quickly, right before them. The heels of his palms smashed the cartilage of their noses up into their brains, and they crumpled at his feet, dead instantly.

Astrid and Donovan had opened fire down below, seeing to more of the men who'd obviously been keeping guard on the ground floor and were now streaming out of the bakery's kitchens, weapons blazing.

He decided to leave them to keep the escape route clear as he went after Ginny.

He ran to the end of the corridor, sidestepping through the door from which the cultists had emerged. The room on the other side was bare and unfurnished, other than an old, bulky wireless, two overturned packing crates they'd obviously been using for chairs, and some takeout cartons, dumped on the floor, their gelatinous contents seeping out onto the bare floorboards. Another door led deeper into the apartment.

He crept forward, trying to get a sense of how far back the place went. It had obviously once been two apartments that had been knocked into one at some point in the recent past, and the work had never been completed. The walls were peeling and bare, and exposed wires peeked out of gouges in the plasterwork. He guessed the cult must have moved in before the work had been finished, and saw no need to make good.

From the other side of the door, someone fired a shot, and it winged his shoulder, burning a line across the fabric of his coat. He flung himself against the wall, shuffling forward, and then went low, ducking out and shooting the man in the kneecaps. The explosion took his legs off, and a final shot to the head put him down for good.

The room beyond was a small kitchen. A kettle was whistling on the stove. He crept forward, heard a noise behind him and grabbed the kettle, swinging it round and cracking another man across the head with the scalding metal. He screamed, dropping to his knees, and the Ghost dropped the kettle and shot him in the throat.

These were the men that had taken Ginny, the men who had turned her into that *thing*. He had no time for mercy, not tonight.

Below, the sound of gunfire came to an abrupt halt. He heard Donovan thundering up the stairs, Astrid in his wake. They'd find him easily enough by the trail of corpses.

Another doorway took him through to what he assumed was the hallway of the adjoining apartment. Here, the décor was dated but still largely intact: exuberant wallpaper covered in fleur-de-lis, an old chandelier, a grandmother clock that hadn't chimed in years. Everything was covered in a thick patina of dust. It was a relic from before the war.

He heard a rustling sound from one of the rooms up ahead, and started for the door. He buckled a second later when something heavy struck him on the back, and he stumbled forward, barely maintaining his balance. It screeched angrily in his ear, clawing at his face, trying to pull his goggles off and get to his eyes.

The baboon.

The thing had incredible strength. It had obviously been lurking above, out of sight, and had dropped onto his shoulders as he'd passed beneath it, wrapping its legs around his neck. He could feel it beginning to constrict his breathing, crushing his windpipe as it gave up trying to get at his eyes and started pounding his head with its fists instead.

He charged backwards, slamming the creature against the wall. It bellowed angrily, but didn't release its grip.

Ahead of him, the door opened and two cultists rushed out, laughing at the sight that presented them. The Ghost put a flechette in the face of one for his trouble, and another in the gut of his companion.

He was gasping for breath now, his head swimming, his damaged ribs stabbing with pain. He staggered forward, grasping at the baboon's legs, but it was too strong, and he couldn't prise it free.

There was a loud shot from right behind his head, and suddenly the creature's muscles went slack, and the weight of it slid from his back, striking the floor with a thud. He turned, gasping, to see Astrid standing behind him, lowering her gun. Her face was spattered with the creature's blood.

"I'm glad I gave you that thing," said the Ghost, through choked tears. "Thanks."

"I think that's two you owe me now," she said, with a cocky grin.

Donovan was already at the other doorway. "In here," he called. "Quickly."

They ran to join him.

Ginny was inside, lying on a mattress on the floor, her hands and feet bound with leather belts. She looked unconscious. Her skin was pale, and she was wearing the tattered rags of the costume she'd had on during the parade. There were dark circles around her eyes, and she clearly hadn't eaten properly in weeks. Around the mattress was the detritus of her captivity—used hypodermic syringes, coils of frayed rope, a potty, the remnants of a sandwich, a stain that looked disturbingly like vomit. It was unconscionable that someone could do this to Ginny; to take such a bright, brilliant woman and put her through this hellish nightmare.

Astrid was at her side before the Ghost was properly through the door. She felt for a pulse. "It's sluggish," she said. "She's been drugged."

"Get those binds off of her," said the Ghost.

Astrid did as he said, and he came forward, scooping her up into his arms. She felt as light as a feather. He cradled her for a moment, and then turned to Donovan. "All right, get us out of here."

"And then where?" said Donovan. "Back to your apartment?"

"No," said Astrid. "My place is closer, and I might be able to help her."

The Ghost nodded his assent, and together, they fled before any of the neighbors could report the disturbance.

TWENTY-FIVE

For a while, he watched her sleeping.

She was curled up in Astrid's armchair like an indolent cat, her breath coming in short, shallow gasps. She looked so fragile, so thin and broken. This wasn't the Ginny he knew, the vibrant, cocksure, self-confident woman who had gone off to Egypt on her own for an adventure. He hoped it wouldn't change her; that she wouldn't become cautious and afraid to live her life in the way she always had. That was what he loved about her, he realized—her ability to turn any situation into an adventure, her fierce independence, her freedom and sense of *being*. He hoped he could help her to heal. He hoped that she'd want him to.

While Donovan put a call in to Mullins to tell him what had gone down above the baker's shop, Gabriel sat with Astrid, talking in hushed tones while Ginny slept. He'd divested himself of his goggles, having already lost his hat during his encounter with the baboon, and was sipping a mug of her restorative tea.

The church still reeked of smoke from their experiment with the Seer that morning, and Astrid—much to her delight— had discovered there were still cold pastries in the bag he'd left on the counter.

She'd taken a moment to clean herself up once they'd settled Ginny in the chair, and now she sat cross-legged on the floor beside him, munching hungrily.

"You're quite handy with that thing," he said, nodding at the gun, which she'd placed on the workbench.

"I've known my way around a few of those in my time," she said. "Hate the things, but sometimes they get the job done."

"You saved my life."

"Mmm hmm."

"I won't forget it."

She laughed. "You make it sound so grand, as if I'm the heroine in a dime novel or something. I did what I had to do. You'd have done the same. I'm sure you'll have chance to pay me back at some point."

"I hope so. Although I'll be honest, I'll be glad if I never see another baboon in my life."

She grinned.

He glanced at Ginny. "You said you had some ideas."

Astrid nodded while she chewed on a mouthful of pastry. "She needs to sleep the tranquilizers off for a start. Aside from keeping her sedated, they'll be suppressing her own personality, allowing the interloper to maintain control. She needs to wake up in order to fight it."

"To fight a goddess?"

"We can help her," said Astrid. "There are techniques for controlling possession. Once she becomes aware of what the other personality is trying to do, instead of being pushed into the background by the drugs, she'll be able to assert herself." She took another bite of her pastry. "There *is* something else, too, but it might not be easy."

"Go on."

"The tomb. That's the source of Sekhmet's power. Remember what I told you about buildings mirroring the heavens, strengthening the links between the different realms? Well, that's exactly what that tomb is doing. It's like a conductor, channeling her power."

"So if we destroy it…" said Gabriel.

"We don't even need to destroy it," she said. "Just disrupt it. Alter the layout somehow, stop it reflecting the design it was built to mirror. That'll weaken Sekhmet, and give Ginny a better chance of asserting herself again."

"Then that has to be a priority," said Gabriel. He started to get to his feet, but felt her hand on his arm, holding him back.

"For tomorrow, yes," she said. "Once we've all had some rest. We've got her back now. We'll be no good to her if we're half asleep."

Gabriel was about to protest, but thought better of it. She was right. It would soon be dawn, and his wounds were beginning to ache again, now that the adrenaline of the raid was wearing off.

"Don't worry. We can take it in shifts. Why don't you get some rest while I wait for Felix to return?" Astrid didn't have a holophone terminal, and so he'd had to head out to find one.

"You should go first," he said.

Astrid shook her head. "I'm not the one who had a baboon on his back." Her face creased into a wicked laugh, and he couldn't help himself from joining in. "And besides—she's not going to want to see you looking like that, is she?" She nodded at Ginny.

"Go on, get some sleep. Take a few cushions and use the other room. I know it's not the height of luxury, but it's safe."

"All right," he said. He could feel his eyelids fighting to close. "But you wake me the moment she stirs."

"Of course," she said, and took another big bite of her pastry, as if to underline her point.

"You were supposed to wake me!" said Gabriel, emerging bleary-eyed from the other room to see Ginny sitting up in the chair, Astrid kneeling on the floor before her. Donovan was propped on a stool in the corner, sipping coffee. Light was streaming in though a small stained-glass window on the far wall, vibrant blues, yellows and reds pooling on the flagstones.

"Shhh," said Astrid, waving her finger before Ginny's face. "I'm busy." She smirked. "And besides, you looked so peaceful."

Gabriel knelt beside Astrid on the ground. Ginny was awake, but it seemed as if Astrid had her in a trance of some kind; she sat stock still, her back straight, her eyes wide and staring.

Astrid was moving her finger back and forth, and Ginny's eyes were following it. He realized after a moment that Astrid wasn't simply testing Ginny's reactions, but was actually tracing shapes in the air—runes that she was presumably attempting to imprint on Ginny's unconscious mind.

"These will help," she said. She didn't elaborate further, and Gabriel decided not to push her—he probably wouldn't have understood anyway.

After a moment, she clicked her fingers and sat back, and Ginny seemed to suddenly snap back to life. She blinked, her eyes trying to focus. Then she saw Gabriel, and her face broke into the most sorrowful smile that he'd ever seen. She flung herself forward, wrapping her arms around his neck and squeezing him so tight that he could barely breathe. He felt her hot tears on his neck, and he just held her for a while, her body wracking as she let it out—the relief, the pain, the horror.

"Oh God," she whispered in his ear, over and over. "Oh God."

"It's all right. I've got you," he said. He didn't know what else he *could* say.

He heard the door click shut as Astrid and Donovan stepped out, leaving them alone for a moment.

"Are you…?" He tried to frame the words. How could he ask her if she was okay? Of course she wasn't okay. She might never be okay again.

"It's me," she said. "It's me." She pushed herself back, her hands on his shoulders, searching his face. "I'm sorry."

"For what? You have *nothing* to be sorry for."

"I almost led them to you."

Gabriel frowned. "To *me*?"

She nodded. "They wanted you. They were going to make you into one of their vessels, like… like *me*. But I wouldn't tell them where to find you. I *wouldn't*."

So that's why they'd turned over her apartment, and why they'd drugged him that first night rather than killing him outright. Suddenly it all made a terrible kind of sense.

"You have to know, whatever I did, it wasn't *me*. I can't control it. It's as if she's somehow able to push me out of the way, and I can see everything that's happening, but I've got no way of stopping her." The tears were still streaming down her face. "Last night outside the museum—I almost killed you."

"No, *you* didn't," said Gabriel. "*She* did." He leaned in, kissing her forehead. "We're going to help you, Ginny. Astrid knows what to do. We'll find a way to get that thing out of you. I won't stop until it's gone. I promise."

She cupped his face in her hands, trailing her fingers down his neck. He felt them close around his throat, her thumbs digging painfully into his flesh. He tried to pull back, confused, but her grip was like a vise, and she clung on, squeezing.

Her eyes had taken on an awful, distant gleam, and the quality of the light around her had shifted, as if she were wrapped in the corona of a distant, pale sun. Her hair whipped up around her face, stirred by a breeze he could not feel. There was only the awful, constant pressure of her hands, slowly choking the life from him.

He tried to stand, his scrabbling foot kicking over a glass, which shattered on the flagstones. She was too strong. He grabbed her arms, trying to lever her off, but she just clung on to him, immovable, deadly.

The door opened and Astrid and Donovan came running in, calling his name, but they seemed to him like a distant memory, slowly slipping away, a half-remembered dream. His eyes were closing, his lungs burning as they fought for oxygen that wasn't coming.

"No!"

He opened his eyes as the pressure suddenly lifted, and he gulped at the air, dragging it down into his lungs. Spots were dancing before his eyes. He fell back, spluttering.

Ginny had drifted up out of the chair, hovering a few feet above the ground. She looked pained, doubling over with the turmoil of her inner battle. "No!" she screamed in defiance, raging against the deity who was attempting to subsume her. "*No!*"

She dropped suddenly, crumpling back into the chair. Slowly, the pale aura began to fade, and her eyes regained their previous luster. Within moments she was Ginny again, hugging her knees to her chest. She looked at Gabriel imploringly. He tried to force a smile.

"You did it, Ginny," said Astrid. "You stopped her. Now you know what you have to do to control it."

"It hurts," said Ginny, her voice cracking. "It hurts so much."

"We've got to put an end to this," said Donovan. "Who did this to you, Ginny? Tell me so I can put a bullet between the bastard's eyes."

"It was Amaury," she said. Her voice was barely a whisper. "Jacques Amaury."

"But Amaury's still in Egypt. Landsworth said as much."

Ginny shook her head. "He was on the ship. He kept me in this little room, done out like the inside of a tomb. It's *all* Amaury. He's going to resurrect Thoth and destroy Manhattan."

Gabriel glanced at Donovan, and their eyes met.

"How, Ginny?" said Gabriel. "How's he planning to do it?"

"He's built a temple beneath the streets," she said. "Somewhere on the Upper East Side. He's going to channel Thoth's power."

"Mirroring another temple," said Astrid. "Right here, beneath our noses."

"But where?" said Gabriel.

Ginny shrugged. "I'm sorry, I don't know."

"The waste ground," said Donovan. "That's what this is all about."

"The waste ground?"

"The reason it all started between the cult and the Reaper. He tried to convince them to sell a patch of waste ground, but they weren't interested. He wasn't prepared to give up. He pushed a little too hard, and woke the beast. That's why they went for his girlfriend, the Allen woman."

"And you're only telling us this now?"

"It's a patch of wasteland, Gabriel. How were we to know? Mullins checked it out, but didn't find anything. Of course, he wasn't looking below ground."

"Then that's where it'll be," said Gabriel, getting to his feet.

"We have to stop them before they manifest Thoth," said Ginny. "If you think Sekhmet is dangerous…"

"All right. We make our move tonight," said Gabriel. "But first, we need to pay a visit to the museum."

"The museum?" said Donovan.

Gabriel nodded. "Astrid thinks a little wanton destruction is in order," he said, with a grin.

TWENTY-SIX

The museum had been closed since the shooting at the parade, and now, following the firefight the previous evening, the police had erected barriers, boarded up the main entrance and cordoned off the street outside.

In the light of day, Gabriel was shocked by the devastation caused by the grenades—whole chunks of the sidewalk had been overturned, the road was completely impassible to cars, and the museum steps were going to need completely rebuilding. It resembled the middle of a war zone rather than the beating heart of Manhattan art and culture.

The bodies had all gone, of course, cleared away during the night by an army of ambulance workers. The remnants of the statues had gone, too, and Gabriel wondered how Mullins had explained them away—he couldn't imagine the Commissioner, or the media, buying into a tale of living idols and resurrected gods. He'd probably found some way to pin the blame on the dead cultists, claiming they'd been trying to steal them.

Arthur was waiting for them on his favorite park bench. He looked thoroughly dejected, sitting in the dappled shadow of an oak tree, his pullover ruffled and his hair mussed. He'd clearly been dragged out of bed in a hurry that morning, and hadn't bothered to straighten himself out since.

He looked up as Gabriel and Donovan approached, Astrid and Ginny trailing behind them. "Next time, just make sure whatever you get yourselves involved in has something to do with dinosaurs, all right?" He looked from Gabriel to Donovan. "Or mammoths, mastodons, saber-toothed tigers... anything like that. The Museum of Natural History *never* has these sorts of problems, and it's only fair." He peered myopically at Ginny. "I'm delighted to see you're back with us, Miss Gray."

Donovan had argued to leave the two women behind at the church, but they needed Astrid with them to oversee any changes they made to the exhibits, and besides, now that Gabriel had Ginny back, he wasn't about to let her out of his sight again. Not for a while, anyway.

"So, what is it you need?" said Arthur, with a heavy sigh. "I've been up since the small hours, cleaning up last night's mess." It was his usual brand of mock-weariness, rather than any real sense of bitterness at the devastation they'd caused, and Gabriel admired him more than ever for his restraint.

"We need access to the exhibition," said Gabriel. "Astrid thinks a few tweaks to the layout might make a difference to Ginny. She's... umm..." He considered for a moment the best way to put it. "Well, let's say she's under a malign influence."

Arthur waved a dismissive hand, letting him off the hook with any further explanation. "I won't pretend to understand," he said, "and you can knock the whole bloody thing down as far as I'm concerned. It's a disaster. Landsworth's disappeared, the Mayor's decided the exhibition will remain closed indefinitely, and the repairs to the museum are going to take weeks." He rubbed his eyes and yawned. "So be my guest."

"You're a good man, Arthur," said Gabriel.

"Well, just you remember that when you're footing the bar bill later," said Arthur. "Then you really will be sorry. Remember I'm an Englishman."

"How could I forget?"

Arthur stood, stretching his weary limbs. "Come on, then. We'll use the side entrance. The front door is out of commission."

They crossed the road, skirting the police barricade, and circled around to the side of the massive building, to a door familiar to Gabriel from many clandestine meetings with Arthur in the past.

Arthur pulled a hoop of keys from his belt, selected one, and let them in. "Hold on a moment and I'll fetch some torches," he said. "It'll be dark inside, and I'd rather not draw any attention by putting the lights on." He propped the door open with a small stone Buddha while he shuffled around inside a cupboard, producing three electric torches. He handed one to Astrid, and another to Donovan, and then slid the Buddha out of the way. The door slammed shut, throwing them into darkness.

Seconds later the torches blinked on, blades of light stabbing into the eerie gloom. "This way," said Arthur, taking the lead.

Gabriel took Ginny's hand in the darkness. Her fingers interlaced with his as they walked, footsteps echoing through the empty halls.

Gabriel had always found the museum intimidating, particularly in the dark; looming, unfamiliar shapes, leaping out at him from across the eons; the blank, staring faces of the long dead, peering out of portraits and busts—a sense of the weight of history crowding in around him, oppressing him. In his world, history was a dangerous thing—his experiences during the war were an indelible stain, but more than that, everything that had happened with the Roman, and then all of this, with Ginny. Now he had her back, all he wanted to do was look to the future, and not dwell on the past.

"It's just down here," said Arthur, leading them along another silent passageway. "On the left."

He lifted the curtain to let them through. He'd left it hanging for the grand unveiling, and had never even had the chance to pull it down. Gabriel wished this whole business had been easier on Arthur. He deserved a break, a little bit of success. He'd joked with them earlier, but in truth, Gabriel knew he was deeply wounded by the failure of the exhibition. It would have put the museum—and him—on the map. Now it had been reduced to one long tale of disaster.

Gabriel ducked under the curtain.

The exhibition looked even more stunning now that it was complete, and in the gloom, he felt almost lost, as if he'd stepped through a portal and out into the desert night. He stood for a moment in the shadow of the monolithic structures, feeling dwarfed.

He felt Ginny stiffen beside him, her grip tightening on his hand. "It's almost a mirror image," she said, "of what I saw in the desert."

He couldn't imagine how hard this was for her, coming here after what had happened back in Egypt. It must have been like returning to the scene of a violent crime, and he kept her close, as much for his sake as hers.

"That's the tomb," said Astrid, running the beam of her torch over a wall on the other side of the exhibition hall. To the left of them was the grand colonnade, the recesses now devoid of statues.

They followed Astrid over to the temple.

"Hang on," she said as she walked, playing her torch back and forth. "There's something in the doorway."

As they got closer, the beam seemed to catch on something white and round. Astrid hurried closer, the focus of her beam widening. When she saw what it was, she screamed, and the shrill sound seemed to rend the air, causing Gabriel's hackles to rise.

Landsworth was hanging in the doorway, his head lolling awkwardly to one side, his neck broken. He'd drooled blood down the front of his pale suit, and his arms hung limp and lifeless by his side. Most disturbingly, there was no rope. He was simply hanging there in the void, suspended as if by supernatural means.

"Oh God," said Ginny, from beside him. "It's started."

A man laughed in the darkness, and Donovan turned, spearing him with his torch.

"Amaury," said Ginny, as the light found his bearded face.

"Hello, Ginny. I knew you'd return, that you wouldn't be able to keep away, no matter what these people put you through." He spoke with a smooth French lilt. "You've brought them back here, haven't you, to your place of power, your place of rebirth?"

"No!" said Ginny. "It's not like that. You're twisting it."

Amaury grinned. "Now, now. You know I don't like liars."

He glanced toward the tomb. "Landsworth was a liar, and look where it got him."

Landsworth's body suddenly slumped to the ground, released from whatever occult grip had been suspending it. "The poor fool just couldn't keep his mouth shut. He did in the end, though, when I fed him his own tongue." He smiled. "Although I think the irony was a little lost on him."

"I saw you," said Gabriel, stepping forward. "In the Café Deluxe. You've been here all along, ever since the *Centurion* arrived. You've played us all for fools."

"Ah," said Amaury. "The man in the bar, searching for his lost love. There were a lot of ghosts there that night, weren't there?"

Out of the corner of his eye, Gabriel noticed that Donovan had been slowly sliding his gun from its holster, and was now pointing it at Amaury. If he could keep him talking for just a moment longer, Donovan would have a clear shot. "You know who I am, then?"

"I know who you might have been. Anubis, Horus, Atum. Ginny didn't want that, though. She didn't want to share it with you. I can't say I blame her. The power is quite beguiling."

Donovan's gun barked as he squeezed the trigger. Gabriel felt Ginny jump at the report.

The bullet struck Amaury in the chest, just above the heart. He staggered back, face contorting, clutching at the entry wound. Then he started to laugh again, and straightened up, lifting his hand away with a magician's flourish. There wasn't even a blemish on the front of his shirt.

Frowning, Donovan emptied the clip, snapping out shot after shot, but every time a bullet struck Amaury, it just...

disappeared. The only sign of their passing was a minute shift in the quality of light, a vague amber glow at the site of impact.

Amaury threw his arms wide, and Gabriel felt a rush of hot air, felt sand stirring around the room, peppering his face. Immense wings of amber light unfurled behind Amaury, filling the chamber with a glare like the midday sun.

He lifted into the air, his eyes shining, his body shimmering as if lost behind a heat haze. In his left hand he carried a long, curved blade, forged from the starlight itself, and in his left a blackened shield, emblazoned with the head of an ibis. He was beautiful and terrifying in equal measure.

"Thoth," said Astrid. "We're too late. He's already done it. He's already been resurrected."

"I see it now," said Ginny. "I've been such a *fool*. He's always been Thoth. Ever since I first met him. It must have happened out there, in the desert, when they first found the temple in the sands."

"Then the complex he's building here," said Astrid, "it's not to resurrect him."

"It's to give him power," said Ginny.

Thoth's voice boomed in a guttural tongue that Gabriel could not decipher. The sound of it seemed to make the very ground beneath them rumble. Behind him, Ginny screamed, her hands going to her head as she buckled, falling to her knees.

"No!" she said, her voice a mere whimper. "No." Her hands had begun to glow with the pale light of elsewhere, and she rose into the air, ribbons of light forming around her trailing arms and legs as she completed her transition into Sekhmet. She hovered in the sky above them, a terrible goddess of death.

Gabriel knew they only had moments to live. Trying to fight was a fool's errand. They'd be incinerated with a single look. There was only one chance...

"Over here," he said, running for the colonnade. The light of Thoth guided his way as he hurtled to one of the columns. "Quickly, help me."

"Help you *what*?" cried Donovan, behind him.

"Help me push it over. *Now!*"

The three of them joined him as he shoved at the column, trying desperately to topple it. He felt it shift, rocking unsteadily on its plinth.

The temperature in the room was rising as Thoth began to boil the air. He was going to cook them alive. Gabriel could already feel it searing the inside of his lungs.

"There! One more push..." He roared as he threw his weight behind it, straining until he felt the muscles in his arms begin to pop. Beside him, Arthur cried out in pain.

The column shook, wobbling unsteadily, and then went over, listing to the left as it fell.

It crashed into the side of the tomb, shattering the wall and sending the crumbling roof into a cataclysmic slide to the ground. Hunks of masonry tumbled to the floor, burying Landsworth's remains and spilling out onto the marble concourse.

Gabriel dropped to his knees, almost swooning with the rising heat. He saw Sekhmet, her arms raised, two ghostly lions forming in the air around her. As he watched, she turned toward Thoth, and set them free.

The lions roared, surging forward and slamming into the other god's chest. They burst into pyres of ethereal blue flame, swamping him utterly, as if she'd doused him in petrol and struck a match.

Thoth roared, tumbling from the sky, his ghostly wings beating ineffectually at the air as he fell.

Gabriel didn't wait to see what he would do next. He was already on his feet. "Go, *now*!" he bellowed.

Behind him, the others scrambled to their feet and ran for the door.

"Ginny! Come on!" He backed away, hoping beyond hope that she would follow him; that there was enough of the woman he loved still left in the apparition to assume control.

She turned, and their eyes met. "Go!" she said. "I'm coming."

That was good enough. He turned and ran.

TWENTY-SEVEN

"I left her there," said Gabriel, as he arrived, panting, at the door of Astrid's church a short while later. "I didn't see her get out."

Donovan was standing on the doorstep, smoking a cigarette, and he held up his hand, appealing for calm. "She's already inside," he said. "We've been waiting for you."

Gabriel heaved a sigh of relief, leaning forward, his hands on his knees. "I haven't run like that in years," he said.

"We took a cab," said Donovan.

"*What*? You took a cab, after something like that? You actually stopped on a street corner and flagged down a cab?"

Donovan shrugged. He took another draw from his cigarette, and then tossed the butt amidst the gravestones. "We were lucky," he said. "And we might not be so lucky next time. We're dabbling in things we don't understand."

"We're protecting our city," said Gabriel. "The only way we know how. We can't stop now. That thing won't let us, even if we wanted to."

"That's what I'm afraid of," said Donovan. He looked troubled. "Come on. She'll want to know you're here. They all will."

Inside, they'd gathered in the old church hall, righting some of the moldy pews to use as seats. Arthur sat by Astrid, while Ginny was pacing, her fingers drumming excitedly against her chin.

"Ginny?"

"Gabriel!" She seemed brighter than she'd been since they'd found her. He wondered if perhaps the tranquilizers were finally wearing off, but he suspected there was more to it than that. "Did you see? Did you see what I did?"

He nodded, slowly. "I saw. But Felix is right. We can't get carried away. We caught him off guard. *You* caught him off guard. That doesn't mean it's going to be so easy next time. Remember, we still need to get that thing out of you, somehow."

"That's just it," said Ginny. "Astrid doesn't think we *can* get it out of me. She says I've got to learn to control it. What you did back there, destroying that tomb—I feel more like *me* than I have in months."

Gabriel glanced at Astrid, who shrugged. "She's right. This isn't the sort of thing you just wheel out an exorcist for. She has a shard of a *goddess* inside of her. Nothing short of a binding ritual would shake it loose, and there wouldn't be anything left of her after I'd finished."

"I can do this, Gabriel. I can take him on. I want revenge on that son of a bitch for what he did to me, and I'm damn well going to get it."

Gabriel sighed. "This complex. We're going to have to do to *it* what we've just done to that tomb. Only, the complex is underground, and probably full of cultists, not to mention an army of living statues and an angry god. Believe me, I know we've got to find a way to end this, but there's four of us, plus Mullins." He looked at Arthur. "Forgive me, Arthur, but I'm not putting a gun in your hand and sending you to your death."

"Fine by me," said Arthur. "I've always seen myself in more of a supporting role."

He dropped onto one of the pews, looking to Donovan. "I hate to admit it, but I think you're right. I'm out of ideas. I've got nothing."

Donovan was frowning. "It's all right. I know what needs to be done." He pulled a notebook from his jacket pocket and scrawled down an address. "Give me until nine, then meet me here. And call Mullins. Tell him to be there too."

"Where are *you* going?"

"To get help," said Donovan. He lit a cigarette, and then turned and left.

TWENTY-EIGHT

"This is a pleasant surprise, Felix. I hadn't expected to see you back so soon."

He was standing in the hallway of Paul Abbadelli's mansion. He'd come alone—not because he didn't feel the need for backup, but because he didn't want Mullins to see how far he was about to fall.

"I presume there's been a development in the case?"

The case. Donovan found it difficult to believe how Abbadelli could speak so nonchalantly of his murdered lover. "You could say that. Things have progressed somewhat since we last spoke. Consequently, I have a... well, a *proposition* for you." The words almost stuck in his throat.

Abbadelli grinned, enjoying Donovan's discomfort. "Oh, now that does sound interesting." He stepped to one side, ushering Donovan into his study. "You'd better come on through and tell me all about it."

Donovan swallowed. He wasn't sure he'd ever be able to look himself in the mirror again after this, no matter how many times he told himself it was the only option.

He took a seat before Abbadelli's desk, while the man himself whispered something to Carlos, before joining him and closing the door. He circled his desk, took a cigar from a wooden box, and offered it to Donovan.

Donovan shook his head. "My taste only runs as far as cheap cigarettes," he said, reaching for his packet.

"Then we shall have to cultivate you," said Abbadelli. He clipped the end with a gilded cutter, and struck a match. "There's a great deal of pleasure to be had from the more luxurious things in life, Felix," he said, between puffs. "You may yet come to realize this."

"I doubt it," said Donovan, pulling the ignition tab on his cigarette. He tried not to let Abbadelli see that his hand was trembling as he took a draw.

"So, my information proved useful, then?"

Donovan could hear Gabriel's warning going around and around inside his head. *Don't allow him to think you're in his debt.* What else could he do, though? Here he was, sitting before the man, about to beg him for help. "In a manner of speaking. As I said, things have progressed."

"You've found out where they're hiding, haven't you?" said Abbadelli. He perched on the edge of his desk. "The Circle of Thoth."

Donovan nodded. "In a warren beneath the wasteland you tried to buy. They've constructed some kind of complex down there, recreating the footprint of an Ancient Egyptian temple."

Abbadelli smiled. "So *that's* why they wouldn't sell." He chewed thoughtfully on the end of his cigar. "I must say, Felix, I'm most impressed. And delighted you've come to me with this."

Donovan plumed smoke from the corner of his mouth. "They're planning something big," he said. "Tonight. They're going to make a play for control of the streets, and I have reason to believe their forces are numerous."

"And so we find ourselves at an impasse, do we not?" said Abbadelli, getting up and pacing the room. "Everyone wants control of the streets. The mob, the cult... I don't envy you, Felix, caught in the middle. There must be an easier way."

"I want to stop them," said Donovan, flatly. "That's why I'm here." He was growing impatient with Abbadelli's games.

"You intend to ferret them out of their warren?"

"I intend to destroy it. Collapse the tunnels. Put an end to whatever they're doing down there. Only... I don't have the resources."

"And I do," said Abbadelli. He laughed. "You must at least allow me to enjoy the irony. So you're proposing a partnership?"

"I'm suggesting that our goals might be... temporarily aligned. With your manpower, and your Enforcers, we could take them down for good." He hated himself even as the words passed his lips.

"And if I agree?" said Abbadelli. "What's in it for me?"

Donovan frowned. "Revenge against the men who killed your lover. An end to the war you started. One less thorn in your side."

Abbadelli shrugged. "In time, I shall claim all of those victories regardless. What else?"

Donovan sighed. This was the moment he'd been expecting. There was no turning back from it now. "I'll be sure to keep my dinner date," he said.

Abbadelli grinned. "Then we have a deal." He thrust out his

hand. Reluctantly, Donovan took it. This time, he was *certain* he was making a deal with the Devil.

Abbadelli dropped into the chair behind his desk. "All right, Inspector. Tell me what you need."

TWENTY-NINE

"Where *is* he?" said the Ghost, glancing at his watch.

They'd been lurking on the edges of the waste ground for almost half an hour. So far, there was no sign of Donovan. The night was still and quiet, punctuated only by the rumble of distant traffic and the sighing of a cool breeze blowing in off the water.

The Ghost and Mullins had already scouted the area and ascertained that the entrance to the complex was most likely in the basement of the adjoining building—an abandoned wheelwright's shop that had been boarded up and marked for demolition. They'd yet to explore more closely in fear of alerting the cultists to their presence, so instead had retreated to a safe distance to wait it out. The more time that passed, however, the more anxious the Ghost had become.

They'd spent the afternoon making preparations. Astrid had once again replaced his bandages and inked his body with the intricate swirls and runes of her protective wards, and this time, she'd shown him how to mark his flechettes with icons that she hoped might allow them to breach some of Thoth's defenses.

Ginny had found two of Astrid's old pistols, testing them in the church hall for balance and weight. She'd always been something of a sharpshooter, and didn't appear to have lost any of her skill. She'd placed two bullets through the same hole in an overturned pew, and declared that she was ready to go.

It wasn't much against a legion of cultists and an ancient god, but it was what they had. They all knew what they were heading into, but none of them were prepared to walk away. They'd be dead, anyway, if Thoth were allowed to rise; they might as well die trying to put him down.

The Ghost had begun pacing. The waste ground really was nothing but a small scrap of scrub—hardly big enough to warrant the animosity and series of scaling reprisals it had engendered between the Reaper and the cult. Of course, whatever was below it was a different matter entirely, and the cult would fight to protect that, no matter the cost.

The Ghost understood that there was more to be read into the Reaper's intent, too. It had never really been about the scrap of land, for him—it was about dominance and power, just as Astrid had said; about demonstrating he was the biggest player in town, and not allowing any other organizations to grow to a size where they could challenge that mantle. To him, the cult was a threat, rivals for control of the streets. It was little wonder he'd felt moved to take them down.

He felt a tap on his arm. It was Ginny. "He's coming," she said, jabbing her finger up the avenue behind him.

Donovan was marching at the head of a veritable army, and the Ghost realized that the sound he'd taken for the rumble of distant traffic was, in fact, the noise of Enforcers' feet, pummeling the sidewalk. He counted nine of them, lumbering along behind Donovan and flanked by scores of men in suits, all of them carrying automatic rifles.

The Ghost's heart sank. He saw immediately what Donovan had done, what the troubled look had been about, back at the church. He'd sold himself to the Reaper to give them a fighting chance. He'd given himself up to save the city, and his friends.

"Sorry we're late," said Donovan, huffing as they came to an abrupt stop in the street. "Took a while to get these guys motivated."

"Felix... what have you done?" said the Ghost.

"What was *necessary*," said Donovan. "This way, we stand a chance against that thing. You said we had to bring the tunnels down." He jerked his thumb over his shoulder. "This is the demolition crew."

There was no point arguing about it now. Donovan was right—with the Enforcers they could strike fast and hard, get in and trash the tunnel system early, minimizing Amaury's power before they took him on. It was the chance they'd been looking for.

They would have to worry about the Reaper another day. For now, they'd make use of the resources at their disposal.

"All right," said the Ghost. "Then I suggest you and Mullins lead the Enforcers while the others scatter, taking out as many of the cultists as they can. Bring down some of those tunnels as soon as you get in there, but remember to leave us an escape route."

"Good," said Donovan. He looked as if he'd been expecting more resistance from the Ghost. "You have your orders, then," he said, turning to face the mob behind him. "Remember, the Reaper wants this place cleaned out. Not a single one of them left. When we're done, get out of there, and head for cover."

There was a murmur of acknowledgement from the men.

Donovan turned back to the Ghost. "It was the only option," he said apologetically. "I couldn't let you go in there alone. Not against that."

"I know." The Ghost patted his friend on the shoulder. "You watch out for yourself in there, okay?"

"You're going after Amaury?"

"Me, Ginny, Astrid. Yes."

"All right. When I've finished trashing the place, I'll come get you." He looked around, frowning. "Now where do we get in?"

"We figure the basement of that wheelwright's shop is the best option. There doesn't seem to be any other route in."

Donovan slid his gun from its holster. "Come on, then. Let's do it, before I change my mind."

They sent the Enforcers in first, thundering through the outer wall of the wheelwright's shop like bulldozers, splintering wood and glass to clear passage for the rest of them.

Shots rang out almost immediately, and the Ghost slid in amongst the chaos, strafing his weapon back and forth and picking off two armed guards who'd come running onto the upper gantry above the shop floor.

Automatic fire belched behind him, dropping more of the cultists as they emerged above, and the Ghost beckoned to Astrid and Ginny, leading them deeper into the dusty old workshop, searching for a way down.

They found it moments later when three men came hurtling up a wooden staircase in the far corner of the main workspace.

Ginny put two bullets in one of them, while the Ghost's explosive rounds saw to the others, opening their chests like glistening, blooming flowers.

"Come on!" he bellowed, stepping over the bodies, leading them down into the darkness. Behind him he could hear Donovan, barking orders at the Enforcers, their ponderous footsteps crunching on the mildewed floorboards that were barely managing to support their weight.

The basement was damp and musty, thick with cobwebs and rotting packing crates. A cool breeze was blowing, however, through a gaping portal in the outer wall that had been opened up to create a doorway to the bizarre complex beyond.

The door had been fashioned to resemble the entrance to an Ancient Egyptian tomb, and reminded the Ghost of the one from the museum—a heavy stone lintel, resting on twin pillars on either side of a yawning hole. The walls had been painted with intricate friezes, depicting scenes of Thoth, standing tall amongst the pantheon of his sibling gods, and two braziers stood just inside the mouth of the entrance, hot coals crackling with heat and soot. Beyond the doorway was a narrow tunnel, its walls lined with further facsimiles of ancient art.

"In there," said the Ghost, "and be on your guard."

Mobsters were hurtling down the stairs behind them now, and the Enforcers were only moments behind. They ran into the tunnel mouth, hugging the walls, weapons ready.

The cacophony above had stirred the men below, like a stick being poked into a hornet's nest. He could hear them buzzing around them, a hubbub of raised voices in the passages ahead. The tunnel veered left, then forked, and he took the left, sensing the slight decline in the floor. They hurried along, brushing against walls colored to resemble the ancient murals that Amaury had found beneath the shifting sands.

Two men lurched into the passage up ahead, and fell almost as soon as they hove into view, the explosions in their chests under-lighting their faces in the gloomy tunnel.

He heard the report of a gun from behind, and swiveled to see Astrid taking pot shots at three black-robed cultists coming up behind them. More were pouring into the mouth of the tunnel ahead, too.

"Behind us!" bellowed Astrid, as the Ghost loosed a volley in the other direction, chewing chunks of plaster out of the wall and felling more of the oncoming cultists.

"Ginny, help her out," called the Ghost over his shoulder. The three of them were standing back to back, weapons raised and blazing.

"What do you think I'm doing?" called Ginny. "Having a picnic?"

He grinned, continuing to spray the tunnel ahead as more and more cultists rose from the depths. He could hear the plodding of the Enforcers in the neighboring tunnels now; the crash of their fists as they set to work, pulling the ceilings down behind them. The walls trembled as, somewhere up above, chunks of masonry slumped across the tunnel ceiling. He looked up to see a crack forming above them.

"Quickly," he said, "the roof's coming down on top of us."

"Oh, perfect," said Ginny. She pivoted, arms outstretched, one gun pointing in each direction. A few more shots and she'd have fully rotated, standing by his side, still firing into the morass of limbs ahead of them.

The ceiling groaned with the rending of stone.

"All right," called Astrid. "Move!"

They surged forward, clambering over the still-warm bodies of the fallen cultists as the ceiling finally gave and the tunnel collapsed, hunks of stone hammering down behind them, blocking their retreat.

Astrid coughed, wiping brick dust from her face as she hurriedly reloaded her gun.

He heard the thud of footsteps in the tunnel ahead and thought one of the Enforcers must have strayed into their path, but when the dust finally settled, he saw it was not an Enforcer at all, but four ebon-black statues, each of them armed with staffs, each bearing the aspect of a different animal—a hawk, a lion, a jackal, a baboon. They marched emotionlessly across the corpses of the dead cultists in their path, crushing them underfoot.

There was nowhere to run. They'd have to stand their ground. The Ghost doused them in explosive rounds, shattering the arm of one, chipping lumps out of the others, but still they came on, arms menacingly outstretched, silent and tenacious.

There was another rumble from the tunnel on their left. Donovan and the Enforcers were moving through, collapsing it behind them.

The statues were almost upon them. Ginny loosed a couple of shots, catching two of the statues square between the eyes, but the bullets barely scratched the ancient stone, and the statues, undeterred, lumbered on.

"Get back!"

"There's nowhere to get back to!" called Astrid.

"Just give me some room!" said the Ghost. He leaned forward, powering his boosters, and shot at the hawk-headed statue, presenting his shoulder as he tried to bowl it into the others. He hit it like a wall, his shoulder rebounding painfully, and the statue, unmoved, swung at him, its staff striking him painfully across the side of the head. He dropped to the floor, his boosters still firing, and slid into the tunnel wall on the opposite side.

A massive *crump* from the other tunnel caused the wall to tremble, and further cracks crept like jagged spider legs across the walls and ceiling. The hawk-headed statue raised its staff again, and brought it down, just as an Enforcer's gauntleted fist burst through the wall, snapping the thing in half. It crumpled to the floor, sending its baboon-headed kin tumbling over beside it.

The Ghost saw their chance. "Through there!" he bellowed, pointing to the gaping wound in the wall. On the other side he could see the Enforcer stomping away, moving further into the complex.

Ginny lurched for the hole, jumping up and through, Astrid behind her. The Ghost scrambled to his feet, leaping up just as the jackal-headed statue grabbed his ankle, dragging him back.

He twisted in its grip, crying out as its ebon fingers tore his flesh, and fired a volley up at its face, showering its neck and torso.

The arm blew free, fragments of jagged stone showering him, burying themselves in his clothes and flesh. The statue toppled backwards, striking the opposing wall and splintering into fragments.

He shook his ankle free, scrambling up and through the hole as the fourth statue swung its staff, narrowly missing the back of his head.

He landed heavily, crumpling onto his side. Ginny and Astrid helped him to his feet, and he dusted himself down, picking a fragment of stone out of his cheek. Behind him, the lion-headed statue was scrabbling at the hole, its arm grabbing frantically at the air as it tried to reach them. They left it there, hurrying after the Enforcers, anxious not to find themselves trapped in another collapsed tunnel.

Up ahead the passage branched again. The Enforcers had gone left—he could tell from the thundering footsteps and the tide of rubble they'd left in their wake. He pressed on ahead, winding ever deeper into the complex. Here, the tunnel sloped dramatically, and they each had to keep one hand against the wall for balance.

They were deep below the streets of Manhattan now, and the Ghost could sense they were nearing their target. Ginny had sensed it too; he could tell by the sudden hesitation in her step, the way she was cocking her head, listening intently.

Below, the sloping passage terminated in an open doorway, dressed in smooth, dark stone, and engraved with a frieze of Thoth and Sekhmet facing one another across the disc of the sun.

Ginny glanced at Gabriel, and their eyes met.

He was about to say something encouraging when two sword-wielding cultists burst from the doorway, hurtling up the slope toward them. Ginny dropped them both with a single action, both pistols barking in her fists. The men slumped to the ground and slid back toward the doorway, their swords clattering on the stone.

"Ready?" said the Ghost.

"Stop asking that, and just get on with it," said Astrid.

Laughing, the Ghost ran on down the slope and through the door.

The chamber beyond showed the true scale of the construction work that had been carried out down here, and equally, the scale of the devotion necessary to pull it off.

The space was pyramidal, the walls sloping in as they rose, reaching a pinnacle over sixty feet above them. In the center of the room, a huge set of stone steps led to a distant dais, upon which more flaming braziers stood, casting light that glimmered and reflected off the smooth, polished stone of the walls.

Above and behind them, the Ghost could hear the wanton destruction of the Enforcers as more and more tunnels collapsed. Soon the whole complex would be destroyed, buried once more beneath the detritus of the city.

Something stirred in the shadows to his left, and he spun, expecting to see Amaury. It was too big for Amaury, though— perhaps twice, even three times the height of a man. It crept forward, its feet scuffing against the stone steps, moving with an odd, awkward gait.

Ponderously, it emerged into the light.

It was covered in gray downy fur, with an elongated nose and two beady red eyes that flicked from side to side, taking them in, one at a time. It opened its mouth, flashing sickly yellowed jaws that could take a man's head off in one terrible bite.

"Oh, great," said the Ghost. "Another baboon."

"Not just any baboon," said Astrid, slowly moving around the other side of him, her gun arm raised. "A bloody massive baboon."

It moved across the steps on its knuckles, crawling higher, circling as if making ready to pounce. The Ghost could sense the power behind its limbs just by watching it move; its chest was so dense with rippled muscle that it was practically armor-plated.

It pounced, and he raised his flechette gun and fired. Shots exploded against its breast as it flung itself at him, each detonation tearing fist-sized lumps of meat out of the thing, but still it came on, screeching as it hurled itself down the steps toward him. He moved, but too late, and its fist knocked him sideways, lifting him from his feet and sending him careening into the wall. He slid to the ground, spitting blood, as it lurched at Ginny, who dropped to the ground and rolled to avoid it. Far from dissuaded, it twisted, plucking her off the ground and tossing her like a ragdoll. She struck the steps and fell limp and still.

Roaring in frustration, the Ghost fired his boosters, soaring over its head, causing it to swing wildly for him with both fists, as Astrid, below, emptied round after round into its face and throat. The bullets were nothing but irritants to it, like buzzing gnats, and it ignored her, still trying to grab for the Ghost.

He dipped, going low, coming up under its arm and twisting in the air, so that his boosters were pointing directly at its face. He hovered there for a moment, the flames scorching its eyes until they blackened and burst, and the creature screeched, thrashing out and catching him on the hip. He spun, his boosters guttering, and collided with the doorway, dropping to the floor.

Astrid had reloaded her gun, and she emptied another round, trying to catch it in the throat.

The baboon, infuriated and blinded, punched out, bowling her over. She screamed, and its head twitched, its nostrils flaring. It had her scent. It padded down the remaining steps, scratching around for her on the ground. She shuffled backwards, trying to get away, but it was on her now, and it crept forward, looming over her, its yellow jaws dripping.

The Ghost cast around, searching for anything he could use as a weapon. The swords of the two dead men lay on the ground close by. He rolled, snatched them up, and jumped to his feet, boosting into the air. He climbed higher, trying to give himself enough momentum.

As the creature lowered its jaws, he cut the power and dropped, a blade in each hand, tips pointing low.

He soared through the air, keeping his legs together and his back arched, plummeting at the baboon's back.

Astrid screamed again just as he struck, the swords sliding to the hilt in the baboon's neck.

The Ghost bounced off its back, the wind knocked out of him, his broken ribs smarting. He struck the stone steps and fell, tumbling down to the bottom, bashing his elbow and finally coming to rest a few feet from Astrid. The dead baboon was on its side, slumped on the ground, its tongue lolling from its open jaw. He'd almost severed its head with the force of his blow, and the tips of the blades had erupted from its throat, jutting like a bizarre necklace.

He looked across at Astrid. She was slowly pulling herself to her feet.

"*Now* we're even," he said, with a crooked smile, "and we've both got baboon stories for next time we're in the bar."

She shook her head in exasperation.

On the steps, Ginny was stirring. The Ghost went to her, helping her to her feet. "Are you all right?"

She nodded. "Just a knock to the head. I'll be okay."

He could feel the whole room shaking now, and knew they didn't have long before the roof started to come down. The Enforcers had done their job too well, and he only hoped Donovan and Mullins had remembered to keep an escape route clear.

"Up there?" he said.

"As good a place as any."

Astrid joined them, and together they mounted the steps, onwards toward Amaury, and Thoth.

"So, you are true to the spirit of Sekhmet, even as you deny her," said Amaury, as they reached the top of the steps a few moments later. "You make quite the warrior, Ginny Gray."

He was standing at the foot of a large altar, watching them as they fanned out around him, weapons drawn. On the altar, an ibis-headed statue of Thoth presided over a stone lintel with a concave base.

"You know it's over, Amaury," said Ginny. "The temple is destroyed, your cultists are dead. There will be no empire of the gods, not here, not now."

Amaury shrugged, a gesture so familiar, so human, that the

Ghost almost found it difficult to believe he carried the spirit of a vengeful god inside of him. "We are *gods*, Ginny! We have infinite patience. It is a simple matter to rebuild, to find slaves willing to bend their knee. Can't you see that? That's all these people are." He waved dismissively at the Ghost. "That's all *he* is. He claims to love you, but humans cannot know true love. You've bewitched him, is all, *enslaved* him."

"Your words are poison," said Ginny, "but they mean nothing to me."

Amaury sighed. "Must we dance again? I grow weary of all this fighting." He threw his head back as his body began to shimmer with the familiar amber light.

The Ghost raised his arm and loosed a shower of flechettes into Amaury's chest. His head came forward and he took a step back, surprised, glowering at the Ghost.

Astrid's runes had worked, although the weapon seemed to have done little damage.

Amaury sighed, and his breath was the hot wind of the desert. His wings unfurled, translucent and glittering with the light of stars, and his sword and shield formed from the swirling aura of light around him. His wings beat, and he rose into the air above them, looking down upon them like a man might peer down at ants.

Ginny, too, was undergoing a similar transformation; this time—the Ghost hoped—at her own behest. The pale light swirled around her, forming ribbons, the sun disk glowing bright and pure behind her head.

He backed up, holding out his hand, guiding Astrid away from the dais.

Ginny spread her hands low, and the light stirred, boiling furiously as Sekhmet's lions took shape.

Thoth watched impassively, waiting for her to make her move.

She thrust her hands forward, loosing the lions, and they roared, charging for Thoth. This time, however, he was ready for her, and he raised his blackened shield, battering them away. They burst into clouds of ethereal light, fracturing into tiny sparks that blew away on the hot desert breeze.

Thoth lurched, then, his sword arm thrusting upwards, so that his blade speared Sekhmet through the gut. She buckled, gagging, gasping for breath, her light suddenly dimming. The tip of the starry blade was jutting from her back, and she clutched at her chest, her face creased in pain.

Thoth slid the blade free, and she dropped to the ground, crumpling into a heap upon the steps.

"No!" All sense of reason fled the Ghost's mind. He boosted high, spraying Thoth with round after round of flechettes, firing again and again, until there was nothing left, until he'd emptied the entire ammunition tube into the god's face.

Still Thoth hovered, impassive. "Puny thing," he said, in a voice that resembled rasping sand blowing across dunes. He held out his hand, and the Ghost felt something close around his throat.

He choked, scrabbling, but there was nothing there, no physical limb to grab hold of. He could feel the life being squeezed out of him.

This was it, he realized. He was going to die here, in a vault beneath Manhattan, killed by an angry god for trespassing upon his temple.

And then suddenly Thoth was burning, wreathed in blue flame. The pressure lifted from the Ghost's throat, and he fell to the floor, watching through tear-streaked eyes as Sekhmet rose, her fists doused in flame. She thrashed out at Thoth, striking him across the face, knocking him back. She struck again, and again, furious and beautiful, her eyes glowing with untold power, the distant light of the heavens.

Thoth roared, raising his sword, but she batted it away with a swipe of her arm, grabbing him round the throat, forcing him lower, until his back was pressed against the concave slab on the altar.

"Now, Astrid!" croaked the Ghost, rubbing his throat. "Do your thing."

Around them, the walls were beginning to crack as the weight of the collapsing structure bore down on them.

Astrid ran forward, throwing open her coat. She reached the altar and pulled a tattered scroll from her pocket, along with a fistful of bone runes. She tossed the fragments of bone at Thoth, and they scattered around him on the dais.

He howled, struggling to get free, but Sekhmet held him firm, blue flame still searing his wings, coursing over his flesh.

Hurriedly, Astrid intoned the words on the scroll—the ritual of binding she'd spoken of, back at the church—and then dropped the scroll to the ground, standing back.

The bone fragments began to glow, hot and amber, as the light of Thoth poured into them, streaming out of his body, siphoned off by the binding ritual.

He screamed, kicking out at Sekhmet and sending her sprawling back, but it was too late. His light was already fading, and Amaury, at the centre of it all, was burning, still wreathed in Sekhmet's eternal flame.

The Ghost watched as his features withered, his human form crumbling to ash. The light faded, and all that was left on the altar was dust.

The Ghost ran to Ginny, whose own light was already beginning to fade. He searched her chest, looking for any sign of the puncture wound, but could see nothing. She glanced up at him, smiled deliriously, and then collapsed into his arms.

He scooped her up, calling for Astrid, and together they ran for the exit as the sky began to fall in around them.

Donovan and Mullins were waiting for them on the waste ground outside the wheelwright's shop. Donovan was pacing, while Mullins was calmly smoking a cigarette. It was a strange reversal, and the Ghost laughed when he saw it, eliciting a look of surprise from Donovan, who rushed over, helping him with Ginny.

"I thought you were coming for us?" said the Ghost.

"I couldn't find you," said Donovan. "Everything was coming down around us, and we had to get out." He looked at Ginny, his face creased in concern. "What happened? Is she okay?"

The Ghost nodded. "I think she's going to be fine," he said.

"And Amaury?"

"It's over," said the Ghost. "Thanks to Ginny and Astrid."

"Thank God," said Donovan.

"I'd rather not," said the Ghost. "I've had enough of gods to last a lifetime." He looked around. "What happened to the Reaper's men?"

"Gone," said Donovan. "The Enforcers, too. We lost two of them down there, but the others all made it."

"More's the pity."

Astrid was standing by his elbow. "Where to?" she said. "My place?"

The Ghost shook his head. "No. Long Island, I think. It's time to rest. You're all welcome."

"Maybe next time," said Mullins. "I've heard about your parties."

The Ghost laughed. "Thank you," he said. "All of you."

Donovan clapped him on the shoulder. "You're the one who said it. We're a team."

"We are, aren't we?"

The ground shuddered beneath them as the last of the subterranean tunnels finally gave way.

"Come on, time to go home. We'll worry about the rest of it tomorrow."

"Yeah," said Donovan, with a sigh. "We will."

Ginny was beginning to stir in his arms. He set her down, and held her to him for a moment. Then, as the others began to peel away into the night, he took her hand, and started out on the long journey home.

THIRTY

The Ghost stood on the lip of the precinct building, basking in the twinkling lights of the city. The crosswinds whipped his coat up around him, a rippling black wing at his back. He longed to soar above the rooftops once again, to enjoy the majesty of his city for a short time, with no thought of angels and demons, gods and men.

Tonight, everything felt fresh and renewed. The pain in his chest was finally starting to subside, and Ginny was back at his house in Long Island, no doubt stirring up all manner of difficulty for Henry as they saw to the packing. He smiled at the thought.

He felt that if he could only capture that feeling, find some way to hold onto it, then he could find a way to be happy. And if a man like him could do that, then anything was possible.

Behind him, Donovan was studying the smoldering tip of his cigarette. There was nothing triumphant about his demeanor. He looked thoughtful, standing amidst the ruins of his favorite rooftop.

"You're thinking about the Reaper again," said the Ghost, hopping down beside him.

"What?" Donovan looked up. "Oh, yes," he said. "You know, he's already purchased that plot of land. He's backfilling what's left of the tunnels with cement."

"A man who's learned to cover his tracks," said the Ghost.

"Now I have to live up to my side of the bargain." Donovan scratched at his beard. He wouldn't meet the Ghost's eye. "How am I going to live with myself, Gabriel? How can I show my face in that precinct building, when that man is undermining everything I believe in, and using *me* to do it?"

"You did the right thing, Felix. The only thing you could. You saved the city."

"And damned myself."

"Sometimes there's no other way. That's the world we live in. And besides," he put a hand on his friend's shoulder, "you're only damned if *you* believe it, too. This is our chance to bring him down. Don't forget that. To work from the inside, get to know his organization, the major players. Once we know enough about how he operates, we'll dismantle the whole lot, piece by piece."

"And in the meantime?"

"In the meantime we do what we can to protect the people we love. That's all any of us can do. They're alive because of you, Felix. Never forget that. Thoth would have leveled this entire city if we hadn't stopped him. We'd have nothing left to protect. Everything else has to seem small against that."

Donovan had allowed his cigarette to burn down in his fingers. He tossed it aside, dusting the ash from his sleeve. "All right. You've said your piece. Now tell me, how's Ginny?"

"Remarkably well, considering what she's been through. But I... I can't forget about that thing inside of her. What if she loses control again?"

"She won't," said Donovan, with such conviction that the Ghost was taken aback.

"How can you be so sure?"

"Because she's got you looking out for her. That thing, it might seem like a curse, but if she can learn to use it, Gabriel, think of the good it could do. If anyone knows what it's like to have demons, it's you. Teach her what you know. Don't try to make her hide it. Help her embrace it instead."

"You're a wise old fool, you know."

"Less of the old," said Donovan. "Fool, I'll give you."

They stood in silence for a moment, neither of them feeling the need to fill it.

"So what's next?" said Donovan after a while. "I mean, I know there's the Reaper and all."

"I'm going away for a while," said the Ghost. "Ginny needs time, and so do I. I'm taking her to London tomorrow."

"Tomorrow!" said Donovan. "You can't just go running off, Gabriel. This city needs you, now more than ever. Christ, *I* need you."

"It's only for a few weeks," said the Ghost. "While she heals. No boats—we're going by airship. Thought we might look up an old friend while we're there."

"So you've finally taken your own advice," said Donovan. "A bloody vacation. I can't say I blame you."

"You'd better not," said the Ghost, "or it'll be a miserable journey."

Donovan frowned. "Now what are you on about?"

"Here." The Ghost reached inside his coat and withdrew a small paper wallet. He handed it to Donovan.

"What's this?"

"Tickets, you fool. You and Flora are coming with us."

Donovan stared at him, wide-eyed. "I can't accept these! There's work to be done here. Just look at this place, for a start." He made a gesture that seemed to take in the entire city.

"And Mullins can take care of it. Just for a little while. It's time to slow down, take a break. We've earned it. When we come back, we'll start work again. What do you say?"

"I say you're a bloody fool yourself," said Donovan, and he stepped forward and clasped the Ghost in a firm embrace. "But I'm grateful to call you a friend."

"Well, I wouldn't go *that* far," said the Ghost, laughing. "Now get home and pack. The car's coming for you at two."

He turned and hopped up onto the ledge.

"What about you, don't you need to pack?"

"I just need a little while." He reached inside his jacket and pulled the cord, his boosters kicking to life with a sudden roar.

"Be seeing you." He stepped off the ledge, momentarily dipping out of sight, before riding high on a plume of flame and sailing off into the night.

Donovan lit another cigarette as he watched him go. Then, when he was sure he could no longer see him amongst the hazy lights of the city, he stubbed the cigarette out on the ledge, and set out for home.

ACKNOWLEDGMENTS

So many people helped in so many ways, but specific thanks this time to: Cath Trechman, Cavan Scott, Paul Magrs, Stuart Douglas, Andy Smillie, Manuela Clausi, the timeless special effects of Ray Harryhausen, the music of David Bowie, and, of course, my remarkable family.

ABOUT THE AUTHOR

George **Mann** was born in Darlington and has written numerous books, short stories, novellas and original audio scripts. *The Affinity Bridge*, the first novel in his Newbury and Hobbes Victorian fantasy series, was published in 2008. Other titles in the series include *The Osiris Ritual*, *The Immorality Engine*, *The Casebook of Newbury & Hobbes*, *The Revenant Express* and the forthcoming *The Albion Initiative*.

His other novels include *Ghosts of Manhattan*, *Ghosts of War*, *Ghosts of Karnak* and the forthcoming *Ghosts of Empire*, mystery novels about a vigilante set against the backdrop of a post- steampunk 1920s New York, as well as an original Doctor Who novel, *Paradox Lost*, featuring the Eleventh Doctor alongside his companions, Amy and Rory.

He has edited a number of anthologies, including *Encounters of Sherlock Holmes*, *Further Encounters of Sherlock Holmes*, *Associates of Sherlock Holmes* and the forthcoming *Further Associates of Sherlock Holmes*, *The Solaris Book of New Science Fiction* and *The Solaris Book of New Fantasy*, and has written two Sherlock Holmes novels for Titan Books, *Sherlock Homes: The Will of the Dead* and *Sherlock Holmes: The Spirit Box*.

GHOSTS OF EMPIRE

GEORGE MANN

In the aftermath of the events surrounding the Circle of
Thoth, Gabriel takes Ginny to London by airship to
recuperate. But he isn't counting on coming face-to-face
with a man who claims to embody the spirit of Albion
itself, sinister forces gathering in the London Underground
and an old ally—the British spy, Peter Rutherford—who
could desperately use his help.

AVAILABLE OCTOBER 2017

THE CASEBOOK OF NEWBURY & HOBBES

GEORGE MANN

A collection of short stories detailing the supernatural steampunk adventures of detective duo, Sir Maurice Newbury and Miss Veronica Hobbes in dark and dangerous Victorian London. Along with Chief Inspector Bainbridge, Newbury & Hobbes will face plague revenants, murderous peers, mechanical beasts, tentacled leviathans, reanimated pygmies, and an encounter with Sherlock Holmes.

SHERLOCK HOLMES
THE WILL OF THE DEAD

GEORGE MANN

A young man named Peter Maugram appears at the front door of Sherlock Holmes and Dr. Watson's Baker Street lodgings. Maugram's uncle is dead and his will has disappeared, leaving the man afraid that he will be left penniless. Holmes agrees to take the case and he and Watson dig deep into the murky past of this complex family. Is it connected to the robberies being committed by the enigmatic iron men?

SHERLOCK HOLMES
THE SPIRIT BOX

GEORGE MANN

Summer, 1915. As Zeppelins rain death upon the rooftops of London, eminent members of society begin to behave erratically: a Member of Parliament throws himself naked into the Thames after giving a pro-German speech to the House; a senior military advisor suggests surrender before feeding himself to a tiger at London Zoo; and a famed suffragette suddenly renounces the women's liberation movement and throws herself under a train. In desperation, an aged Mycroft Holmes sends to Sussex for the help of his brother, Sherlock.

For more fantastic fiction, author events,
exclusive excerpts, competitions,
limited editions and more

Visit our website
TITANBOOKS.COM

Like us on Facebook
facebook.com/titanbooks

Follow us on Twitter
@TitanBooks

Email us
readerfeedback@titanemail.com